A Lovely Dream

A Seneca & Michael Novel

Barbara Cutrera

Published by On My Way Up, LLC

Cover Photography: Sherri Proctor www.SherrisIslandImages.com

ISBN: 978-0-9913642-4-4

For Andre, my father who is an Air Force veteran, and for Jim and all of the other spies who risk their lives and sanity in an attempt to make the world a better place.

Chapter One

"The best way to make your dreams come true is to wake up."
–Paul Valery

I had a lovely dream in which a smart, handsome, dark-haired man loved me passionately and unconditionally. He told me how beautiful and intelligent I was and how he never wanted to be apart from me. I felt joy, desire, and a sense of security I'd never before experienced in my life. I had no way of knowing I'd soon find that connection with the man of my dream. Our union would also bring with it pain, fear, and danger.

I woke the following morning feeling wonderful and humming a little to myself as I got ready for work. Nothing in my life had changed. I was still Seneca Jones, a twenty-seven year-old divorced, childless social worker. However, I felt different. I felt special.

As I brushed my long, black hair before leaving my house, I tried to push aside my thoughts of the lovely dream and focus on my busy day ahead at Hearts at Home, a company located in Bradenton, Florida that specialized in providing caregivers for new mothers, the elderly, people recovering from surgery, and the terminally ill. I coordinated services for the clients and managed the caregivers. I also maintained a small caseload in order to keep myself in touch with the practical and emotional aspects of my job.

I spent that Tuesday morning in the office doing necessary but unexciting administrative work then drove to my friend Tom Langston's for lunch. I'd met Tom at a local art gallery where we'd literally bumped into one another and then struck up a conversation about the merits of the Surrealism Movement. We'd quickly become close friends. Tom was eighty and lived in nearby Palmetto. Inside his home was an odd assortment of expensive artwork and sculpture. Pictures of his ever-absent children were interspersed throughout the collection, displayed on bookcases, shelving, and accent tables.

Tom himself was an unassuming older gentleman. He frequently became so engrossed in a book or in a series of movies that he forgot to eat. Since he suffered from arthritis, high cholesterol, diabetes, and COPD, forgetting to eat at regular intervals was not an option. Neither was forgetting to take his medications, which was why I talked with him in person or by phone every day.

I parked my car and enjoyed the beautiful April day as I walked to Tom's front door. I knocked out of politeness and then used my key to unlock it. When I entered the living room, Tom immediately stood to greet me. I'd told him long ago that he didn't need to do this, but he insisted that a gentleman should always stand when a lady came into a room. After our customary hug, we went through the usual exchange regarding whether or not he'd eaten that day and if he had taken his medications. He told me that he'd had breakfast and his pills for the morning.

We moved to the kitchen. When I opened the refrigerator, I was horrified to see that the large jar of fig preserves a neighbor had given him the previous week was already gone and exclaimed, "That's so bad for your sugar levels!"

"I know, but they were so good," Tom said with a twinkle in his eyes. "I haven't had figs like that since I was in Libya in the 1960s. It's 2005, for Christ's sake! I couldn't resist."

"You could try."

"I'm old and have had a more adventurous life than most people ever dream of. If I want to eat a jar of figs and shorten my life a little bit, then I will."

As I withdrew the makings of a salad from the fridge, I said, "It's your life. It's only that I don't want to lose such a good friend."

Tom grew serious and gently took my hands in his. He lightly squeezed them before saying earnestly, "If you'd been alive when I was younger, then I think we would have made a good match for one another. I think I'd have found in you what I was searching for in all the other women I've had in my life, and I hope you would've found the same in me. I would've wanted nothing more than to have you for my very own and for you to want me that way, too. It's a shame that wasn't meant to be, but at least we know each other now."

"If we'd been contemporaries and had gotten together as a couple, would you still have been a spy?"

I wasn't teasing Tom. He'd been a bona fide intelligence agent for over three decades of his life. The first time he'd mentioned this, I'd thought he was joking. However, he produced several books by reputable authors that listed him as a former intelligence agent for the United States government. Further research on my part confirmed that his claims were not an attempt at bravado by an old man. He'd worked all over the world as a spy then retired from that life and gone back to school in order to get his Ph.D. in art history. After teaching for over twenty years, he'd ended up in my little corner of the world along the Gulf Coast of Florida.

"I was destined to be a spy," Tom declared. "I would have become a spy whether or not you and I had married."

"Would I have made a good spy?"

"Not at all. You would have made a hell of a good director for the Red Cross or the Peace Corps or something like that."

"Was being a spy worth it?"

"It was, but my views on government certainly aren't now what they were when I was an idealistic young man. I did good work for the good of my country, and I loved the life I led doing it."

We ate in companionable silence. Once we'd finished our lunch, Tom stood painfully, put his plate in the sink, and then motioned me back towards the living room. His limp was becoming more pronounced. He retrieved a book from one of his many bookcases and handed it to me. It was a compilation of poems, folktales, and nursery rhymes written for children. I opened the front cover and scanned the contents. I didn't recognize any of the titles listed.

"Seneca, I know you have to leave soon, but I wanted to ask you a favor. Would you do me the honor of letting me read to you? It's been decades since I've read nursery rhymes to anyone, and I used to enjoy doing that with my sons and daughters when they were little."

"That would be nice. No one's ever read to me before. How about if you read some to me each time we visit?"

"Your parents never read to you?"

I laughed at how astonished he sounded and said, "My dad never read anything that I can recall, and my mom read magazines but no books."

"A smart girl like you with no one to encourage you."

"My parents encouraged me to do well in school. They were proud of me, even if they didn't really understand me."

"Well, it's past time someone read to you. It's not only the learning that's important; it's also how you go about it that counts, too."

Tom read me several poems involving Jack and Jill, another Jack who was nimble and quick, and another Jack who could eat no fat but whose wife could eat no lean. I was about to ask Tom whether every male character in these old nursery rhymes was named Jack when he moved on to Peter the pumpkin eater and Mary and her little lamb. He finished by singing a funny song about an old lady who swallowed a fly.

I left Tom's house looking forward to the next performance. As I drove to my first appointment of the afternoon, I found myself singing the song about the old lady and remembering Tom's baritone and the odd drawings that accompanied each line. It was amazing how my mood had been so positively affected by some simple nursery rhymes and a children's song.

I arrived at Walt and Sheila Hummel's penthouse condo on Anna Maria Island. We discussed the need for a new caregiver for Sheila, whose dementia had recently worsened. Walt struggled with his wife's continuing decline, and I suggested he try a local support group. He agreed to think about it although I doubted he'd attend.

Next, I met with Adiba Salah and her newborn daughter, Hadeel. Adiba was an Iraqi landscape architect who was very nervous about caring for her baby. Her first child, a son, had died at birth a year before she and her husband had immigrated to the United States. Adiba was not fluent in any language except Arabic. This made communication a challenge, so I'd decided to show her by example how to care for Hadeel. Adiba and I were getting along well, despite the language barrier.

My final appointment that afternoon was with a seventy-eight-year-old short, stocky, gray-haired widower named Alfredo Benedetto. He was a wonderful man who owned a huge house on Siesta Key. His many children, grandchildren, and great-grandchildren visited from all around the country whenever they were able. Family meant everything to him. I always enjoyed Al's company although I was not so enamored of his seventy-five-year-old girlfriend, Diane, who was rather abrasive.

He and I reviewed his dwindling need for services from Hearts at Home, which had been initiated after hip replacement surgery. Al had worked hard at physical therapy and continued to enjoy life to the fullest. I was happy for him. He'd earned his fortune the hard way, starting as an Italian immigrant who'd become a delivery boy and ending as the owner of a chain of very successful grocery stores. He deserved to reap the benefits of his persistence and sacrifice.

"My grandson, Michael, is coming soon. I have not seen him in ten years."

"That's an extremely long time for you. Usually everyone in your family is in and out of here several times a year, no matter where they live."

"Michael is different. He has been in the military and was deployed in Iraq, Afghanistan and other places. He is undoubtedly my favorite grandchild although I know one should not say such things."

"What branch of the military?"

"The Navy." Looking directly at me, Al confided, "I think he was one of those SEALs, but I cannot be sure."

"What makes you think he was a Navy SEAL? I don't really know too much about them, but I've heard it's a pretty elite group."

Al nodded and explained that he'd done some research on the subject. Michael fit the profile of the perfect man for such a specialized outfit – highly intelligent, dedicated, perpetually striving to push himself to surpass the limits of his endurance, and wanting to make a valuable contribution to humanity no matter what the cost to his own life. The intermittent communication over the previous decade also seemed to support the idea that his grandson was involved in missions where regular contact with relatives wasn't possible.

"Do not get me wrong," Al hastened to say. "He calls, but it is often not on the appropriate date. For example, he phones to wish me a happy birthday, but it might be a month before my birthday and he is apologetic but says he has no choice. A Christmas call might come three weeks late, again with similar apologies. You understand?"

I did, although I wasn't certain if this infrequent communication meant anything other than that this man had the stereotypical male tendency to not remember important holidays or celebrations except at opportune moments.

"I know what you are thinking," Al said seriously. "But Michael is not a man who forgets anything. He reminds me of myself. I have an excellent memory, but Michael has an eidetic memory."

"He has a photographic memory?"

"Yes, although there are many misconceptions about the whole thing. Having a good memory or being able to recall certain things does not mean one has eidetic memory. It is complicated. Michael has more of the gift than anyone I have ever read about or encountered."

"When does your grandson arrive?"

"This weekend. He will be here when you come to check on me for the last time."

"I'll look forward to meeting him." As I stood, I asked, "Where is Diane today?"

"Ah, my bella Diane is at the salon having her hair done for our attendance at a special performance of Mozart's The Marriage of Figaro. Have you seen that opera?"

"I've never been to an opera in my life." When he appeared startled by this admission, I hurriedly added, "I have heard it though."

"Really?"

"Of course. I grew up watching Bugs Bunny. He did all the great operas, didn't he?"

Al laughed heartily but shook his head and declared that one day he would take me to an opera. When I made a face, he laughed harder and insisted I would appreciate it, even if I didn't particularly care for the music.

I called the office before starting my car and explained that I was just leaving my last appointment and was heading straight home. It was already after four-thirty. I reminded the receptionist that I'd be in the office most of the following day and asked her to transfer me to my voicemail. Since there were no urgent messages, I simply saved them all and vowed to return calls in the morning. Then I relaxed and enjoyed the thirty-minute drive home.

My little beach house was unusual in that it was tucked away from other properties along the coast. While most houses or condos were built practically on top of one another, my bungalow could only be reached by following a long and winding road. Edged by thick plantings of palms, sea grape trees, and tall grasses, it was completely secluded. I'd had friends ask me whether or not this frightened me, but the truth was that I felt more safe at this home than I had anywhere else I'd lived before.

Another question I'd been asked was how I'd managed to purchase such a property on my salary, which was good but not enough to afford such a house. I usually replied I'd caught a lucky break, which was not exactly true. The reality of the situation was that I'd received a substantial check two years earlier from the estate of the man who'd owned the farm where my father had died. The owner's widow had included a note stating their family had always felt badly about what had happened and wanted to somehow make it right. I'd accepted the check and hopefully assuaged their guilt. Fighting the urge to hold onto the funds, I decided to use them to purchase my first home.

I loved my house. It had been built in 1955 and was painted Caribbean blue. At eleven-hundred square feet, it was definitely big enough for me with its two bedrooms and one bathroom. The former owner had painted each interior room a different color. Therefore, I'd selected furniture that was white so that it stood out in stark relief from the colorful walls. I'd deliberately placed prints of some of my favorite paintings throughout the home. A huge lanai, otherwise known as a screened-in porch, ran the length of the back of the house and looked out onto the beach. This was a tremendous bonus, especially for a woman who'd spent her first eighteen years in a tiny mobile home in central Florida. The place was my house, and I never intended to leave it.

When I arrived home, I ate a light dinner as I sat and watched my blue Siamese fighting fish, Doc, swim in his tall glass bowl that rested in the center of the dining table. I reflected on the day's successes and failures. When I was finished, I went to take a hot bath, watched a movie I'd received via Netflix, got ready for bed, and then went to sleep.

That night I did not have a lovely dream. I awoke shaking, screaming, and horrified. Sitting up, I twisted from one side to the other, not certain of where to go or what to do. Finally, I scooted to the right side of the bed and braced my hands on the mattress while I tried to slow my breathing. Lifting my left hand, I covered my eyes before switching on the lamp.

I felt tears falling on the exposed flesh of my thighs. I removed my hand and rose unsteadily from the bed, as I tried to clear my head and recall where my Cookie Monster doll was. I walked through the house to the living room and found the stuffed toy nestled in one of the niches of the white, built-in wall unit. I picked it up and held it tightly against me as I returned to my room and crawled back into bed. Pulling the covers up to my chin, I hugged Cookie Monster to my chest and stared blindly at the lamp. Gradually, the shaking lessened although I found that the terror and grief refused to recede.

I glanced at the clock. It was 5:30. My alarm would be going off at 6. I wondered if I could get my emotions under control by then.

I have to go to work, I told myself. I have too much to do. Adiba Saleh and her baby are literally depending on me. Tom needs me to take him to the store. I have reports to work on and paperwork to process.

I squeezed Cookie Monster tighter and attempted to wipe away the tears and the dream. I wanted to call someone and have them tell me it was going to be all right, that I'd just had a nightmare and would forget about it soon enough. Unfortunately, there was no one to call. I had male and female friends, and any of them would have gladly listened and offered kind words of encouragement if I chose to share my personal problems with them. But I didn't want my friends at that moment; I wanted my family and knew I had no one.

I relaxed my hold on the doll and began to sing the silly song Tom had taught me. I was relieved when it helped to distract me from the nightmare.

I can't go to work. It will take me all day to get over this.

However, as I thought of baby Hadeel, I knew that staying home was not an option. I had to put on my Big Girl Panties and get moving. Perhaps that would help me to stop crying.

I sat up and held Cookie Monster in front of me then said, "Get a grip, Seneca. You haven't had this nightmare for at least two and a half years. You'll feel better if you just get ready and go to work."

Cookie Monster had always been my favorite Sesame Street character, and my father had borrowed a car and driven from our rural Florida area to a large toy store in Tampa in order to purchase the doll for my fifth birthday. My mother had baked a sheet cake and awkwardly cut it in the shape of a cookie with a bite taken out of it before adding frosting. I had no idea how they'd managed to pay for the gas for the ride to Tampa, the toy, or the cake. We never had money for extras. We rarely had the money for necessities.

All of the kids in our mobile home park had attended my party and played in the kiddie pool donated for the occasion by a neighbor. It was my most memorable birthday celebration, and the Cookie Monster toy had instantly become a prized childhood possession. Aside from a scrapbook, the stuffed doll was the only material evidence that I'd had a childhood.

When I shut off the clock alarm, I was pleased to see that my hand was only trembling slightly. This bolstered my self-confidence, and I gave Cookie Monster one last squeeze before placing him on the nightstand and rising from the bed.

As I got ready for work, I wondered how I could have the best dream of my life one night and the worst the next. Perhaps my brain was subconsciously reminding me that the man from my dream would not be part of my future, and I could never escape my past.

Chapter Two

"Are you coming down with something?" my co-worker, Krystal, asked when I passed her desk. "You don't look like yourself."

I suddenly realized I had forgotten not only to put on make-up but also to don any jewelry. I was grateful at least I'd brushed my teeth and hair.

"I'm just really, really tired. I'll warn you now I'm going to be crabby today."

"Why did you even come in to work? You have more leave time than almost anyone else here. You could go home and get some more sleep."

"I'll go home if I start to feel worse. I promise."

"If you're sick then we can go to the Less of You meeting another Saturday," she offered sweetly.

Krystal, who was blonde, blue-eyed, and a hundred pounds overweight, had recently found out I'd lost sixty-two pounds eight years earlier by going through the Less of You Weight Loss Program. She'd shyly approached me and asked whether or not I'd go with her to a meeting. I'd been thrilled for her and had readily accepted. I would *not* miss this Saturday's meeting and told her so. After all, it was only Wednesday.

"You're not getting burnt out are you?" she asked worriedly. "Being a social worker can be tough. I don't want to see you quit."

"I'm not burnt out. I'm not quitting. I just didn't sleep well. I'll be fine. Really."

Placated, she returned to her payroll work and left me alone. For the next four hours, I threw myself into my administrative duties. I was so engrossed that I lost track of time and was only dimly aware of phones ringing and people passing by my office. I was startled when the alarm on my phone chimed, signaling that it was noon and time to eat before leaving the office for Mrs. Saleh's house.

I quickly went to the lunchroom, ate a turkey sandwich and some fresh vegetables, and then hurried back to my desk. I shut down my computer, grabbed my purse and satchel, and left the building. I was exhausted.

The two hours I spent with Adiba and Hadeel were productive if alternately gratifying and frustrating. At least Adiba's English was rapidly improving. She seemed truly happy throughout the course of the conversation and effusively thanked me before I left. Well, I assumed that her words were words of thanks.

"You look really good today," I told Tom as we exchanged our customary hug. "You had a good morning?"

I'd expected Tom to say yes. Instead, he frowned and asked me what was wrong with me. When I told him I was very tired, he snorted derisively and remarked that I was more than tired.

"Something's bothering you deep down inside," he said seriously. "Tell me what's the matter. I could make it better."

"Leave it alone, Tom."

"If something was really wrong with me, you wouldn't let it lie."

He was right, but I wasn't going to talk with him about my nightmare. I'd never told anyone and never planned to change my mind.

"What happened will fade, and things will return to normal."

"You're exhibiting symptoms of Post-Traumatic Stress Disorder."

"I have one bad night, and you're labeling me as someone with PTSD?"

"It's not only one bad night. I've seen the signs of depression, anxiety, and avoidance before in myself and others. Denying it and running away isn't going to make it better. Take it from one who knows."

"We should leave for the store," I told him, ignoring his comments.

Tom grumbled just loudly enough for me to hear, "Goddamned fool."

My temper ignited, and I snapped, "Me or you?"

"Both of us," he shot back. "When I became a spy, it wasn't only because I wanted to serve my country. I was running from someone who abused me greatly when I was younger. I thought if I went far enough away, it would mitigate my pain, my shame, and my anger. I was wrong – even though I was an excellent operative if I do say so myself."

"But –"

"You're doing the same thing and are too young and self-absorbed to see it."

"I wasn't abused and have only been out of Florida once in my life," I argued. "And self-absorbed? I couldn't care less about vanity or status or anything like that. I chose to specialize in my field because there was a need."

"A need in the community or a need within yourself?" he demanded. "There's no fault in doing it for either reason. The fault lies with your not allowing yourself to admit the truth."

"Truth?" I echoed.

"You might not have run away to the Middle East, but you escaped into the world of academia." Tom actually shook his finger at me and said, "You had no way to get away except through your studies."

"Wanting to get out of poverty and get my master's degree proves your theory that I was some sort of victim?"

"You are a victim!" he cried. "It's as plain as the nose on your face! As for self-absorption, that term doesn't make you some stuck-up, vacuous, vain bitch. It means you're scared and are trying to find protection from whatever's hurting you so badly. You need a man who can take care of you and who'll let you take care of him. That and some therapy!"

I was stunned into silence. Tom had never spoken like this to me, nor did I want to acknowledge his interpretation of my life. I was trying to absorb what he'd said only minutes before about his childhood abuse, and I was feeling queasy and emotionally off-balance.

"I work with my clients –" I began, but he cut me off.

"Because through your clients you find grandparents, parents, siblings, and children. You give comfort to the sick, the dying, the newborns, and those who are mentally unstable. It doesn't take a secret operative to figure out that these people represent –"

"We should go to the store," I said deliberately. "Then I'm going home."

"To sleep?" he goaded. "To whatever you dreamed about last night that made you look like the ghost of yourself today?"

There was silence between us for some time. Eventually, I said quietly, "I didn't come here to argue with you. I came to take you to the store. You need groceries."

"To hell with the groceries! Your life is worth more than a trip to Publix."

I knew that if I didn't take Tom to the store soon I was going to burst into tears. I needed the routine, the return of our relationship to where it had been before I'd arrived at his home that afternoon.

"Have you taken your medications today?" I asked. "Did you eat?"

He sighed deeply and said, "Yes to both."

"Good. I'd like to go to Publix with you right now. Will you get your list and come with me?"

Tom watched me for a while, and I was under the impression that he was studying me and calculating how I'd react depending on his answer. I didn't like the idea that he was scrutinizing me.

In the end, we went to Publix and spent an hour getting the items on his list and picking up a prescription from the pharmacy there. Usually, we had a fun time shopping together, but that day's excursion felt more obligatory on both our parts.

I glanced at the clock on my dashboard before I left Tom's driveway. It was 4:40.

Well, I didn't really want to go home early anyway, I thought. *I don't want to go home now.*

Having no place else to go, I resigned myself to simply returning to my house. Once there, I made a chicken salad sandwich, got a bottle of red wine and a glass, then put on a jacket and went out to the beach with a towel and a blanket. I ate slowly, hardly tasting my food. My first glass of wine was quickly followed by another and then another. Since it was evening in April, it was chilly on the beach. I wrapped the heavy wool blanket around me and watched the sunset while I sipped more wine.

I considered seeing a therapist. I pondered this option long after the sun had set, finishing the bottle of wine in the process. I woke the following morning feeling sick. One glass of wine was usually plenty for me, so consuming an entire bottle didn't agree with my head or stomach. I called the office and said that I must have caught a virus, then I went back to sleep, waking only to go to the bathroom, feed the fish, eat some crackers, and sip some water. I moved from the bed to the couch at 6:00 and called Tom to check on him.

"Yes, I took my medicines and even ate a bowl of soup for dinner."

"What did you have for breakfast and lunch?"

"Cereal for breakfast. I don't think I ate lunch."

"Two out of three isn't so bad," I told him. After downing an Advil, I asked, "What time is your appointment with the internist tomorrow?"

"Let's see. I wrote it down somewhere."

I heard him rummaging through the articles on his desk for a short while and pictured him looking for the paper. It brought tears to my eyes. He was such a smart, capable man, but I could see that his memory was failing more and more as the days passed. He knew it too, and he despised it.

"Here it is. I see her at 11:00."

"Do you want me to go with you?"

"No, dear girl. You and she can have a chat about it later. I'd rather go alone."

"Tom, I didn't mean to –"

"Stop right there, young lady. What happened yesterday is in the past. I stand by what I said, but I don't want it to undermine our friendship. I won't talk about it anymore if you don't want me to. If you change your mind, you let me know."

"Thank you."

"You are so very welcome. Get some rest. You still sound very tired."

The next morning I woke feeling fine, and I enjoyed my drive to the office. The high temperatures were projected to be in the mid-sixties. I worked in the office all morning, went to visit Adiba then returned to the office to finish some paperwork before the end of the day. I verified with Krystal that we were still meeting at the Less of You center the next morning, then met some friends whom I hadn't seen in a while at our favorite restaurant, Ceviche, where I thoroughly enjoyed excellent Spanish food, good music, and dancing. I arrived home at midnight, tired but happy. It was a wonderful end to an odd week.

The Saturday leader of the Less of You sessions was great, and Krystal continued to be extremely enthusiastic about the program. I asked her if she wanted to go shopping and have lunch with me, and she readily accepted my offer. During the course of the next three hours, I discovered she'd always been a shy girl, had been teased about her weight since childhood, and had parents and brothers who demeaned her on a regular basis because of her appearance. Her description of her past made me sad and angry, and I told her how I felt. She said that she appreciated my concern and interest. Then we started to talk more about our lives and dreams. Our main goal, we both agreed, was to be happy.

"Easier said than done," I remarked.

"Isn't that the truth?" Hesitating, she asked, "Have you had a lot of boyfriends?"

I shrugged and told her I'd been married and divorced young and that I had dated, but not frequently, since then. I refrained from sharing with her that I hadn't been sexually involved with a man since my divorce. I nervously asked her how many boyfriends she'd had. She stared at her lap and said she'd had quite a few, but all they seemed to want was sex.

"None of them wanted me for who I really am. They all thought that I'm easy because I'm overweight and desperate. I guess they're right. I kept hoping one of them would want me for more than sex."

I fought the urge to lecture her and simply said, "I think losing the weight will give you the confidence to stand on your own and not feel as if you have to sleep with any man who asks you. That's not the way it should be."

"I know. Thank you so much for helping me do it, Seneca."

"Thank you, Krystal."

"For what?"

"For being such a sweet person. I'm glad we're friends."

Once we'd gone our separate ways, I called Tom for our typical exchange regarding whether or not he'd taken his medications and eaten. Then I went to the gym, where I worked on some resistance training and walked on the treadmill. I returned home, showered, and put on my pajamas. My plan was to relax and read a book I'd bought about new theories in physics regarding the possibility of time travel. I was four chapters into the book when my cell phone rang. The Caller I.D. showed the number for the office answering service.

"A Mr. Hummel insisted I call you," the operator told me. "He sounds frantic and was crying while he talked to me. I couldn't quite make out what he was saying, but it had something to do with his wife. I couldn't reach their aide, who's off-duty. He begged me to call you. He said you had to come to their condo right away, that he didn't think he could take anymore. Then he hung up, and I couldn't get him when I called back."

I checked the time. It was 6:15. After informing the operator I'd go to the Hummels' to see what was wrong, I hurriedly dressed in jeans, a sweatshirt, and tennis shoes then drove to the condo.

Walt was practically sobbing when he opened the door for me. For a split second I wondered if Sheila had died. Then I saw her standing in the doorway behind him.

Sheila was wearing light blue satin pajamas and matching slippers. Her face and hands were covered with something brown. Whatever it was had gotten on her nightclothes and in her hair. I suddenly realized she was coated in peanut butter.

"I only went in the bathroom for a minute, and when I came out, she was like this. She said she'd forgotten to wash her face." Wiping futilely at his tears, Walt said, "I can't do this anymore. I've been watching her disappear, and I can't stand to see it any longer. I don't know what to do."

I understood completely. All of the money Walt had couldn't make it right and bring back his beloved wife's mind. She existed in blissful oblivion, while he was forced to watch her become the shell of the woman she'd once been. It was tearing him to pieces inside.

"Let me get her cleaned up, then we can talk. Why don't you get a glass of water and wait for me on the balcony?"

I led Sheila to the bathroom and tried to wash the peanut butter off her skin. I finally gave up and helped her into the shower, which worked much better than only using the wet washrag. Once she was clean, I handed her a towel and instructed her on how to dry herself.

"Have we met before?" she asked, as I assisted her in dressing in a pair of silk pajamas. I assured her that we had as I threw the washcloths and dirty nightclothes in a plastic bag I found under the sink.

"You're a very nice girl," Sheila told me. "I wish I had a daughter like you. You make me feel safe."

"I'm so glad. Why don't we get you to your bedroom now?"

I helped the woman to bed, and she instantly fell asleep. Then I retrieved the bag of stained rags and clothing before going to the balcony. Looking dejected, Walt sat at the patio table.

"Throw away whatever's in the bag," he muttered. "It doesn't matter."

I followed his instructions, and then I went to sit at the table. I'd had these conversations before with relatives of dementia patients, and they were never pleasant. They were, however, necessary and usually beneficial.

"I can't put her in a nursing home," Walt insisted. "She had asked me never to do that to her. I also can't stand to live with this any longer. She's not my Sheila anymore. It's killing me."

I folded my arms in front of me on the table and said, "I have a suggestion. You and Sheila have been blessed to have a lot more money than most people. Are there any other condos in the building that might be for sale? It wouldn't have to be large, since Sheila doesn't really know where she is most of the time. You could purchase the condo or rent one if you didn't want to buy, then have full-time caregivers stay with her. You could visit whenever you liked, but you wouldn't have to bear the brunt of the burden every moment as you do now."

I waited patiently while he thought about my idea. The tension in his shoulders seemed to lessen, and he leaned back in his chair.

"I – I think I could resign myself to that arrangement and not feel such guilt."

Walt seemed to become ten years younger as I watched the notion take root in his mind. He proceeded to ask me questions about full-time companions, and I reviewed the various types of care available. He hugged me when I left, which came as a total surprise. He also vowed to attend the support group meeting for partners of those with dementia as soon as possible. I believed him this time.

The following Monday, I went to see Adiba, who was eager to practice her English with me. She was doing much better at caring for her daughter. I liked the woman and enjoyed playing with the baby in-between instructing her mother. Adiba thanked me in English when I left for the day.

My lunch break consisted of "The Children's Hour" with Tom, who read me more nursery rhymes, fables, and folk tales. Again, he sang me the song about the old woman who swallowed a fly before I left. Then I headed to Al's.

"The opera was magnificent last week," Al told me in his thick Italian accent as he let me in through the gate. "I will take you soon since today's visit ends my Hearts at Home care, and there will be no conflict of interest. What do you think?"

Knowing that he wouldn't relent, I agreed and promised to attend whatever upcoming opera he chose for us to see.

"Promise me you will attend at least three operas with me. There is a performance of *zarzuelas* that is a special program in two weeks."

"*Zarzuelas*?"

"*Genero chico* or *genero grande*."

"The little genre or the big genre."

"You speak Spanish."

"I was raised bilingual."

"Excellent. You will enjoy the *zarzuelas*, then. They are Spanish operas rooted in musical theater. Since you speak Spanish, perhaps starting with that would be best. If you like it, we could try something more traditional like Puccini or Verdi. Our area has so many opportunities to attend the theater, opera, and ballet. You could come with me, my Diane, and Michael."

"That's right; your grandson is here."

"He is. I would very much like for you to meet him."

As we walked into the house, I asked Al questions about his physical therapy and overall health. I set my purse and satchel on a chair and allowed him to lead me to the kitchen, where he insisted on getting me a glass of a new fruit drink he'd "fallen in love with" over the weekend. Once I tasted it, I agreed that the drink was delicious.

We were reviewing his long-term, post-Hearts at Home goals when Al stopped mid-sentence, looked up, smiled, and said, "And here is my Michael! Michael, please come and meet Seneca Jones. She is my angel here in Florida."

I turned and rose from the chair to greet Al's grandson. Knowing that the man had been in the Navy for ten years, I'd expected a stern military type with buzzed hair and an emotionless expression. Instead, I saw before me a man with a gentle smile, olive-colored skin, black hair, and deep blue eyes. He was at least six feet tall and wore khaki shorts and a close-fitting shirt that conformed nicely to his muscular frame. I doubted there was an extra ounce of fat anywhere on his body. He exuded an aura of power and sexuality without apparently any effort whatsoever on his part. He moved languidly towards me, extending his hand.

"It's a pleasure to finally meet you, Miss Jones," Michael Benedetto said by way of introduction. "Thank you so much for helping my grandfather."

His voice was soft, low, and utterly masculine. It was the voice of a man who was totally in control of himself, knew what he wanted, and knew where he was headed. It somehow reminded me of the voice of the man in my lovely dream.

Quit romanticizing, I told myself. *He's a sexy guy. That's it. You've already established that there is no dream man, so stop gawking and talk.*

"Call me Seneca. As for helping your grandfather, it's been my pleasure. He's a joy to be around, and coordinating his P.T. has been an interesting process."

Michael grinned at his grandfather and said, "I can only imagine. I know how resistant he must have been in the beginning. If you hadn't been so persistent, he would have discontinued the P.T. altogether, which would have been a mistake."

We shook hands, and I had the distinct impression that the man's true essence was almost too great to be contained within his body. It was an odd thing to sense, but was something I'd never encountered in my life. His touch was virtually electric, and I had to fight to remind myself what we were discussing.

Looking to his grandson, Al said, "It is so good to have you home. Why do you not sit with me and Seneca and listen to our plans for my future now that I will no longer be her client?"

I had expected Michael to make his excuses at this point, but he poured himself a glass of the fruit drink, refilled our empty glasses, and then joined us at the table.

"You're great with Nonno," Michael told me as he escorted me to the gate half an hour later.

"Nonno?"

"It's Italian for grandfather. Nonnie is what you call a grandmother."

"Al is quite an unusual client. I typically oversee caregivers and their caseloads, but I have my own special clients like your grandfather." When Michael and I reached the gate, I asked, "Will you be staying with Al long?"

"Indefinitely. We're going into business together."

"Really. What kind of business?"

I easily pictured Michael running some sort of adventure tourism company. Since Al loved boats and Michael had been in the Navy, they could combine their interests into a potentially lucrative enterprise.

"We're starting an organization that will help veterans who've fallen on hard times get back on their feet. The Veterans Administration does a good job but not everyone can make the hour plus trip to Tampa to the nearest facility. The V.A. can't reach everyone and do everything. We want to provide assistance with vocational training or helping vets further their education, aiding those who are homeless, mentally ill as a result of service, or have become substance abusers. Physically disabled vets have special needs, too. Because of our veterans, those in the U.S. have the opportunity to be free. We owe these men and women a huge debt. I want to spread awareness and enlighten the average person. It's a big undertaking, but I think it's truly worthwhile."

I stared open-mouthed at him. His bemused smile turned into a grin and then into a chuckle. I exclaimed, "You're a bigger idealistic bleeding heart than I am!"

"See you later, Seneca."

Michael Benedetto was not at all what I'd expected. He seemed to be easy-going, provided pleasant conversation, had an unexpected career agenda, and was what I considered to be extremely attractive both physically and intellectually.

If only he could be the man from my lovely dream, I thought. *Who am I kidding? It was a dream, a subconscious wish for something I'll probably never have. That doesn't mean I can't enjoy spending time with Michael. After all, I have nothing to lose.*

Chapter Three

The next couple of weeks seemed to fly by. My friendship with Krystal grew as did her excitement over her steady weight loss. My work schedule was more hectic than ever. On top of everything else, Tom had been hospitalized with pleurisy.

I helped Walt Hummel rent one of the empty furnished condos in his building and move Sheila into it. It was emotionally traumatizing to him in the beginning, but he adjusted quickly once he saw that his wife was completely oblivious to the change in her surroundings and was being well cared for by the private duty nurses. I went with him to his first support group meeting, and he told me afterwards it had been a life-changing experience.

Adiba was blossoming into a self-confident mother. Her hesitation at learning English had all but vanished, and she was now speaking to her baby in Arabic and English so the child would grow up bilingual. Adiba and her husband were looking forward to the opening of the new Mosque in Sarasota. Yet, for all of her progress, she declared she still needed my help and guidance. So, I went.

Al was doing well post-Hearts at Home and was ecstatic to have his grandson living with him. He was thrilled with the new business venture and was totally beside himself when he talked of the upcoming opera I would be attending with him, Diane, and Michael.

As for the younger Benedetto, I hadn't had any contact with him since our initial meeting. I was hoping to see him when I dropped in to visit Al at the older man's request, but Michael wasn't home. I hid my disappointment.

"Michael is very organized and single-minded when he has a particular goal in mind," Al told me during that visit the Monday before our outing. "He has done much research and inherited my good business sense. His dream of making a difference person by person is thrilling to me. It makes me feel as if I have done a great job of raising him."

"You raised him?"

"His parents were killed in a subway accident when he was small. My wife and I raised him together until she passed from her heart attack. Then it was only me as the parent. Seeing how he has turned out gives me the feeling that I did all right. When my own children were growing up, I was involved, but not like that. I was working hard to make my business grow. I went to Mass, ball games, recitals, dinner with my family as often as I could, and those sorts of things. However, my wife was the one who did all of the day-to-day raising. With Michael, I got a new opportunity. I guess I am proud of both of us."

"You should be," I said firmly.

He thanked me for the compliment, and then he asked what was bothering me.

I felt my face flush and stammered, "I...I don't know what to wear to the opera. We live in Florida, and things can be pretty casual here. Do I wear a long dress, a cocktail dress, a sundress, or something like one would wear to church?"

"Do not worry my angel. I can tell you that Diane will wear a long gown and pearl or diamond jewelry."

I smiled ruefully and said, "The only long gown I've ever worn was for my prom. I have no pearls or diamonds, other than the little diamond stud earrings I wear at the tops of my earlobes. Somehow, I don't think those will count."

"I will get my Diane. She will help."

He called out for her before I could object, and she quickly appeared in the room. His lady friend might have been in her mid-seventies, but she looked ten years younger. She had dyed blonde hair and was adorned with exactly the right amount of makeup, jewelry, and perfume.

As Al explained my predicament, I groaned inwardly. Diane was tolerable, but she'd never been one of my favorite people. I could have done without her involvement – or so I thought.

Diane checked her watch and asked, "Are you going home after this, or do you have other appointments?"

"Home."

"All right. You and I are going to my house first."

"Oh, I couldn't," I protested.

"You must," she insisted, but there was a softness in her tone I'd never heard before during her previous conversations with me. "It wouldn't do for you to go to your first opera feeling uncomfortable. You want to appreciate the entire experience. Don't argue. Just come with me."

Although not quite as large as Al's home, Diane's place was more ornately decorated. Like Al's mansion, it sat along the water's edge. The woman led me to a closet larger than my living room that was filled from top to bottom with clothing, shoes, purses, and accessories. An oversized, full-length mirror was positioned in one corner.

"Where are those gowns?" Glancing back at me, Diane said, "I have several I purchased and haven't worn, yet. Maybe there's one you'll like, and we can have it tailored to fit you." Before I could comment, she pivoted and said, "Don't say a word. You and I may not be the best of friends, but we both want the best for Al. You let me do this for you whenever he asks you to go somewhere with us. Al is a great man, and we're good for each other in our old age. He's good for you, too. Are we clear?"

I fought the urge to say, "Yes, ma'am." Diane and I might have different approaches, but she was correct in her reasoning that we both wanted the same thing when it came to Al.

"What do you think of Michael?" I asked, as she sorted through one section of the closet.

"I truly like him. He's Al's pride and joy." Pulling out one gown, she said, "Hold out your arms so I can pass you some dresses. I see a few different selections here."

Although they were too long and loose for me, three of the five dresses were flattering and to my taste. Diane called her tailor, a tall, heavyset man who arrived at the house a short-time later, took my measurements, and made a few marks on the dresses with some chalk.

"That's all?" I asked, once the tailor accepted the final gown from me. "You don't have to use pins or something?"

The man rolled his eyes at me. Mentally, I transformed into a four-year-old wearing worn shorts with frayed edging and a faded pink shirt my mother had gotten from the thrift shop. My tennis shoes had been bought at a garage sale. My hair was falling out of its ponytail, and I was hot and dusty from playing in the field behind the trailers.

"I expect these back day after tomorrow," Diane sternly told the man. "Come at six-thirty."

Once the tailor had gone, Diane leveled her gaze at me and ordered, "Stop feeling inadequate. It doesn't become you. I saw the way you reacted to that look my tailor gave you. I'm certain it's the same look I had on my face when I was your age." Crossing her arms over her chest, she said, "You and I are very different, but we're also very much alike. You remind me of me fifty years ago – a pretty woman with above-average intelligence who came from a below-average upbringing. I was motivated, respected, and had a history of feeling insecure about my background. I discovered, as I'm sure you already have, that the only way to surmount a childhood spent in poverty is to constantly work on bettering oneself. I worked hard at it, and it paid off. I built a supremely successful business conglomerate involving freighters, cruise ships, and all sorts of boats in-between."

"Boats?"

"My father was a fisherman. I learned about boats from him and built upon that knowledge in order to make millions. I met my husband through a meeting about venture capital, and we had five years together before I lost him to kidney failure that resulted from diabetes."

"Why are you so interested in suddenly sharing your personal life with me?"

"For the majority of my life, I allowed old insecurities to shadow me. Don't waste your days running from who you are. Embrace everything about yourself and build on it."

I left Diane's with a new respect for the woman and returned two days later to try on the altered gowns. I was amazed that they fit as if they'd been made for me. I'd never worn such expensive, beautiful formalwear. As I studied my reflection in the mirror, I felt like Cinderella sans the glass slippers.

"Shoes," I said aloud. "I forgot about the shoes."

"You and I are going shoe shopping right this second, but we're not leaving this room. I bought several different styles of shoes I envisioned would match with each of your gowns. I didn't know your shoe size, so I bought multiple sizes for each style. I'll return what doesn't work."

Diane's fashion sense was unquestionable, and I quickly had a pair of shoes to wear with each evening dress.

"Now, for the rest," she announced. "You'll come to the salon with me and have them arrange your hair and do your nails."

"I can do that myself," I informed her. "My mother worked as a hair stylist and did manicures and pedicures."

"And I'm sure she did a beautiful job on her clients. She obviously taught you well, because your hair is done nicely, no matter how you wear it. Your make-up is simple, but flawless. You do a lovely job of your nails, too.

"Regardless, I want you to join me and grant someone else the privilege of doing your hair, make-up, and nails. Allow yourself the luxury of being pampered. A massage wouldn't be a bad idea either. You need to let yourself feel like a woman and be treated as such. Respect the possibilities and help someone else earn a living."

She's like a fairy godmother with attitude, I thought.

"Meet me here at one. We'll go to the salon, then come back to dress before dinner."

"Dinner?"

Diane muttered, "So much like me that it's scary, I tell you." Looking up from her jewelry box, she said, "Dinner usually precedes the opera. The entire evening is a grand affair, especially for Al. His mother loved opera and raised him on a musical diet of the great composers. He knows more about opera than any man I've ever met. It's a passion for him, and the whole night will revolve around getting the most out of the before, during, and the after. Learn from it."

"Do you even like opera?"

"I like Al, so I like opera," she confided. "I myself prefer ballet." Focusing on me, she asked, "Have you been to the ballet?"

"I saw a professional production of *Swan Lake* when I was thirteen."

"How did your family manage that?"

"They didn't. I took ballet for eight years through a deal my mother worked out with the local ballet school director. She gave her free haircuts, pedicures, facials, and manicures in exchange for my lessons."

"Were you good?"

"I was the star pupil of the school."

"Did you find joy in dancing?"

"Yes."

"So, why did you stop?"

I didn't want to talk about my dancing or why I'd stopped, but Diane was like a bloodhound on a scent trail once she latched onto a line of questioning.

"The director had retired to Florida from Houston. She still had connections to the Houston Ballet and took me there for an audition. I was invited to join the Junior Company. While we were there, she took me to see *Swan Lake*."

"Why didn't you join the Junior Company? Being asked is a great honor, especially for one so young and from a rural area."

"My family didn't have the means for me to go, and they couldn't survive without my help on the farms when I wasn't in school or taking dancing lessons."

"What did you do on the farms?"

"It depended on the season."

Diane merely nodded. She understood that no one cared about child labor laws or working conditions or living hand to mouth. She had done it herself. People did what they had to and were thankful when there was food on the table and a roof over their heads.

"Certainly you could afford to see ballets as an adult," she prompted.

"I could, but I don't want to. Once I turned down the invitation to join the Junior Company, I never wanted to see another ballet. Just the thought of it made me sad."

Again, she merely nodded. I wondered what childhood dreams she'd had to let go of during her younger days.

"I do still love to dance," I hastened to say. "I go out dancing with friends and have a great time doing it. I just don't do ballet."

"Maybe someday."

"Maybe."

During the night, I woke, calling out for my mother. I was in a panic and turned over to bury my face in the pillow before I began to cry. I reached over and lifted the Cookie Monster doll from the bedside table where he'd remained since my nightmare three weeks earlier. Drawing him to me, I sobbed into the pillow and wished more than anything that I could have my mother's arms wrapped around me. I wanted to talk to her, to hear her voice, to smell her skin, and to listen to her tell me I was the prettiest, smartest, and sweetest girl in the world. I missed hearing her say it and being able to say back that I loved her and that no one could ask for a better mother.

I eventually quieted and lay in my bed, remembering our preparations for my senior prom. My mother had already been told by her doctor that she had pancreatic cancer and would not live long, but she'd kept that news from me until after my high school graduation. Looking back on that time period, I marveled at how my mother had been able to disguise her true state of mind and body.

It had taken us weeks of going through clearance racks to find an attractive prom dress in my size that fit our twenty-dollar budget. The deep purple gown was long, sleeveless, and had a sweetheart neckline and flared skirt. I was lucky enough to locate a pair of black patent leather pumps for five dollars and a black patent evening purse for two dollars at Goodwill. My mother borrowed some sparkly costume jewelry from a friend of hers so that I had a matching set of earrings and necklace.

The afternoon of the prom, she cut and styled my hair in a trendy up-do then gave me a manicure and pedicure before applying my make-up. I carefully put on the dress so that nothing was smeared or knocked out of place. I donned the earrings and necklace before stepping into my shoes and getting my little evening purse.

A neighbor who owned a camera had come over to our trailer to take pictures before we started the transformation. The woman came back periodically and snapped candid photos of me and my mother throughout the process and then of me standing alone when I was completely ready. Once my date arrived, the neighbor was called back to take pictures as my boyfriend slipped the wrist corsage on and as I pinned the boutonnière to the lapel of his suit.

We left laughing and had a wonderful night at the school gym eating, dancing, and being goofy teenagers. Afterwards, we'd gone to a couple of parties where the kids were drinking heavily, but neither of us was into getting drunk. We wound up at a nearby park, sat on a bench by the river, and talked about our respective futures before kissing for what seemed like an eternity. I was home by two a.m. and regaled my mother with stories of my exciting evening until almost dawn. She drank in every word.

How wonderful and heartbreaking for her. She had to be thinking how lucky she was to be there for my prom but also how she'd never see me graduate from college, get married, or have children.

Little had my mother known I'd accidentally become pregnant the first time I had sex and would be married less than three months after her death. I'd lost the baby a few months into the pregnancy and divorced my husband. I'd desperately wished she'd been around to offer me her support.

Maybe you wouldn't have had sex if you hadn't been so alone after Mommy died, I told myself. *I wonder how many other girls get pregnant the same night they lose their virginity.*

I got out of bed, slipped into my robe, and went to the living room to pull out my scrapbook. Switching on the lamp, I curled up in a chair and opened the cover. On the first page was the typical baby picture given to new parents before they leave the hospital plus a paper that displayed the imprints of my tiny newborn feet.

On the next page, there was a photo taken at a church Christmas party. I was four and was sitting on Santa's lap. My mother, who was short, pudgy, and black-haired, and my father, who was tall, sturdy, and black-haired, stood on either side of the chair. My diminutive maternal grandparents stood beside my mother, and my paternal uncle stood beside my father. It was the only picture I had of those family members I'd known as a child.

On the following pages were snapshots of my Cookie Monster birthday party. I smiled as I studied the images of the children playing in the little pool, the homemade cake with its five candles, and of me holding my doll.

I flipped the page and stared at a professional photo taken of me in ballerina mode. I was Giselle, wearing a costume provided by my instructor. She had paid for the costume and photo session, so the pictures could be included in my submission to the Houston Ballet. Tears clouded my eyes, and I quickly turned the pages that held the pictures of Giselle/Seneca in various poses.

The next series of pages showcased the pictures related to my senior prom. My dying mother appeared healthy and radiant in the photos, and it made me surprisingly happy to take my time examining each one.

The final page of the scrapbook had a picture of me in my cap and gown taken for the high school yearbook. My sense of accomplishment was evident in my expression. My smile was genuine. I had no idea that my mother would be dead in a few weeks.

I liked to think that both of my parents would be proud of me. I had graduated as valedictorian of my high school class and with high honors from college and had gotten my Master of Social Work degree a year and a half later. I had a good job that I was good at, and I owned my own home. I drove a nice car and had nice friends, although I didn't see many of them as often as I'd like. I had money in savings and lived comfortably. I had achieved what they'd only imagined.

So, why can't I move on?

I slipped the scrapbook back into the bookcase and returned to bed. I dreamed of nothing except fluffy clouds and rainbows and woke wondering what was wrong with me. I lay in bed for a long time and attempted to talk myself into contacting a therapist. I failed.

Typically early, I was five minutes late for the Saturday Less of You meeting. I skulked in and sat beside Krystal. After apologizing for being late, I asked her how she'd done during her weigh-in that week.

"I lost another two pounds," Krystal whispered back. "That brings me to eight pounds lighter."

I congratulated her and then we both ceased talking for the remainder of the meeting. When awards were given out, Krystal beamed as she got a gold star and a round of applause to acknowledge her efforts. As everyone rose to go, a blonde man about our age came over to us and congratulated Krystal on a job well done. He was a little taller than we were and looked trim and fit. Krystal blushed and thanked him.

"I'm Greg and have been doing this for a few years. It's inspiring to see someone new who's so enthusiastic about getting healthy."

"I'm loving it," Krystal admitted. "I'm so thankful to Seneca for being my weight-loss buddy."

"You can never have too many of those. A friend kept me motivated during the weeks when the scale wasn't going the way I would've liked."

"If you don't mind sharing, how much weight did you lose?" I asked, knowing he'd be proud to tell us.

"A hundred and fifty-five pounds."

"There's no way you could've weighed that much!" exclaimed Krystal.

"Yes, way. It took me almost four years, but I did it. I've kept it off for six years. It's like I'm a different person now that I'm not carrying around the weight of another human being."

I could tell Greg and Krystal were attracted to each other, so I made my apologies before heading to my car. If Greg turned out to be a nice guy, he would be great for my new friend. I could only pray he was sincere and that Krystal wouldn't hop into bed with him at a moment's notice in hopes of keeping him interested.

Diane and I went to the salon after lunch. We were given massages, facials, waxing, manicures, pedicures, and had our hair arranged in classic styles that would complement our eveningwear. A make-up artist provided the final service for the salon. I had never been so pampered by others in my entire life. It was relaxing and invigorating at the same time. I guesstimated that our afternoon had cost Diane four to five hundred dollars apiece, although there was no way to be certain without being gauche and requesting a price sheet. I couldn't imagine spending that kind of money on such things every week, but then it was difficult for me to conceive of having that much disposable income, period.

We returned to Diane's. The dress I'd selected for that night's adventure was a long-sleeved black sequined gown with a V neck and fitted waist. It wasn't flashy, but the sequins gave the dress a slightly playful look. It exuded femininity without being demure. It made me feel powerful.

Diane surprised me by wearing an ivory gown that had straight, simple lines and a lace jacket. The dress was sleeveless and no-nonsense. After seeing most of the gowns in her closet, I had expected a more elaborate outfit for our excursion.

The doorbell rang. A chauffeur stood on the top step. As Diane and I came out through the front, Michael and Al exited the limousine and stood beside it. Both were wearing black tuxedoes and well-shined black shoes. Al appeared very dapper, but it was the sight of Michael that took my breath away. He looked more amazingly sexy than any man I'd ever seen.

Diane was walking ahead of me, and Al gave her a kiss before taking her hand as she stepped into the back of the limo. Then he turned to me and said something with great flourish in Italian. Michael said something in Italian to his grandfather then extended his hand to me as he remarked, "Nonno says the sight of you has caused him to forget how to speak in English for the moment. He says you look beautiful, and I wholeheartedly agree."

I thanked both men in Italian as I climbed into the limo. Once they were seated with Al beside Diane and Michael beside me, Al said, "You did not tell me you spoke Italian."

"I don't, but I do speak Spanish, remember? *Gracias* and *grazie* are pretty similar."

"Very true," he said appreciatively. "Perhaps you could learn Italian from me and Michael. I raised him to speak the language, and then he has picked up other languages during his years in the military."

When I asked Michael what other languages he spoke, he answered, "Greek, Croatian, and several Arab dialects."

I smiled and thought of Tom. I had no way of knowing if Michael had actually been part of Naval Intelligence, but I suspected he had. Michael and Tom could talk about their military experiences in a language none of us could understand and not feel compromised. Tom would be ecstatic.

After a delicious dinner at Fleming's Steakhouse, we headed for the opera. The beauty of the Sarasota Opera House was beyond anything I'd imagined. I felt as if we'd been transported back in time. Al, Diane, Michael, and I shared a balcony to the right of the stage. It provided the perfect vantage point in order for us to see all of the action and yet be close to the performance itself. As I took my seat next to Michael, I wondered idly how much Al's season tickets cost, although I certainly didn't begrudge him his attendance. He was supporting the arts and gaining great personal satisfaction with each opera he viewed.

Michael continued to be a perfect gentleman as we waited for the opera to start. He was good company, but he seemed to be holding back in some way when it came to me. I didn't want to throw myself at him, but I did want more from him than simply good company. Perhaps it wasn't meant to be. Maybe he liked me but not in a romantic or sexual way.

I looked at the slick cover of the program. It read *El barberillo de Lavapies*. I scanned the synopsis of the plot and waited. Soon, the lights dimmed, and the action began. For the duration of the performance I was enthralled by the costumes, the singing, and the story. The production was well-executed, and it was nice that I could understand what the characters were saying as they sang. I speculated as to whether or not I would enjoy a performance in a language I didn't know.

When the lights came up, Al turned to me and asked, "So, what did you think?"

"I loved the entire experience. I was glad I could understand it all though. How do you appreciate something if you don't speak the language?"

"You will tell me after the next opera, for it certainly will not be in Spanish. We were fortunate to have this *zarzuela* being performed this season. It is the first time I have seen one."

I was shocked. I'd assumed that Al, being an opera aficionado, would have seen every opera ever composed. I wondered how many there were.

"Now we will go out for coffee and dessert," Al announced. "It will be a lovely end to a lovely evening."

As we rode back to Diane's house later, Michael said casually, "You know I was wondering something, Seneca. Are you Spanish or Hispanic? You obviously speak the language fluently. You're definitely not Asian or Scandinavian or Indian." When I laughed at his selection of ethnicities, he went on, "Your surname is Jones, but your first name isn't a typical Celtic, Welsh, or English name. It's not Hispanic or Spanish either. So, what *are* you?"

"A woman of mystery." With a shrug, I admitted, "Actually, I have no idea."

"But how is that possible?" Diane queried. "Everyone has some idea of where they came from."

"Not me. My father's grandfather was apparently a well-educated man who liked to gamble, was a great marksman, and had a huge stubborn streak. His troubles with the law drove him out West. He died in the late 1800s.

"For whatever reason, his son saw his father's education as his downfall and dropped out of school early. He legally changed his name from whatever it was to Jones, was an itinerant farmhand, and worked on farms his whole life. He basically told my father and uncle that education was a waste of time and pushed them to drop out of school and work on farms with him. He refused to tell them what their actual surname was or where he'd been born, so my father never knew the truth."

"And your mother?" Diane asked.

"She was left at a church as a newborn and was adopted by a nice Hispanic couple. So, she had no idea who her parents were or where they came from."

"How tragic," Al said soberly. "To have no connection with one's family heritage is a sad thing."

I stared at the mansions as we passed and thought, *No, to have no family is the sad thing.*

"And your name?" Al prompted. "Where did that come from?"

"My grandfather picked Jones because it was such a common name. He told my father and my uncle once that it was a lot better to be every man than to be the son of a brilliant, good-for-nothing gunfighter with a bad reputation."

"And Seneca?" Diane asked with interest.

"My mother told me she'd read the name in a magazine article and thought it pretty and unusual. She said the moment I was born she took one look at me and felt I was destined to be pretty and unusual and decided to name me Seneca."

"Was it because of her that you learned Spanish?" asked Michael.

"That and the fact that I grew up in the midst of a large migrant community. I know this may come as a shock to you, but there are lots of Spanish-speaking people working as tomato pickers and such," I said wryly. "On the farms and in the groves, Spanish tends to be the primary language. Both of my parents were fluent, and I was raised speaking English and Spanish. It's been very useful being bilingual."

When we arrived back at Diane's home, Michael and Al exited the limo first. Al extended a hand to Diane, while Michael did the same for me. I felt a tingle run up my fingers, hand, and arm as I took it and stepped out of the vehicle. As the older couple made their way towards the front door, Michael made no move to follow but said simply, "I enjoyed tonight."

"Me, too. The food, the opera, and the company were exceptional."

"I couldn't agree more. Do you have plans for tomorrow?"

"Sleeping late is on my list. I'll visit a good friend I see almost every day, but I won't go over to his place until lunchtime. Maybe you could join us and then we could hang out somewhere afterwards."

"I'd like that. Where should we meet?"

"Are you okay with going straight to Tom's if I give you his address?"

"Sure. What should I wear?"

"I'm wearing shorts and a casual shirt. He's a really good friend. You'll like him."

He grinned and nodded before lifting my right hand with his left and kissing it. My brain went fuzzy, and I was momentarily at a loss for words. Finally, I managed to say, "I'll get a piece of paper and write down the address."

"No need. I have an eidetic memory."

"Oh, right." I gave him the address then said, "Is 1:00 good for you? I'm going to make a Sunday dinner. Tom loves to eat but never eats enough."

"He'll be all right with me just showing up?"

"It'll be great. Tom is always thrilled to see me."

Michael intertwined his fingers with mine and leaned closer before saying in a husky voice, "So am I, and I've only seen you twice."

I wanted to kiss him so badly, but my mind overrode this irrational urge and reminded my body that I barely knew this man and should take things slowly. My body rebelled and all but demanded it be satisfied in some way. I lifted my chin and put my mouth close to his left ear before saying, "Good night, Michael Benedetto. Sweet dreams." Then I kissed him lightly on the jaw and stepped back.

The intensity of *him* made me weak in the knees. I could feel the sexuality radiating in waves towards me. I realized I was in deep, deep trouble, as he said nothing, but lightly took my elbow and led me to Diane's open front door. When we reached the top step, he tightened his hold ever so slightly, causing me to pause and turn towards him. He lowered his lips to my left ear and whispered, "Sweet dreams, Seneca Jones." Then I felt his mouth on my neck. It moved downwards until it reached the base of my throat.

As Michael took a step away from me, Al emerged from the house and thanked me again for accepting his invitation and talked of our next operatic adventure. I found my voice and thanked him again for everything then bid both men a good night before retreating into the house. I was already wishing it were 1:00 on Sunday afternoon.

Chapter Four

Tom sat at the kitchen table and gave me his full attention as I recounted the previous day's activities while I cooked. I answered his occasional question or remarked on any comments he made, but I was doing most of the talking. It almost seemed like I was a kid again, telling my father or mother about something that had happened at school. It made me feel good.

"What a spectacular day," Tom said as I finished my explanation. "I'm so pleased for you. You deserve to have more days like that." He paused then continued, "And you really like this Michael Benedetto. I can't wait to meet him, although he'd better pass muster if he's interested in courting you."

"Courting? I don't think people court each other in today's society."

"Well, they should. He should. I won't see you treated with any less respect."

"I'm a grown woman. I can take care of myself."

"Yes and no."

I was about to ask him to elucidate when there was a knock on the front door of the house. Tom insisted on answering it, struggled up from his chair, and slowly made his way out of the kitchen. As I stirred the contents of a pot, I listened as he opened the door. There was a very long pause, and then he and Michael exchanged introductions before Tom led Michael back to where I was standing in front of the stove. As Michael and I greeted one another, I felt the electric charge that seemed to surround him at all times.

Unlike Tom, who was wearing long pants and a Polo shirt, I was dressed in khaki shorts and a bright pink knit top. Michael wore knee-length, dark brown shorts and a close-fitting blue t-shirt. It was certainly different from the tuxedo he'd worn the previous night, but I thought he looked extremely sexy both ways.

I suggested that the men get comfortable in the living room while I finished preparing our lunch. At first, they spoke in English.

Tom was pleasant enough but was firing off questions at a rapid rate. Michael responded courteously but held his own with no effort. This obviously impressed Tom, who suddenly switched from speaking English to what sounded like Arabic. The two of them carried on quite a long conversation while I took my time cooking. For better or for worse, I wanted Tom and Michael to become well-acquainted. Not only did I value Tom's opinion, I also wanted the two men to like one another. I wasn't certain what I'd do if they didn't.

When I could delay things no longer, I called out that the meal was ready. Once they returned to the kitchen, I instructed both men to take a seat then prepared their bowls and plates, telling them there was more if they wanted.

"What's on the menu today?" Tom asked, as I put his food in front of him. "It looks deliciously bad for me."

"Yes and no," I said, eliciting a smile from him. "The soup is called *Churpe de Camarones*, which is shrimp chowder. Then there's shredded chicken in a creamy yellow pepper sauce over potatoes called *Aji de Gallina*. On the side you have marinated tomatoes with cheese."

He thanked me for my culinary efforts, as did Michael once his bowl and plate were in front of him. I took my place at the table before realizing I hadn't gotten anyone's drinks.

"I'll get them," Michael insisted. "What would you like?"

"There's a container of *Chicha Morada* I brought with me," I told him. "Tom and I both love the drink, but you may not care for it. It's made of Peruvian purple corn and tastes sweet, spicy, and fruity all at the same time. I have to limit Tom's intake or else he overdoes it and drinks it all at once."

"I'm always up for new experiences. I'll definitely try it."

We ate, drank, and chatted about past and present politics. Both men had second helpings of everything and highly praised the quality of the meal. I thanked them as I rose and insisted on clearing the table while Tom took his medications.

"She's a spectacular cook!" Tom said enthusiastically. "I get a treat every Sunday that tastes great and isn't always healthy for me. The rest of the week she's a real taskmaster and fusses if I eat too much sugar or salt or anything else I really like. I have to sneak in candy bars here and there just to survive!"

Michael laughed and asked me, "Are you this strict with all your friends?"

"Only those whose doctors tell them they can't eat whatever they please without shortening their lives."

Tom said something in Arabic that sounded sarcastic to me, but Michael merely sobered and nodded. He said something in response, and Tom nodded back.

"You two can't use my inability to speak Arabic in order to make fun of me while keeping me ignorant," I protested. "That wouldn't be fair."

"I would never in a million, trillion years make fun of you," Tom said indignantly.

Michael echoed Tom's sentiment. Standing, he announced he would clean the kitchen and suggested I relax with Tom. I objected but not too strenuously. Tom and I went out onto the back porch and sat on the swing while Michael began the clean-up.

"He appears to be a keeper," Tom said quietly. "Reminds me of myself when I was his age, although I don't know if he's quite the romantic I was."

"You're still a romantic," I pointed out.

"Too true."

"Tom?"

"Yes, my lovely Seneca?"

"Was he a spy?"

"That's not for me to say. He'll tell you what you need to know if you two continue to get on well."

"Can I trust him?"

"I thought you were a grown woman who could take care of herself."

"I can. Sometimes I don't want to, but I don't have any other choice."

"You can trust him implicitly. Even though he barely knows you, that young man would die for you. He would die for me, and we've only become friends today."

I was relieved to hear Tom say he thought of himself and Michael as friends and that he approved of the man. I knew he would give me his honest opinion if he disliked Al's grandson or mistrusted him or his motives.

"I'd like to spend more time with your Mister Benedetto. We have a lot in common."

"Invite him to visit," I proposed. "He doesn't only have to come when I'm here. He's starting a new business, so I have no clue as to what his schedule might be. Work something out."

"I believe I will. It's nice to have someone I can really talk to, someone who understands what my old life was like. I haven't had that in a long time. Well, not face-to-face."

From this commentary I deduced that Mister Benedetto had been in Naval Intelligence. It would be beneficial for Tom to have someone like him to speak openly with and to stimulate his memory. Perhaps it would keep his mind a little sharper and slow the mental deterioration.

Michael soon emerged from the sliding door. The three of us spent the next hour talking on the back porch. Tom began to look tired, and I suggested we move inside to the living room. Once there, Tom lowered himself into the recliner and requested the large children's book. Michael looked confused.

"It's storytime," I told him. "We've been filling in the gaps in my childhood education. We read a story or some nursery rhymes each time I visit."

After he'd completed reading "The Three Billy Goats Gruff" to us, Tom announced, "I think I'm ready for a rest. Thank you for your company and the wonderful meal, Seneca. It was delicious, as always. And thank you so much for coming, Michael. I would appreciate further contact with you."

Michael said, "Thank you, sir. I'd like that, too. If you'd give me your phone number, then I can call you and drop by off and on. It's good to have someone I can actually talk to about certain things."

"Understood."

Tom rattled off his phone number, and Michael repeated it back to him before the two of us prepared to leave. We stepped out through the side door of the house shortly after four.

"I'd like to spend some more time with you today, unless you're too tired from yesterday, "Michael said.

"No, I feel great."

"Good. What do you want to do?"

I knew what I wanted to do, but I wasn't about to do it. Not yet. I needed to get to know Michael a lot better before I went any further with emotional involvement and physical entanglements.

"How about the beach?" I suggested.

"Sure. I always carry a pair of swim trunks, a towel and water shoes in my vehicle."

"Swim? Honestly? The water's still freezing!"

"When do you normally go in?"

"The end of May, unless it's unusually warm."

"That's only two weeks from now."

"Two weeks makes a world of difference. I was thinking we could sit on the beach behind my house and talk."

"Talking would be nice. You want to give me your address, so I can plug it into my GPS?"

"My house is sort of set back. Maybe you should just follow me in your car." I glanced at the curb then corrected, "Your SUV."

Michael drove behind me from Tom's to my house and parked outside of the garage when we arrived. As I emerged from my car, I noticed him scanning the area with what looked like approval. I bit my lip in order to hide a self-satisfied smile. As the garage door automatically closed, I asked him whether or not he thought his GPS would have been able to locate my house without difficulty.

"Probably, but that long driveway and the way this place is tucked away might have thrown it off." As he studied the house and the deliberate plantings, he said, "This is amazing. Have you lived here long?"

"I bought it a couple of years ago."

As we walked through the front door, he said, "Either you make a fantastic salary or your family has money."

"Neither. Something good came out of something bad."

"There you go again with that woman of mystery thing."

"You're a man of mystery. Two can play that game."

He was oddly silent, and I hoped I hadn't offended him. I gave him the tour of the house and ended with the lanai. He was obviously taken with the whole place, but the view of the beach and flora along the sides seemed to surprise him.

"You're really, really lucky to have found a place like this."

"That's an understatement. I know how fortunate I am to have all this for my very own."

"For my very own" was a phrase Tom liked to use whenever he spoke of things near and dear to his heart. I realized I had subconsciously picked up the expression and used it here and there when I spoke. I enjoyed the quaintness of the phrase.

"Why don't you have a seat while I grab a few things? Then we can go sit near the water."

When I returned a few minutes later with a picnic basket, two towels, and wearing gray sweatpants, a lightweight, long-sleeved, purple top, and flip flops, Michael grinned and asked, "Anticipating a cold snap?"

"The wind makes it chilly near the water in the evenings right now," I protested with an exaggerated pout. "Maybe *some* people can handle cold better than me, but they certainly don't have my cuteness or talents."

"I'd have to agree with you there."

Blushing, I went on, "If you don't mind getting those two folding chairs that are stacked in the corner, I'll carry the basket and towels."

"I can carry all of it if you like."

Michael easily carried the wooden chairs with their fabric coverings plus the basket, while I carried the towels. I wasn't quite certain why I'd brought those. I supposed I was so used to going out to sit on a towel that it had become second-nature.

He set the chairs a few feet away from the water's edge and put the basket beside one of them. I put the towels down between the two chairs; then we took our seats.

"What do you want to know?" Michael asked suddenly.

"What do you mean?"

"I'm a man of mystery. What do you want to know?"

I shrugged and said, "What do you want to tell me?"

"Everything, but that's impossible."

"Tell me what you can then. I've heard the spy speech from Tom before, so don't worry about any of that." I hesitated before adding, "Unless you're going to tell me you weren't in Naval Intelligence and so none of it's even an issue."

He reflected on this while I got out two glasses and a bottle of wine. After I'd poured us each a glass, he began by saying, "Nonno and Nonnie were my parents for all intents and purposes. They were great at raising me. When my Nonnie died, it was devastating for me and for my grandfather. In the end, it actually brought the two of us closer together."

"Did you play sports growing up?" I asked, as I removed a box of multi-grain crackers, a Ziploc bag filled with Laughing Cow cheese, and a freshly rinsed bunch of grapes from the picnic basket. I placed these items on the top towel between us and opened the box of crackers before saying, "Perhaps you were part of the Glee Club instead."

"Chess club," he corrected. "Although I did sing at Mass in the choir on Sundays. As for sports, I played baseball and took karate. I was on the Honor Roll, was an Eagle Scout, and tutored other kids after school twice a week. I was valedictorian of my senior class."

"Your typical overachiever."

"It takes one to know one," he shot back.

"There was no chess club at my school."

"But...?"

"I was president of the Book Club, was the president and valedictorian of my senior class, and worked with 4-H." After taking another sip of my wine, I asked, "What did you do after high school?"

"I was a dual enrollment student, so when I graduated from high school, I already had my associate's degree. I finished my last two years of college at Princeton, then got my M.B.A. from Harvard. A week later, I joined the Navy. My parents had been Naval officers, and I had this notion that I should honor their service to their country in some notable way now that I was out of school."

"How long did you serve?"

"Close to ten years. I loved it, although I wasn't your typical military man."

"So, why'd you leave it?"

Michael ate some cheese and crackers and sipped his wine before saying, "It was time for me to move on to something else."

"Meaning you can't tell me. It's okay." I ate a few grapes before asking, "Have you ever been married?"

"Never. You?"

I nodded and offered, "I was eighteen and had recently lost my mother to cancer. My father had been dead for four years. There was this guy –"

"You don't have to tell me everything either," Michael interrupted.

And I never will, I thought.

What I said was, "I'd like for you to know this. I'm a pretty private person, and I don't share a lot of intimate details with others."

"But you want to share with me?"

"Yes."

He nodded and asked for the wine bottle before pouring himself another glass. I refused his offer to top off mine.

"So, this guy in my English class had lost both parents to cancer earlier that year. We already liked one another, and when we found out our mutual connection regarding the effects of cancer on our family lives, our bond grew stronger. We were talking in my dorm room one night, and we…well, it just happened. Neither of us had ever…you know…and we weren't ready. I got pregnant that first time, and we decided we should get married for the baby's sake. I lost the baby four months into the pregnancy, but we tried to make our marriage work. We divorced before we started our sophomore year. I never saw him again, although I think of him once in a while, especially on our anniversary. I hope he's happy wherever he is. He was a nice person."

"But you didn't love him."

"I've never loved anyone, not in that way. You?"

"My career didn't lend itself to relationships, but that wasn't the only thing."

We watched the waves for quite some time before I asked, "What do you want, Michael?"

"You."

Although hearing him say this thrilled me, I laughed and said, "You don't even know me."

"I know enough. I know that I'm attracted to you all the way around. The first time I saw you I wanted you more than I've ever wanted any woman, and I've met lots of women all over the world."

"How many have you slept with?"

"Three." I must have given him a dubious look because he said, "Not all men are pigs, Seneca. Sex is great, but it's not great if it's just for sexual gratification. How many men have you slept with?"

I looked out across the vast expanse of water and said, "Only the one. I've dated other guys, but sex for me is such an intimate thing."

"As it should be," he said quietly. "I think it should *mean* something."

"So, what do you propose?"

"That we get to know each other better and decide how much we like each other. Maybe we're completely incompatible. I don't know. What I do know is that you're the first woman I've really wanted to try this with, so I'm thinking that's an excellent sign."

"I feel the same, but I'm kind of scared about the whole thing."

"You're only scared? I'm terrified."

I giggled, since he sounded anything but terrified. I figured that was the effect he'd been aiming for, and it had worked.

"Tell me about your childhood," Michael prompted. "I know what you said about your questionable ethnicity and your name, but what kind of a childhood did you have? Were you a happy little girl?"

My throat tightened, and I swallowed hard. Michael took my hand and opened his mouth to speak, but I shook my head and stopped him.

"There were happy moments. I loved my parents, and they loved me," I finally managed to say. "They loved each other but had a very volatile marriage. They divorced when I was fourteen."

"What were their professions?"

"My father was a farm worker, and my mother was a hair stylist. We lived in poverty for my entire childhood. My parents weren't...."

I struggled with verbalizing the truth. I knew it would sound bad if I said what I knew I should.

"They weren't as intelligent as you," Michael said matter-of-factly.

"They were always so proud that I did well in school. Neither of them had finished high school. They were both very hard workers, but it was never enough."

"You said your mom died of cancer when you were eighteen. Did your dad have cancer, too?"

I looked away and said, "No. I don't want to talk about that, Michael."

"Then we won't."

In an attempt to change the direction of our conversation, I asked, "You said you sang at Mass when you were younger. Are you Catholic? Do you go to church?"

"I went with Nonno when I lived at home, but I personally don't believe God has a denomination. You?"

"My parents were Christians. Church was never my cup of tea. For me, God is in everything around us and inside of us. Each person has to decide what God means to him or her and go with it."

"I like that. It's a good explanation of what I've felt most of my life."

I withdrew my hand from his and ate some more cheese and crackers before announcing I was going back to the house for some water. The sun would be setting soon, and I did always love a good sunset. I didn't want to miss one when I had the opportunity.

"Do you mind if I swim?" Michael asked. "I'll get my stuff out of the SUV and change while you're inside. I can put my dry clothes back on afterwards."

"Brrr. It's fine with me, and there's no one else around to care. We're completely isolated here. So, be my guest."

I made a trip to the bathroom, got two bottles of water out of the fridge, and headed back for the lanai. The moment I opened the door, I stopped. I thought my heart would stop, too.

From his position near the edge of the beach, Michael was unaware that I was standing in the doorway to the house. He slipped off his shirt and placed it on one of the chairs. He then undid his belt buckle, unbuttoned the top button on his shorts, and then unzipped them. Once those were placed next to the shirt, he took off his black boxers. I watched as he pulled on his swim trunks, slipped on his water shoes, then walked into the water and began to swim.

The image of Michaels naked body lingered in the forefront of my brain. His muscles were well-defined but not overly so. His butt was not flat but not too rounded either. And the glimpse I'd had of his....

You need to be very careful or else you know what's going to happen. Then where will you be? What if he is really like the man from your dream and you have sex with him too soon and ruin everything?

45

Sighing, I made my way down to where our chairs were set up and took the same seat. I was so engrossed in watching Michael's powerful body as he swam that I forgot about looking at the sunset.

He continued to swim as the stars came out, and I wondered how he could enjoy being in the cold, dark waters. I had never been in the Gulf after sunset even when the waters were warmer. I didn't like not being able to see what was around me in the depths.

I handed him a towel when he emerged, and he dried off quickly and reached for his clothing. As close as we stood, he smelled of salt water and looked like a dripping Adonis. The physical ache in me was strong and continual.

"Let's bring the chairs and basket back, and you can shower before getting dressed," I suggested. "Are you hungry?"

"I'm fine. You?"

"I'm craving hot chocolate. You want some?"

I tried not to think of Michael Benedetto showering in my bathroom as I got out the hot chocolate mix, milk, and mugs. It was pointless. I would be showering in there the next morning and knew what would be in store for me then.

Michael came into the kitchen clean, dressed, and carrying the Target bag I'd given him to hold his swim trunks and water shoes. He placed the bag on the floor near the table as I stirred steaming 2% milk into a mug filled with hot chocolate mix.

"Will you let me help you with something?" he asked. "You never want to let anyone do anything when you're around."

"I'm used to taking care of things," I answered.

"So am I. We're going to have to trade off on this control issue if we plan on making it work between us. I've been deferring to you out of courtesy, but I can't do it forever. It goes against my nature. We need to have some balance when it comes to who's in charge."

"I don't know how," I said truthfully.

"Just tell me you'll work with me on figuring it out. That's all I need to hear."

"I'll do my best. I did allow you to clean up at Tom's," I reminded him.

"I don't want you to *allow* me to do anything. I want things to be a team effort. Would you want me to *allow* you to do something?"

"Definitely not."

As we took our seats at the kitchen table, Michael asked, "How long have you had the Siamese fighting fish?"

"About six months."

"And his name is…?"

"Doc."

"As in Bugs Bunny?"

"As in Doc Holliday."

"Interesting. An extremely intelligent gambling man and excellent marksman who died in the late 1800s. Kind of sounds like your description of your great-grandfather. Do you think Doc Holliday was your mysterious relative?"

"I doubt it, but there are a lot of similarities. I'd say it was highly unlikely but possible."

"So, why name the fish Doc?"

"Since Siamese fighting fish are tenacious and known for their tempers so to speak, I figured it was a fitting name. After all, Doc was a very hot-headed man who wouldn't stop until he got what he was after."

"Very apropos."

Michael washed our mugs and the spoon I'd used to stir the mix. I showed great restraint and did not leap from my chair and insist on taking over. I merely thanked him, and he replied with a proper, "You're very welcome."

We'd barely taken our seats on the couch when Michael turned towards me, cupped my face in his hands, and kissed me passionately. A low groan came from somewhere deep within his chest, as he slid one hand down the side of my neck and the other behind my head. I wrapped my arms around his waist, let out a soft moan, and pressed my chest against his. He shifted his weight, and I moved my legs until his hips were tucked between my thighs. I could feel him hard and ready between the layers of clothing that separated us. I was hot, throbbing, and wet and would have easily offered him what I'd offered no other man besides my ex-husband.

So much for taking it slowly, I thought through a haze of arousal. *We should stop.*

But I didn't want to stop. I wanted to grant him the privilege of entering my body with his and to give him the gift of surrounding that part of him with the primitive essence of my inner self.

"Michael, we –"

"Can't," he agreed, although he didn't move away. "I know. God, I want to make love to you so badly, but it's too soon. I –"

He stilled as I rubbed against him. Then he took me by the shoulders and declared that we were *not* going to have sex. When I conceded that it would be too early and added that we had no protection against pregnancy, he pulled back. When it looked like he wanted to disengage himself from me, I tightened my hold and shook my head.

"What is it? What's wrong?"

"Pregnancy's not an issue."

"What in the world are you talking about? When people have sex pregnancy's always an issue."

"Not for me."

He looked wary, and it made me uneasy. I told him softly that if he wanted me to trust him then he had to trust me. I kissed him lightly on the lips and encouraged him to share whatever was bothering him.

"I can't father any children." Averting his eyes, he said, "I should have told you right away. I'm sorry. I didn't want you to lose interest immediately. I swear I would have said something once I knew you were really serious."

"Michael, look at how we're positioned. I haven't let any man get this close to me since I was nineteen. How much more proof do you need that I'm serious? And you really think I'd lose interest because you can't have kids?"

"Seneca, most women want children. If they know right from the get-go that a man can't provide them with that, then they move on."

"Shallow, stupid, selfish women might move on. Real women don't think like that."

"How do you think?"

"I think that if I want children there are other options. Do you want kids?"

"Yes. Do you?"

"Sometimes. The thought of having kids scares me because I don't want my children to grow up in a house with parents who fight all the time and not have enough food or clothes and –"

"You and I are different from your parents."

"I'm still afraid."

Michael shushed me then kissed me again. He began to move his hips so that his erection was rubbing against the juncture between my legs. I pushed hard against his chest with both hands, which did get his attention. He paused.

"What are you doing?" I asked, my heart hammering in my chest. "If you keep this up, we'll be naked in minutes."

"I have more self-control than you give me credit for."

"More than I do, obviously."

We separated and sat slightly apart from one another on the couch. I rose and got each of us a glass of cool water then took a seat on the chair beside the sofa and tucked my feet underneath me as we drank. Once the glasses were empty, I asked, "What's next?"

"How about dinner tomorrow night?" he proposed. "We could eat and talk. Maybe if we were in a public place we wouldn't be as apt to end up like we did tonight."

"I'd hope not. I doubt if the patrons or staff at any restaurant would appreciate that."

"Where do you want to meet?"

"How about the restaurant at Holmes Beach? We could eat, talk, and then take a walk and watch the sunset together."

"Sounds good. What time do you want to meet?"

"6:00?"

"6:00 it is."

He stood and returned to my kitchen to retrieve the bag that held his swim trunks and water shoes. We exchanged cell phone numbers. Then, I escorted him to the front door. We kissed one more time before he wished me a good night and walked to his SUV. Once he started the engine, I shut the door and went to bed.

Sleep proved elusive. Not only did I continue to feel tingly all over, but I also couldn't stop thinking about the conversations I'd had with Michael. There was so much we didn't know about each other, but it appeared that we both wanted to overcome our natural reticence regarding exposing our vulnerabilities. I reminded myself that if we added up all the time we'd spent together, it wouldn't equal a full twenty-four hours, but I already couldn't conceive of a future without him in my world.

And speaking of conceiving, how did I really feel about his admission of sterility? If he'd never been married or had a serious long-term relationship, then how did he know he couldn't produce children?

The military, I thought. *If one applied for some sort of Special Forces then the Navy probably tested everything regarding each candidate before making selections for high security programs and positions. To those in charge, it may have been a huge plus that Michael couldn't get any girl pregnant. One less thing to worry about with a spy.*

But how did I really feel about it? Did I want children? If Michael and I actually ended up together, then would I want to have a biological child with some donor? Perhaps a member of his large family would be happy to contribute. Or would adoption be preferable? There were so many children out there who needed good homes. I chastised myself for reflecting on such things when the simple thought of spending my life with another human being terrified me.

I'd made a mistake by marrying my first husband for the wrong reason. I didn't want to rush into anything with Michael, no matter how I felt about him. I was only twenty-seven, and he was probably thirty-one. We had plenty of time.

"You'll know when you meet your soul mate," my mother had told me once when I'd been about sixteen. "You'll sense it."

"But what if I don't find him?" I had asked. "You still haven't found yours."

She'd given me a hug and said, "Your Poppy and I were soul mates."

"But you fought all the time until you got divorced."

"Because neither of us was willing to bend. I always had to be right, and he always had to be right. It made us both wrong."

I fell asleep pondering her words. Sage commentary from a poor, hard-working hair stylist who had never graduated from high school. What a shame that people dismissed those who didn't measure up to their standards. The way I saw it, those judgmental people were the losers.

Chapter Five

Krystal appeared in my office Monday morning. She was glowing and gushing about Greg and how he was such a gentleman and hadn't even asked her for sex. I congratulated her and listened as she quickly reviewed her lunch with him after the meeting and then her acceptance of his invitation to the movies. They had another date scheduled for the coming weekend.

"He says he's old-fashioned and wants to get to know me and treat me right," she confided. "When he says he thinks I'm pretty and nice, I feel like he's telling me the truth. I've never gotten that feeling from any other guy I dated. I hope he's for real."

"I do, too. Keep me posted, and I'll keep my fingers crossed for you. He sounds genuine."

"He does, doesn't he? He'd better not break my heart."

"He'd better not or he'll have to contend with me," I said with exaggerated bravado that made her laugh. "See you at the picnic table out back for lunch!"

"How was the salon, dinner, and the opera?" Krystal asked once we sat at the table with our food. "Tell me all about it."

I told Krystal everything – excluding certain details like Michael's possible former occupation as a spy, his confession of sterility, my unexpected view of his naked body, and our near-sex experience. The rest of my tale was enough to keep her hanging on every word. When I finished, our lunch hour was almost over.

"And you're going to see him tonight?" she asked, as we cleared the table. "It sounds as though the two of you are serious about this." I nodded, but she frowned and asked, "Why do you look so worried? From what you've said, you were made for each other!"

"That's why I'm worried." I checked my watch and said, "We'd better get back."

"No, this is more important. Seneca, what is it? You can tell me."

It struck me then. The reason I trusted Krystal was because she reminded me of my mother. Their coloring and features might be different, but both were utterly giving and sincere and gave good advice although they didn't always take it themselves.

"I have a hard time letting people into my personal life. You're one of the few exceptions." My eyes welled with tears as I said, "What if I can't completely open up to Michael or if I do and then he throws what I've shared back in my face? I don't want to be alone forever, but at least when you're alone, you know what to expect."

"You have to try this. Maybe you'll get married –"

"I was married very young. It didn't work out."

"Maybe this time it will. You and Michael will get married and eventually get pregnant –"

"I was pregnant. That didn't work out either."

"Maybe next time it will."

"Or maybe I'll make another mistake: have a bad marriage like my parents, get divorced again, have no children, and die alone."

She squared her shoulders and said, "You gave me the encouragement to take a chance and be the person I really was inside. Now it's my turn to do the same for you."

I wiped at my tears and said, "I know you're right, but I'm so afraid."

"You think it's easy for me to trust Greg after all the men who've used me? Growing up in a family that treated me like I was less than them because of my size didn't make it any easier. Like you, I want to be happy. So, I have to take a chance on Greg and hope he's not a jerk who's playing around with me. You have to hope the same with Michael, but you can't play around with him either, or you might lose him."

Some co-workers emerged from the back door with their lunches, and Krystal and I threw our trash in the garbage can and went back inside. I thanked her for the advice and her friendship before returning to my desk. Then I put aside my personal concerns and did my job.

I called Tom at four to check on him.

"Your young man and I had lunch together today," he informed me. "We went to the Woody River Roo, and I had a wonderful meal of fish and chips and took all of my medications. Then he took me to the building he's purchased for this business venture of his. He asked me to work with him on developing some of the programs. I told him it would be an honor."

I was totally surprised by all of this news, but I was also tremendously pleased. I could hear the determination and confidence in Tom's voice, but most of all, the return of satisfaction at having great purpose in his life.

"He's quite taken with you," Tom said cheerfully. "I certainly hope you like him, because I think he'd be good to you and for you. He says you're meeting him tonight. Let him into your heart, dear girl. I may be an old man with four ex-wives and children who don't ever think about me, but I know a few things about life. I know what I did wrong, and what's right. You and this fellow are right for each other, so make it work. Don't end up old and alone like me. Carpe diem! Have fun tonight, and I'll see you tomorrow."

At 5:00, I went into the restroom and changed out of my work clothes into a pale green top, a long, flowing, white cotton skirt, and flip flops. After pulling my hair back into a ponytail, I touched up my lipstick and headed for the café at Holmes Beach.

Michael was already there, wearing long khaki shorts, a white Oxford shirt that had the sleeves rolled up to his forearms, and flip flops. He exuded such self-confidence that every woman who passed by was glancing admiringly in his direction. He seemed oblivious to this, and I wondered if he was simply used to it or if he was actually totally unaware.

He smiled when he saw me smiling at him. Taking my hand, Michael led me through the breezeway that ran beside the gift shop and out onto the side of the building that faced the beach. We walked up to the window where the orders were placed and money was exchanged. I ordered a turkey club sandwich and he asked for a cheeseburger with fries. We took our bottles of water and the long silver stand that had our order number on it to one of the outdoor plastic tables, placed it in the center, and then took our seats. Within five minutes we had our food. Neither of us spoke much as we ate, although Michael did ask me if I wanted some of his french fries and I accepted a few.

Once we'd finished eating, Michael said, "I spent a good part of the day with Tom. He's one remarkable man. I asked him to work with me, and he was eager to accept." Pausing, he added, "He's not well at all, is he?"

"This is his fourth bout with pleurisy since I've known him, and he has other challenges with his failing health." Looking up at some seagulls, I added, "His mind is starting to fail, too. It's hard for me to watch but harder for him because he knows it's worsening."

"He said he has four children. Where are they? I saw their pictures all over his house, but I didn't hear him say any of them were coming to see him anytime soon or that any had been here recently."

"The daughter he was closest to was killed in a car accident before I met Tom. The remaining girl talks to him on the phone once in a while, but the sons never call. None of them has come to see him since I've known him. From what he says, he was close to the children when they were small."

"What changed?"

I shrugged and said, "His absences from the family took their toll? They grew apart? His ex-wives poisoned the children's minds against him? He's never really shared any explanation with me. It makes him cry when he tries to talk about that."

"What you described happens to a lot of military families when the parents are away for long periods. No matter what caused it, it's too bad. He's a living treasure." After I had agreed, he added, "He loves you, you know? He thinks of you as his daughter as well as a friend."

"I feel a lot like his daughter. It's a privilege to be able to spend time with him, especially since my father's been gone for so long."

"What was your father like?"

"Strong as an ox. He had black hair and brown eyes like I do and was loving and caring with me. I worked with him on the farms from the time I was little. When the electricity hadn't been cut off, we'd watch whatever was on TV together. He liked to tell me stories about his life growing up on farms, and I used to enjoy those whether they were happy or sad. They were good stories."

"What was his name?"

"Robert Jones."

And your mother? What was she like?"

"Kind of short and pudgy, no matter how little she ate. She had black hair and brown eyes, too. She was the most selfless person, and she did everything she could to make my childhood happy despite our lack of…everything. Our tiny trailer was always spotless, because she took pride in what few things we had."

"And her name was…?"

"Christina Rosa Gonzalez Jones."

"They were good parents?"

"Individually. Together, they were a disaster. They fought all the time even though they loved each other as much as they loved me. When they did that, then I think they were bad parents. They should have divorced when I was a lot younger or, better yet, they never should've gotten married no matter how passionate they were about each other." Staring pointedly at Michael, I asked, "How were your parents?"

"They were strict, no-nonsense types."

"What were their names?"

"Giuseppe and Melissa."

"What did they do in the Navy?"

"They were in Communications. I'm sorry they died, but I'm also thankful that Nonno and Nonnie raised me. I think I had a much happier childhood with them than I would have had with my own parents." Rising, he asked, "You want to walk along the beach for a while?"

I slipped off my flip flops and carried them in my right hand as we walked towards the water. Michael took my left hand in his right, and we wandered along the water's edge at a snail's pace as the time passed. We were quite a distance down the beach when we stopped to watch the sun set. The wind was strong, and I shivered as the stars came out.

"You're cold," Michael noted. He immediately unbuttoned his shirt and took it off before draping it around my shoulders and saying, "See if that helps to make you warmer."

I wasn't about to tell him that it was helping to make me hot. Now that I was wearing his shirt, I had the pleasure of seeing his bare torso once again. I forgot about the cool breeze, the cool water, and the beauty of the night sky. All I could see was Michael Benedetto's muscular chest and arms and his toned belly.

"Do you want to look at the place we bought for our project?" he asked with anticipation in his voice.

"I'd love to. Where is it?"

"Downtown Sarasota."

I followed his SUV to the large three-story building that housed his new business. The sign outside read *John's Place: A Place of Honor for Veterans and Their Families.* It had a fair amount of parking on all sides. The exterior was in good shape and was painted a tan color with white trim. As we stepped out of our respective vehicles, I slipped his shirt off and passed it back to him with my thanks. He put the shirt on but neglected to button it and withdrew a digital key from his wallet. He slid it through the keypad next to the entrance, and the door lock clicked open.

As we stepped inside, I could hear the beeping of an alarm system. Michael punched in a code, and the door lock clicked again and the alarm reset itself. Then he reached over and flipped on the lights.

I had expected an empty shell of a building that needed carpet, interior paint, furniture, and all of the other things that would be required to make the space functional. Instead, the inside of the building appeared to be completely finished and furnished. As we walked through the first floor, Michael showed me the lobby and downstairs offices as well as the physical therapy area. We took the elevator to the second floor, which housed the educational advancement division, computer lab, more offices, and a small library. The third floor was comprised of two meeting rooms, a conference room, an art therapy area, and areas devoted to mental health services.

I wanted to ask Michael about the name of his business. Who was John, and why was this place named after him? However, I sensed that now was not the time and decided to ask some other questions instead.

"When did you do all of this?" I asked as we stood looking at the downtown skyline out of one of the windows in the conference room. "Didn't you just move here a couple of weeks ago?"

"Yes, but Nonno and I have been talking about this since I knew I was leaving the military. That was a year ago. I gave him a detailed business plan, and he handled the legalities involved in starting this enterprise, including finding and purchasing this building. The company that was slated to use it went under right before it was scheduled to open. All of their furnishings were sold to go towards their debt, but the structure and parking lot were completely finished. All it needed was a little construction on that one half of the first floor for the physical therapy area. The rest was perfect for our needs. We got it for a steal, since it's such a buyer's market at the moment."

"Who's funding all of this? Al?"

"He's made a sizable investment, which is tax-deductible since this is a nonprofit organization. The rest of the money is coming from grants, donations, and some state and federal funding."

"It's wonderful. How long have you been planning on doing something like this?"

"Since my first deployment in Iraq. I saw firsthand what men and women were sacrificing for their country and knew that I owed it to every one of them and those who came before and after to make a difference to all veterans. I spent years formulating and refining my vision. I did a lot of research. I talked to people in all branches of the military about what was needed, what was feasible, and what could be accomplished. I know we can't help everyone, but being able to help as many vets as possible will make a huge difference for them and their families. I also want to remind civilians about what they owe to those who've served their country by being in the military."

"That's very admirable."

"It's what's right."

"Not enough people do what's right anymore."

"You want to see my office? It's the one place I haven't taken you, yet."

I had expected Michael's office to be huge and have nice, big windows. Instead, the room was located in the center of the building on the top floor. It was about sixteen feet by sixteen feet and was furnished with a mahogany desk, a leather desk chair, a mahogany filing cabinet, two chairs that faced the desk, and a bookcase that filled one wall. A framed oversized print of a Frida Kahlo painting hung behind the desk.

"*Roots*," I said with interest.

"What?"

"The Kahlo painting. It's called *Roots*."

I stared at the self-portrait of Frida lying prone in a long, orange dress with her long, black hair falling loosely around her and the vines that grew out of her body. There were no thorns extending from the vines, only leaves and flowers. A stony landscape was the backdrop beneath and behind her.

"A very close friend mailed me that print for my birthday a week before he was killed in action," Michael told me. "I never understood why he picked that as a gift, and he died before I could ask him about it."

"Not too long ago the original garnered the highest amount for any Latin American painting ever auctioned."

"You follow the art world?"

"Not really. I like portrait paintings and surrealist artists. Frida Kahlo did both. I like her work, and I've read her biographies and saw a movie about her life. She was quite a woman.

"This is one of the few self-portraits where she actually looks happy. She's nourishing the earth, not taking from it. She had an extremely strong personality. If she'd been weak, she wouldn't have survived."

"Survived what?"

"Parents who fought all the time. Polio as a child. A terrible bus wreck that broke most of her body when she was a young woman. A tumultuous love life. Her inability to successfully carry a baby to term because of the damage done by a steel pole that went through her during the bus accident. Surgery after surgery. Constant pain. And still she kept painting and living. Although she died fairly young by today's standards, she was quite determined."

Michael looked at the print with what seemed to be new appreciation for the work. He asked me for the names of the books I'd read so he could read them, too. He said he wanted to watch the movie afterwards and told me that what I'd explained made it clear as to why his friend had chosen to give him the print, although he didn't share that with me. I wondered if he couldn't or wouldn't.

His arms were suddenly around my shoulders and his mouth pressed against mine. I put my hands on his chest and touched warm flesh since his shirt had remained unbuttoned. I felt one of his hands move up to my ponytail and gently tug at the elastic cord until my hair was released. Then he wove his fingers into the loose strands, as I slipped mine up into his hair and deepened the kiss.

I rubbed my palms across his naked torso and enjoyed the definition of his muscles and the feel of his nipples before sliding my arms around his waist. He moved his mouth to the nape of my neck and murmured, "We're not going to have sex, Seneca. When we do go to bed together, I want it to be *in* a bed, not on a desk, in a chair, or on a floor. That can come later."

"But I want you to touch me now."

"I can touch you and not have sex with you," he said with a twinkle in his blue eyes. "I'll show you."

I opened my mouth to protest, to point out that my resolve was not as strong as his, but his tongue blocked my words. His hands moved from my hair to either side of my neck and then down to the buttons at the front of my shirt. He deftly undid them and pulled my arms away from his waist so that he could remove the garment and toss it onto one of the chairs in front of the desk. He then unhooked my bra and tossed it onto the chair with my blouse before taking a step back.

My breathing was rapid, and my face was flushed. There was a smoldering sexual energy that he was containing somehow, even as his eyes roamed over my exposed flesh. I blushed as he took his time and allowed his gaze to wander from my face to my neck then to my shoulders and arms and finally to my bare breast and belly. My nipples were hard with a combination of excitement and the coolness of the air in the room.

"You're so beautiful," he said with what sounded like awe in his voice. Coming close to me again, he placed his left hand on my back and cupped one breast in his right before repeating, "So beautiful."

"Make love to me," I whispered. "I want you in me."

"Not yet."

"But being this close to you without making love to you is torturous."

"This is nothing like torture. Take it from one who knows."

I wrapped a hand around the wrist that was cupping my breast and asked, "You were tortured?"

"Others have had worse."

"Michael –"

"I don't want to think about anything just now except how beautiful you are and how soft your skin is and how much I want you, body and soul."

I was about to tell him that I wanted him in the same way but found myself unable to speak as he lowered his mouth to my left

59

nipple and slid his free hand down my belly and then around my waist. After a moment, he stopped sucking and straightened. Pulling me tightly against him, he actually lifted me up until I was sitting on the edge of his desk. As he moved his mouth to my neck, Michael slid both hands to my knees then gathered the material of my skirt and pushed it up until he was able to wedge himself between my thighs without interference from my clothing. He then returned his mouth to mine and rubbed what was very obviously the head of his erection between my legs. My fingers were back in his hair, and my body was pulsating with waves of longing.

"We have to stop," I feebly protested. "I'm going to come if we don't."

"Come then. There's no one around to hear you."

He tucked me closer to him and increased the friction between us. I tightened my fingers in his hair and cried out his name as I gave in to the first orgasm I'd had in eight years. My panties were soaked with my own wetness, and I reached down and slid my fingers under the thin elastic band at the top. I wanted to push them off so I could take Michael inside of me.

"No."

I already knew him well enough to know that he wouldn't give in once he'd made up his mind. That didn't stop me from reaching for his belt. He grabbed my hand and held it as he proceeded to draw his tongue along my collarbone. He kissed me again then announced, "We have to leave."

"W-why?"

"Because I've hit my limit. It was reckless of me to bring you here alone. I don't want to stop."

"What do you want then?"

"At this moment? I want to pull off your skirt, rip off your panties, and strip before making love to you all night all over this office. That wouldn't be right, and I so want to do this right. I think we've already stretched our boundaries with what we've done yesterday and today, but I find it difficult to cease and desist where you're concerned." Looking plaintively at me, he said, "I don't know you; I don't understand you; but I already love you." Shaking his head, he swore and admitted, "I'm so overwhelmed by you that I can hardly think straight most of the time."

"It's comforting to know that someone else is in the same boat I am when it comes to you and me and whatever it is we're doing or not doing together."

He sighed and handed me back my bra and blouse before suggesting, "Why don't we take a few days to regroup then go out on a date this Friday? Didn't you say you usually go with friends for dinner and dancing each week?"

"I do. A break might help us not…push our boundaries quite so much."

"Okay, here's the plan. Dinner and dancing on Friday night, then we have the opera coming up with Nonno and Diane on Saturday. Then we'll see."

As I hooked my bra and slipped on my shirt, I said, "Deal."

"I'd still like to talk to you at night, if that's all right."

"That'd be great. You can catch me up on this place and Tom and tell me lovely things besides."

"Like what a wonderful woman you are and how I feel when I'm around you?"

"Exactly."

"Only as long as this is a mutual appreciation society."

The man of my dreams, I thought. *Maybe he really does exist in this man.*

I could only hope and pray I wasn't wrong and that I had the strength to allow myself to love and to trust.

Chapter Six

Michael met me at the front doors of Ceviche that Friday night at seven. He was wearing tan pants, a black shirt, and black shoes and looked amazingly sexy as always. I had chosen to wear a pair of cute but comfortable brown sandals and a sleeveless orange dress that reached my calves and flared at the hem. When he complimented me on my outfit, I told him truthfully that I loved to dance in that particular dress because of the way the material flowed with my movements. He nodded, and then said I looked like Frida Kahlo in the print that hung in his office. I smiled and thanked him before leading him upstairs.

I introduced Michael to "The Gang," a group of friends who habitually gravitated to the restaurant and bar at the end of each work week to unwind, vent, eat, drink, and dance. The Gang included social workers, physical therapists, administrative staff, occupational therapists, and nurses. We were part of a haphazardly formed network of dedicated people whose membership fluctuated at times but whose core group stayed the same.

"He is *hot*, girlfriend!" was the prevailing comment I heard from my female friends throughout the evening when Michael was out of earshot. Even my male friends told me he was "quite a guy" and expressed their approval. I was pleased at their ready acceptance of him and the fact that he seemed to enjoy their company as much as I did. I was also thrilled to discover that he was an excellent dancer.

As the evening wore on and members of The Gang began to drift home, Michael and I sat at one of the rooftop tables and continued to talk. He updated me on the rapid progress of his developing business, his contacts with Tom, and Al's decision to take a trip to Sicily in the near future. I talked about my hectic work week and my concern about attending *La Traviata*, the opera we were scheduled to see the next evening.

"I don't speak Italian," I reminded him. "How will I appreciate something I can't understand?"

"There'll be a synopsis in the program," Michael reminded me. "Just think of it like ballet except with singing in a foreign language. You get the story with the ballet even though no one talks, right?"

I stared at the glass of water in front of me. Michael lifted my chin and asked me why I suddenly appeared so downcast. At first I wasn't going to say anything, but once I began explaining about my years of ballet training and then my inability to pursue my dream of dancing professionally, I couldn't stop talking. To make matters worse, I started to cry. Michael dabbed at my cheeks with a paper napkin and told me it was okay and to cry all I wanted, which made me cry harder.

Michael escorted me out of the restaurant then led me to a deserted area down the street where there was a bench. He sat beside me while I wept. All the while, he kept me in his protective embrace, occasionally offering me some of the small paper napkins he'd taken with us when we'd left Ceviche.

"I'm here," he murmured. "You're not alone."

"I'm used to being alone, and our whole lives before now have been so completely different. You come from money; I come from poverty. You had the benefit of a good home life; I didn't. We don't know if we like the same things or have the same sense of humor or are going to agree on what we want out of the future."

"I don't care. I want to try to have a relationship with you."

The tears stopped flowing, but neither of us moved. I enjoyed the feel of his chest under my cheek and his powerful arms holding me. It was the first time we'd come into physical contact that I didn't want to drop to the ground and have sex with him on the spot.

"How about if I drive you home, then I can get you in the morning and we can come back for your car?" he suggested.

"I can't. I need to go to Tom's and then meet Krystal at the Less of You meeting before I head to Diane's."

He stroked my hair and kissed the top of my head before proposing, "How about this? I'll take you home and then pick you up early and go with you to Tom's. You can take my SUV to your meeting, and I'll stay and talk with Tom while you're gone. Then you come back for me, and we'll drive here to get your car. Then you go to Diane's. Nonno and I will pick the two of you up like we did last time."

"I'm sure you have a lot to do before tomorrow evening and –"

"And I'll work on it tonight. You're more important to me than anything, Seneca."

I laughed. I couldn't help myself.

"What's so funny?" he asked with a combination of perplexity and irritation.

"No one's ever said that to me except my mother."

"That's a damn shame."

"It's reality. I haven't been truly important to anyone since Mommy died."

He looked as if I'd slapped him, and I instantly wondered what I'd said wrong.

"Not important to anyone," he repeated slowly. He muttered something in Arabic before continuing, "Look around you. I've just told you that you're more important to me than anything else in this world, and you didn't even hear it. Tom loves you like a daughter, and Nonno practically wants to adopt you. All of the clients you help…your friend Krystal…your other co-workers…all of the people we just spent the evening with…and even your fish…." He sighed before declaring, "You're obviously important to everyone who knows you except yourself. What happened that –"

I fought to extricate myself from his embrace as I simultaneously demanded, "Stop! I am *so* not going there." Standing, I ordered, "Leave it alone, Michael Benedetto. You can't talk about your secret missions? Well, there are things I can't talk about either."

"That's different."

"Not to me."

I expected him to argue, but he merely sat contemplatively as I stood resolute before him. Eventually, he got to his feet and said, "All right."

His reaction threw me emotionally off balance. I was briefly consumed by anxiety and concentrated on remaining composed. The sensation passed, but my heart continued to race for a short time afterwards.

"I'm going to drive you home," Michael said, as he put an arm around my shoulders and directed me back towards the parking area. "What time do you want me to be at your house in the morning?"

"I was going to leave at 7:00."

"Then I'll be there at 7:00, and we'll follow the plan."

I opened the door to my house at midnight, downed a glass of wine, and went straight to bed dressed, still wearing my make-up and jewelry. It was something I had never done in my life, and I woke feeling grimy at 5:30 the next morning. I stripped the sheets and put on fresh ones before stripping off my clothes in order to shower and prepare to leave. I was ready and dressed in jeans and a black tank top just before 7:00.

When I opened the door and saw Michael, I felt guilty. He wore rumpled shorts and a faded Navy t-shirt and looked tired and tense. I imagined he'd stayed up most of the night working because of his altered plans for the morning. When I offered my apologies for causing a disruption in his life, he told me, "If I look tired it's because I didn't sleep at all last night, and it had nothing to do with work. It had to do with you. I couldn't stop thinking about what you said when we were at the bench."

"You've been stressing and wide-awake all night because I made you worry?"

"I've actually gone for days without sleep, although I wouldn't recommend it. I'll catch a nap later this afternoon and be fine for tonight. Right now, I just want to go with you to Tom's and enjoy my time with him and you."

We rode in silence all the way to Tom's house. I simply couldn't think of anything to say, and I assumed that Michael was in a similar predicament. I began to wonder if our relationship was over before it had even really begun. I was caught in the conundrum of being afraid to be alone for the rest of my life and being afraid to be with Michael for the rest of my life.

Once we arrived at our destination, everything changed. Tom was in a fabulous mood and seemed to feel wonderful. Both Michael and I instantly relaxed and sat with him in the living room and chatted for an hour before the older man announced that he had a surprise in store for me before we began storytime. He slowly rose and went into the bedroom area of the house. Michael looked questioningly at me, and I shrugged.

Tom returned to the room holding a thin box that measured about eight inches by ten inches. The box had seen better days. It was covered in something like red velvet but appeared worn and faded. A shiny iridescent bow had been stuck to the top. He handed the gift to me with the words, "For you, my dear."

I had no idea what to expect. I carefully lifted the front of the box. The top was attached to the bottom by a hinge of some sort. There were four items inside – a necklace, a pair of earrings, and a ring. All of the pieces of jewelry appeared to be made of platinum that was in good shape but needed to be polished. A sapphire and diamond pendant hung on the necklace. The earrings matched the pendant, as did the ring. The entire set looked antique.

"Tom, I can't accept this."

"Poppycock." As he rocked slightly back and forth in his recliner, he said, "I want to tell you a story today instead of reading you one." Looking at Michael, he asked, "Is that okay with you, Michael?"

"Yes, sir."

"Good. You know I never talk about my military work with those who weren't…similarly employed. This morning, I'm making an exception." Directing his gaze at me, he began, "Here's how it goes. I'm in Turkey on a job, and I save the lives of a very wealthy, important man and his young daughter. His wife had been assassinated the year before by militants, and their little girl was the most precious thing he had. Well, that's what he told me anyway, and I have no reason to doubt him." Closing his eyes, Tom said, "I can still picture both of them so clearly. The man was tall, strong, and highly intelligent. The child was about three and had some sort of mental retardation issue. She had a sweet soul, and her father, who was an extremely hardened man, was unfailingly gentle with her." Opening his eyes, Tom said, "After I prevented their murders, the father came to me and said he wanted to give me something of his wife's out of gratitude. I thought this odd and told him he owed me nothing; I was simply doing my job. He insisted and produced this box. He asked me not to open it but said I should present it to a woman who would someday save my life with her kindnesses just as his wife had done for him. I didn't understand at the time, and I've kept the box all these years without looking inside. I put it away when I moved here and forgot about it until I stumbled across it last night. Once I found it, I immediately knew to whom it belonged."

"Tom –"

"Accept the gift, my lovely girl. Let the old romantic fool have his way for once."

I stared at the jewelry and asked, "So, you never looked in the box for all these years?"

"No. Four decades have gone by. You mind if I see what's inside now?"

"Oh." Passing him the box, I stammered, "I – I don't know what to say."

"I'm thanking you for your unending kindnesses, so you should say 'you're welcome.'"

I swallowed the lump in my throat and said, "You're welcome."

Tom smiled and glanced from the contents of the box to me and back again. He nodded with satisfaction and asked if I'd mind trying on the jewelry so he could see me wearing it. I excused myself to go to the guest bathroom where I removed my bottom earrings. I cleaned the hooks of the platinum earrings with some rubbing alcohol then put them on. I slipped the ring on my right ring finger and was surprised to find that it fit. Then I put on the necklace and looked at myself in the mirror. Although the articles definitely needed to be cleaned, the simple elegance of the jewelry was breathtaking.

"This would go perfectly with the dress I'm wearing to the opera tonight," I said, as I walked back into the living room.

"You look stunning," Tom observed. "This was meant for you all along."

"Very fitting," was Michael's initial comment. "You look more beautiful than ever."

I blushed and said, "Thank you to both of you. I wish I had time to get it all cleaned."

"I'll take care of that," Michael remarked. "I'm sure Nonno knows someone who can have it done in a very short time."

"That would be splendid!" Tom exclaimed. "Then you can take a picture of her in the dress with the jewelry on so I can see it."

"I have a better idea," Michael said. "How about if you come with us? I'm sure we could get an extra ticket."

"I appreciate that, Michael, but I get very tired lately if I'm out for too long. I have to lie down early for the night or my old body gives me hell for days."

Michael nodded, but I could tell that his mind was working on some alternate plan. Despite the brevity of our "relationship," I was beginning to quickly and correctly assess his moods and reactions to things. Once an idea got lodged in his brain, he wouldn't rest until he'd worked out the best possible solution. I recognized that same tendency in myself and smiled slightly.

When it came time for me to leave in order to meet Krystal, I removed the sapphire jewelry and put my silver hoops back on. I hugged Tom, and Michael escorted me to his SUV and handed me the key before kissing me and telling me to be safe. Once I recovered from the kiss, I promised I would do my best and would return in an hour and a half.

When I arrived at the Less of You meeting, Krystal was in her usual spot. Greg sat beside her. I greeted both of them, and we chatted about our weekly challenges and triumphs before the leader began her presentation. Afterwards, the couple left hand-in-hand for their lunch and the movie theater. I was very happy that things appeared to be working out for Krystal and Greg and prayed that they continued to be good for each other.

When I arrived back at Tom's, I parked the SUV and went to the side door. I was about to knock, but I could hear the men talking and hesitated. They were speaking in Arabic, and whatever they were discussing seemed extremely serious and urgent. I debated about whether or not I should sit on the step and wait for a while in order to let them continue their conversation, but then I checked my watch and noted that there really wasn't any time to spare. I knocked out of politeness and waited.

Michael came to the door and informed me he and Tom had ordered pizza, which had been delivered not long before I'd arrived. This answered my unspoken question about what we were doing for lunch.

"One vegetarian and one supreme," Tom told me, as we moved to the kitchen table. "You know which one I want. I don't care if the pepperoni is terrible for my blood pressure. I'm eating it."

I laughed and said, "You know I'm going to be good and have the vegetarian."

"I'm having some of both," interjected Michael. "What would you two like to drink?"

After our meal, Michael and I said our goodbyes to Tom and headed for Sarasota to pick up my car. On the way, Michael outlined a plan that would allow Tom to see me dressed up and wearing the jewelry he'd given me. I thought his idea was perfect and told him so before thanking him for picking me up, taking me to Tom's, lending me his SUV, and having the jewelry cleaned. Before I got out of the vehicle, I leaned over and kissed him but didn't linger. I knew what would be in store for both of us if we stayed in close physical contact for long.

My afternoon at the salon with Diane was a repeat of our previous visit. It was enjoyable, but I decided I wouldn't want weekly salon treatments, especially with the high cost involved. A massage once a week wouldn't be bad, but I speculated that to sit for hours and go through the rest of the process would become tiresome.

I had instructed the hair stylist to leave most of my hair down and to pull back the front and secure it with combs that were unobtrusively placed towards the base of my skull. The dress I was wearing that evening was white, strapless, had a gathered bodice and a straight skirt – sort of. The material of the skirt folded over in the front on the left side so that it separated somewhat when I walked, making a slit. I could show as much or as little of my legs as I chose, depending on how I sat and arranged the fabric. The white heels and evening purse Diane and I had chosen went perfectly with the gown.

Diane had selected a long, iridescent silver evening gown that was sleeveless and had a high neckline. She'd decided to accent the dress with a strand of pearls and pearl earrings. Her matching shoes and bag looked like they'd been made to match the gown, which they probably had. To this ensemble, she added a feathery blue wrap that somehow seemed to blend well with the dress.

When the doorbell chimed, Diane went to greet the men and then ushered Al and Michael into the living room. Both were wearing their tuxedoes. They froze when they saw me. I looked down at my dress to make certain I hadn't spilled something on it, but it appeared clean. I wondered if I'd smudged my make-up and wished there was a mirror within viewing distance.

"You will give an old man heart failure," Al said as he placed one palm across his chest. "Mama mia!"

I breathed a sigh of relief and exclaimed, "You scared me! I thought something must be wrong with the way I looked!"

"You could never look anything but beautiful," Michael proclaimed. He glanced down at the worn red velvet box in his hands and added, "I don't' know if I'll be able to handle the sight of you once you put on the jewelry Tom gave you."

I accepted the box from him and said mischievously, "I guess we'll find out."

I went back to the large dressing closet. When I opened the box I was almost overwhelmed. The platinum shone in the light of the room, and the sapphires and diamonds sparkled brilliantly. My hands trembled slightly as I worked the clasp of the necklace. Getting the ring and earrings on was much easier.

When I returned to the living room minutes later, Michael, Al, *and* Diane were speechless. I took that as a good omen.

"How's Tom's heart?" Michael finally managed to ask with a grin.

"In better shape than most of his other organs. Did you call him?"

"I did, and everything's set. He'll be waiting for us, although he doesn't understand."

I looked back and forth between Al and Diane and said, "Thank you so much for going along with this. It will mean the world to Tom."

"How could we not be part of this wonderful plan?" Al asked rhetorically. "Michael admires this man very much and says we owe him a great debt for his service to our country. It is a tragedy that his mind and health are failing. Being an old man myself, I can easily empathize."

"We've seen it happen to many friends," Diane put in. "I pray it never happens to either of us, but one never knows what the years ahead have in store. I try not to dwell on that. The present is much more appealing."

We rode in the limousine to Tom's house. Once we arrived and were standing on the sidewalk, the limo driver opened the trunk and retrieved several bags and boxes and followed us up the driveway. In response to my knock, the door was soon opened by Tom, who was wearing a tuxedo that was in good shape but was slightly too large for him. He had obviously lost weight since the last time he'd worn it.

"Oh, Seneca," he said quietly, as tears began to roll down his cheeks. "You look absolutely lovely. Come in, please. All of you, come in."

Withdrawing a handkerchief from his pocket, he wiped at his face and said, "What a wonderful thing. Michael, I can't thank you enough for doing this, although I confess I was a bit flabbergasted as to why you asked me to dress up this evening as a favor to you. Thank you, my boy."

"It was my pleasure, sir."

Tom nodded and looked back to me before saying something in Arabic. Michael responded in kind before introducing his grandfather and Diane. Then Al instructed the limo driver to put the bags and boxes in the kitchen and wait for us outside.

"But what is all this?" Tom asked in bewilderment.

"Since you couldn't come to dinner and the opera with us, we brought dinner to you." Pausing, Michael added wryly, "The opera was a little too cumbersome."

Tom wiped at his face again and said, "You shouldn't have done this. It's a special night for all of you."

"When my Michael told me of your desire to see a picture of Seneca wearing your gifts to her and of his plan to have you see her wearing them in person, he suggested we include you in our plans," Al explained. Putting an arm around his grandson's shoulders and kissing him on the cheek, he proclaimed, "I raised him well."

"That you did," Tom agreed. "He's an outstanding young man."

"Seneca told me you like pasta, so we opted for Italian tonight," the outstanding young man volunteered.

"Pasta! What a treat! She never lets me have pasta."

"I do, too."

"A handful of times a year," he grumbled, but the corners of his mouth were turned up slightly. "I'm like a goddamn prisoner on rations when it comes to pasta."

"We should eat then," Diane prompted. "Enjoy your evening of freedom."

"Before we do, I want to take a couple of pictures," Michael said, holding up the camera he'd brought with him. "Seneca and Tom, why don't you stand over there?"

He was gesturing towards one of Tom's walls filled with artwork. There were no bookcases or family photos on that wall, only paintings and floating shelves holding glassware and sculptures. There was also no furniture to block full-length camera shots.

Tom stood tall and proud beside me and took my hand. Michael snapped a picture then directed that Tom put one arm around my waist and that I rest one arm across Tom's back. After that shot had been snapped, Tom and I looked at each other and laughed.

"I haven't done anything like this since my high school prom," I said with a giggle.

"And I haven't done anything like this since my fourth wedding," he chuckled.

"The food, it is ready!" Al called out. "Mangia! Mangia!"

"Eat! Eat!" Michael translated.

Before Michael, Al, Diane, and I left, I told Tom I'd see him the next day.

"You don't have to come," he said seriously. "We've had dinner tonight and –"

"And tomorrow is our Sunday lunch date," I interrupted. "I'll be here at the usual time."

"I don't suppose we'll be eating anything bad for me tomorrow," he said resignedly.

"No, probably not."

"It's all right, my lovely child. This was well worth it."

Tom effusively thanked all of us as we prepared to leave. He lifted and kissed the top of Diane's right hand, shook hands with Al and Michael, then hugged me, being mindful not to smudge my make-up or muss up my hair. He wished us all a wonderful evening as we walked back to the limo and climbed in.

Al and Diane talked of what a delightful man Tom was and of how they would like to see him again. I was so happy with the way the evening had gone, and we weren't even at the main event, yet. Any opera experience paled in comparison with bringing joy to Tom's life.

I enjoyed Giuseppe Verdi's *La Traviata*, but I found it didn't have the impact on me that the *zarzuela* had. I wasn't certain if it was because I could understand the language of the *zarzuela* or because it had been my initiation into the world of opera. I supposed I would have to see how the third opera impacted me before determining if I truly was interested in continuing to attend such performances.

We went to an Italian restaurant afterwards for dessert. However, upon learning of my love for red wine, Al ordered a bottle of what turned out to be the best red wine I'd ever tasted. Michael and I split a cannoli, and I had a second glass of the outstanding wine. I would have had a third, but I remembered the unpleasantness of my overindulgence not too long before and declined Al's offer to refill my glass.

During the ride back to Diane's, Michael slipped his arm around my shoulders, and I settled against him. It felt so comfortable and right to be in that position, and I wished the ride could take longer. Michael wrapped his free hand around the hand I had resting on his knee and lightly squeezed it.

"You look drowsy," he said into my ear.

"I am. It's a nice kind of drowsy though."

"There is no such thing if one is driving," Al protested. "Michael, you must take her home. She cannot be on the road like this."

"I'll be fine," I objected.

"Absolutely not," he insisted. "You look as though you are about to nod off to sleep at any moment. Michael will drive you."

I wanted to argue, but I was actually extremely sleepy and knew it would be unsafe for me to drive. However, I pointed out that Michael would have to drive my car and would be stuck at my house.

"I could go to Sunday lunch with you at Tom's then you could bring me home," he proposed. "You have a guest room and a couch."

"So, you're going to Tom's in your tux?"

"He doesn't have to since he has clothes at my house," Diane offered helpfully. "He even has a toothbrush there."

Before I could ask why Michael had clothing and personal articles at Diane's, he whispered in my ear, "I'll explain on the way to your place."

When the limousine driver let us off at Diane's, Al dismissed him for the evening and then we went inside. I retrieved my clothing, while Michael collected whatever he happened to have there. Within fifteen minutes, we were ready to leave. I thanked Al and Diane once again for their generosity relating to the day's events, especially the unexpected detour to Tom's house.

"It is our pleasure," Al said warmly. "One more opera to go. I cannot wait to hear your thoughts after you have seen the third performance. As for your friend, Tom, we will all be seeing more of him soon. Perhaps we will go to lunch with him, since Michael says he tires easily if he goes out in the evenings."

Once our goodbyes had been said, I handed Michael my car keys and climbed into the passenger seat. I realized I had never been a passenger in my own vehicle. It seemed strange to secure my seatbelt as someone else sat on the driver's side and started the car.

"I know you're wondering why I have things like clothes and a toothbrush at Diane's, "Michael began before we'd even left her driveway.

"I'm really hoping it's not the first thing that comes to mind."

"Not in a million years," he said with a roll of his blue eyes. "What happened was that Diane asked me Tuesday if I'd mind staying at her house for a couple of days to housesit while she was out of town. I packed a bag and then forgot it when she came back and I went home. Of course, she had her maid wash the clothes and bought me a new toothbrush."

"Of course," I said with mock seriousness. "I'm very, *very* relieved that you're not trying to steal your grandfather's girlfriend."

"I get along fine with her because she makes Nonno happy, but she's nothing like my Nonnie and wouldn't be my first choice for a partner if I were my grandfather. I have seen her do a lot of good though and appreciate her for who she is and what she overcame. She's just a little too abrasive sometimes for my liking, but she obviously has a lot to recommend her."

"I agree," I mumbled, as I fought to keep my eyelids open. "She's like a....like a...."

Chapter Seven

I woke to find Michael reaching across me to unbuckle my seatbelt and asked, "How long was I asleep?"

"You're still asleep."

There was undeniable humor in his voice. He carefully extricated me from the seatbelt then slipped one hand behind my back and the other under my knees before maneuvering me out of the car. Lifting me effortlessly, he pushed the door shut with his hip before walking towards my front door. Light was streaming through the open doorway, so he must have gone in first and switched on a lamp.

"How long was I asleep?" I repeated.

"About two hours."

"Two hours? It doesn't take that long to drive from Diane's to my house."

"I took the scenic route. You looked really cute sleeping like that, and I didn't have the heart to wake you. I was actually hoping to get you out of the car without disturbing you."

I made some little noise that indicated I understood. However, I was too preoccupied by my drowsiness and by the total sense of security I was experiencing at being carried in Michael's strong arms to comment.

I hadn't been held like that since I'd been seven years old, and I'd fallen out of a tree and hit my head. I'd awakened to find adults and children huddled over me. My father had arrived on the scene and had asked me a long list of questions before gingerly lifting me from the ground and carrying me to someone's truck. I'd been driven to a hospital and was examined by doctors and radiologists who determined that I had a slight concussion. When we'd gotten back to the trailer, my father insisted upon carrying me inside and laying me on my bed. My mother fussed over me, and each of them had taken turns waking me up every half hour to make certain I was all right. There hadn't been any shouting between them for over a week after that.

"Seneca, why are you crying?"

I hadn't realized I was until he'd pointed it out.

"I miss my Mommy and Poppy," was all I said, turning my face further into his shoulder. "I was remembering something."

Michael didn't ask for details. When he stepped into the house, he pushed the door closed with his back then locked it without putting me down. He then brought me to the couch and lowered me onto it before pulling several tissues from a nearby box. Sitting on the edge of the sofa, he dabbed at the wetness on my face. As he did so, I drifted back to sleep.

When I woke again, Michael was no longer wearing his tuxedo. Instead, he was dressed in shorts and a t-shirt and was sitting in the chair across the room. Several books lay on the side table beside the lamp, but it was the one in his hands that instantly caught my attention. It was my scrapbook.

I watched Michael's face as he slowly turned the pages of the book. His expression was unreadable. He took his time as he studied the images, and I tried to imagine what he was thinking as he reviewed my life from birth to high school graduation through the photographs I'd painstakingly placed in the scrapbook.

"Did you sleep well?" he asked casually as he shut the book.

Why am I surprised he knew I was awake? I thought. *He was trained to be super observant. It is kind of unnerving though.*

"What time is it?"

"About 8:00."

"Did you sleep at all?"

"From about 2:30 to 6:00." Before I could voice any concern, he hastened to add, "I'll sleep more later." As he placed the scrapbook on the coffee table, he asked, "Are you hungry?"

"Not at the moment. Are you?"

"No. I went for a run when I woke at 6:00 then showered, changed, and grabbed a couple of granola bars from your pantry. I'm not a great cook, but I could make you some eggs and toast or get you a granola bar or a bowl of cereal."

"I'm good for now."

Sitting up, I removed the combs from my hair and ran my fingers through it. Then I excused myself and went to the bathroom.

Before I returned to the living room, I removed my make-up, washed my face, and brushed my teeth. I also slipped off my pantyhose and threw the pair in the clothes hamper. I decided I would call Tom before taking off my jewelry and evening gown. I could then shower, eat a breakfast bar, and talk with Michael.

Tom had eaten breakfast and had taken his morning medications. He said he was tired and that his arthritis was acting up. We agreed I would join him for dinner instead of lunch so that we could discuss the previous night's events. I told him I'd ask Michael if he could come along but would come alone if not. I then hung up the phone and went back to the living room to update Michael, who had moved to the couch and was reading a book about Eleanor Roosevelt.

"You like biographies," he commented as I joined him on the sofa.

"I like all types of books, but I do love biographies," I admitted. "I just finished a great one about Queen."

"Queen Elizabeth? Queen Victoria?"

"No, the rock band Queen. It was extremely thorough and interesting."

"I'd like to borrow it."

"Of course." As Michael went to close the book in his hands, I asked, "Do you want a bookmark?"

"I don't need one. Eidetic memory, remember? I know what page I was on when I stopped."

"Useful."

"Annoying sometimes, too."

"I'd imagine so."

"A lot of people who have photographic memory only retain things for a short time. I'm different. What I do retain is usually there forever, and I retain more than just about anyone else does on a consistent basis.

"When I was in the military, I was a favorite guinea pig for neurologists when I wasn't on assignment somewhere. They did a lot of studies to try to see how my brain worked and how they could use the information they gleaned to advance memory retention in the average person. They were also focused on Alzheimer's treatments."

"Did you enjoy the testing?"

"Some of it was highly intriguing, but a lot of the testing was monotonous and time-consuming. Kind of what you'd expect when you see people doing that stuff in movies with leads stuck to their heads or MRIs or CT scans."

"I know the military must have tested your I.Q."

I knew that on the I.Q. scale anything over one hundred forty was genius or close to it. Between one hundred twenty to one hundred forty was superior intelligence. I suspected that Michael was at least in the one hundred sixty to one hundred seventy range.

"I'll tell you mine if you tell me yours," he said playfully.

"I've never been tested, but I know the scale. Come on. Tell me. I'm curious."

"One hundred seventy. I can't believe you've never been tested. You're so...so...."

"So me," I said with an impish grin. "I don't want to be tested."

"Fine by me. A person's I.Q. number is just that – a number. It's the combination of intelligence and personality that makes a human being who he is. I happen to think you and I have a good combination of both and that your I.Q. is probably as high as mine if not higher."

"Don't offer me any false flattery."

"I wasn't," he countered angrily. "You are so damned blind to your own integral value, Seneca!"

"I am not!"

"You are! I can picture you as a kid living in the stereotypical run-down trailer park filled with mostly uneducated illegal immigrants and their children. I envision you having to hide your naturally superior intelligence in order to be accepted by them. You were already the minority, so how could you show them all just how smart you really were?" When I didn't reply with a snappy comeback, he continued, "Did you sneak books home from the library? Did you watch science and history programs on T.V. and not tell the other kids? Were there highbrow magazines or educational toys in your room that you didn't share with the other little girls and boys?"

My blood was boiling, mainly because he'd been right about his initial assessment of my childhood. In my early years, I *had* hidden my intellectual bent from the other children. I wanted to belong. Most of my friends had parents with little to no education who didn't speak English. The children were learning the basics in the public school system, but no one was facile enough to strive for more. My own parents had not been geared towards academics, and my brain had been practically starved for stimulation.

I let go of my anger and said quietly, "You're right about most of it."

"What did I get wrong?"

"We only got three channels on the T.V., and there wasn't much science or history programming available to me. As for my room…."

I didn't know how to explain without being ashamed. I knew Michael had grown up privileged, although Al had obviously kept his grandson well-grounded. Still, how could he ever understand what growing up impoverished was really like?

Michael touched my cheek with the back of his hand and said, "Talk to me. I want to know."

"Our entire trailer was probably four hundred square feet. My parents' bedroom held their bed and a beat-up dresser, and the space was so tight that you couldn't even open the dresser drawers all the way. Our living room held a couch, a side table with a lamp, and an orange crate that was the T.V. stand. The kitchen was barely large enough to fit more than one person at a time. We had a table that was squeezed in the dining area. The bathroom had a shower, a sink, and a toilet. My bedroom held my twin bed and a chest of drawers, plus the few toys I had."

"Like the Cookie Monster one I saw in your living room here?"

"That one was special because my parents actually managed to purchase it new for my fifth birthday. Most of my toys were donated to me at the yearly Toys for Tots give-away, so that was the luck of the draw. Any other toys I had were from thrift shops or were found items. I was very grateful for anything I got. I did get a Barbie and Ken I wanted from a well-meaning church lady when I was six. I was so happy and thankful that it made her cry."

Looking grim, Michael asked, "Did you have enough to eat?"

"That depended. We got to keep bruised fruit and vegetables, and we had access to the local charity pantry. We had cheap food that went a long way like rice, pasta, and bread. I remember eating mustard sandwiches. We drank water and Kool-Aid a lot, but we did have a decent amount of orange juice because of my father's work in the groves. There was a nun who used to come around to the communities like where we lived and call out she had bread, and we'd all rush out to get some. It was freshly baked and was a real treat. Once in a while, she'd have cookies, too. Chocolate chip were my favorite ones, but those only came around once every few months."

"It sounds like a pretty tough way to live. What about clothes?"

"Garage sales, thrift stores, or donations."

"And electricity?"

"Off and on."

Michael was silent for a long while before asking, "Did you have air conditioning and heat?"

"We had fans for the summer and a space heater in the winter."

"Only one space heater?"

"It was a small trailer. We did have one heater short out and catch on fire the winter I was nine. Luckily, my father woke up and was able to put out the fire. The trailer smelled like smoke for weeks afterwards though. I was scared of space heaters after that, but it was our only option." Curious, I asked, "What frightens you?"

"Nothing."

He was completely serious, and this somehow made me feel calmed and unnerved simultaneously.

"How can you not be afraid of anything?"

"Because in my previous line of work I learned that fear leads to mistakes, which often lead to death."

"But you're not fearful of death."

"No. It is what it is."

"And you're not afraid to see others you love suffer or die?"

"I might feel anger, grief, and loss, but I wouldn't feel fear. That would be pointless."

"I understand, but I don't comprehend."

He nodded then said, "I'm sorry you had to endure a childhood devoid of security, necessities, and the intellectual stimulation you craved."

I turned my head away and blinked back tears. Michael took my face in his hands and urged me to look at him. The love I saw in his eyes was undeniable, and I was afraid. I wanted to tell him that I wished I could be like him, not scared of anything or anyone. I had no words. I got the impression I didn't need to say them anyway. He *knew*.

I felt that electric charge as Michael put his lips to mine and slipped one arm around my shoulders. I moved my hands up under the cotton fabric of his shirt and ran them over his bare flesh. His breathing quickened, as he caressed my breasts through the smooth material of my white evening gown. His hand slipped between the seam where the fabric was overlaid at my waist, and his palm glided along first my outer then inner thigh. He adjusted his hold on me and I felt his fingers slide under the waistband of my bikini underwear. I moaned.

I was dimly aware that I was completely powerless when it came to Michael and reveled in the surrender. He seemed to sense this and once again assumed a totally dominant role in our physical encounter. I had no problem with that. I wanted someone else to be in control for a change.

My panties quickly ended up on the floor. I grabbed at the hem of Michael's shirt and pulled upwards. It soon joined my underwear next to the coffee table. When I reached for his belt buckle, Michael didn't stop me. His mouth was on my shoulder as I undid the belt then unbuttoned and unzipped his shorts. The sensation of his now-wet fingers stroking me was maddening.

"Not here," he murmured between kisses. "We have to do this right, remember?"

Suddenly drawing back, he stood and scooped me up in his arms then carried me to the bedroom. Sunlight was streaming in through the side windows and soft light came in through the windows that opened out onto the lanai. The dark blue walls receded into the background, while the white comforter glowed in the natural light and illuminated the room. The light reflecting off the huge framed mirror propped against the wall beside my bed brightened things up quite a bit as well.

When Michael reached for the zipper on the back of my gown, I tensed. He immediately stopped, kissed me on the mouth, then asked what was wrong. I admitted that I felt self-conscious. He asked me why.

"I used to be really overweight and even though I'm not heavy now and exercise, I'm not in spectacular physical shape like you are. I'm not all muscled and toned."

"I like soft skin, good curves, and nice breasts. You've got a sensational combination of all three. I want you more than I've ever wanted any woman because of your body and your mind. I happen to think you're the one with the spectacular shape."

I blushed and smiled but shook my head slightly. Michael groaned, and it wasn't with desire. He asked me what else was bothering me.

"I've only been with one other man, and neither of us had ever had sex before. What if I can't please you?"

"That would be impossible. Just your touch drives me crazy. Being in the same room with you is almost intoxicating."

I had lingering doubts, but I nodded slowly and lifted my mouth to his. He deftly undid my zipper and placed his palms on either side of my ribcage before pushing downward. As his hands found their way to my hips, the dress crumpled to the floor. He stepped away from me and removed his shorts and boxers then tossed them into a corner.

I stared at his naked body while he stared at mine. Studying it up close made me realize that my first impression had been almost completely accurate. The only difference was that I hadn't been able to see the few scars that were visible on his left side. I wondered how he'd gotten them but decided that was a topic we could discuss another time. At that moment, I was distracted by other things. Well, mainly one other thing.

His was longer and thicker than my ex-husband's. Had it not been fully erect, the term "well-hung" would definitely have applied.

We embraced, and he kissed me with a ferocity I had never experienced in the past. My flesh tingled as we tightly held each other. The hardness of his erection taunted me as it pressed against me. I so wanted it inside of me.

We somehow ended up next to the bed, and Michael peeled himself away from me and folded down the comforter and top sheet. He then gently but firmly urged me to sit on the bed before kissing me again. He moved his mouth down to my neck and cupped both breasts, while I slid my fingers into his wavy, black hair. I realized my eyes had automatically closed while he'd been kissing me, and opened them. I was startled to see our reflection in the standing mirror.

I had placed the mirror against that wall in order to make the room feel larger. I'd had no idea it would be the ideal location to view anything like what I was now seeing since I'd never had a man in my bedroom. Part of me was telling myself I should look away, but another part was asking myself why on earth I'd want to do that. I was transfixed.

I was sitting naked save for my platinum, sapphire, and diamond jewelry on the edge of the mattress with my knees apart. Michael was kneeling between them and was tenderly running his hands over my skin and trailing his tongue across the flesh of my breasts. As I watched, his position shifted slightly as he began to draw on one nipple. Although the reflection only showed the back of his naked body, I found it highly arousing to watch his every movement. His hands caressed my hips then both palms went to my inner thighs. I tightened my fingers in his hair.

As his head lowered further, I felt his lips, teeth, and tongue along my belly and the soft curls below. When I understood what he meant to do, I started to protest. No man had ever touched me like that. The instant his mouth was on my clitoris, all protestations died in my throat.

I watched my breasts rise and fall as my breathing became more labored, saw flashes of the jewelry through the passion that enveloped me, and watched as Michael gently but firmly held my thighs apart. I gave in to orgasm. I put my hands behind Michael's head and urged him on as I cried out and came then came again. I'd never felt anything that intense in my life.

"You're shaking," Michael noted, as he rested his forehead against my belly and wrapped his arms around my hips.

"I've never had…never done that before."

"Had multiple orgasms?"

"That, too."

He looked up at me with knitted brows. When realization dawned, his eyebrows lifted slightly, but he said nothing. Then he excused himself and went to the bathroom.

During his absence, I removed the jewelry and placed it on the nightstand. I lay back on the bed and thought about the woman who'd worn it before me. What had she been like, this supposedly kind woman who'd given her love to a hardened man? If her husband were still alive, he would be old now. What had happened to their child? Was she alive and being cared for somewhere safe? I hoped so.

Michael returned to the room and climbed onto the bed. When he went to kiss me, I pursed my lips. It made him laugh.

"I thought you might react like that the first time, so I brushed my teeth."

"I appreciate that. I...I know it sounds silly, but this is new to me."

"I did the same thing the first time a woman came down on me then tried to kiss me afterwards."

I made a face, which made him laugh again. He explained that one got used to it and that nothing we were touching or doing was unnatural or distasteful. I knew the last word had been said intentionally to make me smile, and it did.

He kissed me lightly at first. Soon, the caring and tender man transformed into a fierce lover as he used his hands and mouth to pleasure me, but I could sense the ever-present self-control that prevented him from going too far and hurting me.

After what seemed like a blissful eternity, Michael guided me onto my back then knelt between my knees. There was an almost predatory look in his eyes, and it made me ache for whatever wildness was hidden inside of him. I moaned. There was another moan as he eased himself inside, but that one came from him, not me. He was almost too big for me to take him in, and I delighted in the thickness of him as he sank in deeper.

Michael placed his palms on either side of my waist and began to thrust in and out. I came quickly, and he made a noise somewhere deep within his chest that was almost feral. Dropping his head, he altered his rhythm. I focused on his face, which was shadowed by some emotion I couldn't quite fathom.

I knew he wanted to release in me and wondered why he hadn't already. Was this some sort of test he'd set up for himself? Was he seeing how long he could push himself without coming? Was I doing something wrong?

I was on the verge of coming again. I wanted him to come, too. When he said my name, it sounded as though he was speaking in some guttural, ancient tongue. I dug my nails into the flesh of his back and said that I loved him and wanted him to fill me. Michael gave one final thrust and succumbed to his own orgasm. I felt the exquisite wetness of his release and held him tightly as we shuddered and rocked together on the mattress. We lay still and quiet for a long time afterwards, his head resting in the crook of my neck and left shoulder. Eventually, Michael kissed my flesh nearest to his mouth and murmured that he loved me. I wasted no time in telling him that I loved him, too.

He slowly withdrew from me and lay beside me. I rolled over, rested my head on his chest, and draped one arm around his waist. The steady beating of his heart was soothing.

"Sex was never like that with my ex," I confided. "Tell me about the other women you've done this with."

"I've never done what we just did with any other woman in my life."

"But you said you'd had sex with three other women."

"I have, but it was nowhere near as powerful an experience as what you and I shared just now. I didn't love them, and they didn't love me. One was in high school, and one was in college. The last for me was in the military. I cared very deeply for each of them, but I didn't really love them. I love *you*."

"I guess I don't understand why."

"I can be your perfect man, but you can't be my perfect woman?" he asked with frustration. "You believe what society told you from birth, that you came from nothing and, therefore, will never be anything. Your parents believed it about themselves and unconsciously passed that load of bullshit on to you. Hell, I'm amazed you graduated from high school, college, and graduate school."

He pushed up suddenly, lifting me with him. Then he effortlessly turned until we were sitting on the edge of the bed again. He sat behind me, his legs resting on the outsides of mine and his arms around me. I could feel his hardness pressing against my lower back and his hot breath in my ear. It was like being surrounded by a security blanket that had been doused in sex, intellect, and pure maleness.

"Look in the mirror," he directed. "What do you see?"

"The two of us."

"Look at yourself. Tell me what you see, not what you think I want to hear. I want to know what you *really* see."

"An okay-looking woman in her mid-twenties who's smart, capable, alone, and afraid."

"There were three things you said that I know were accurate: mid-twenties, smart, and capable. The alone part isn't right anymore since you're not alone if you and I are going to be together."

"If things work out."

"They will," he said with certainty. "Now, tell me what you're most afraid of?"

"We've been over this before. I can't."

"Why not?"

My eyes welled with tears, as I whispered, "Because I can't. Please, Michael. If you keep pushing me to talk about it, I'll ask you to leave this minute and never come back."

I could tell by his expression that he knew I was serious.

"Have you ever talked about it with anyone else?" When I nodded quickly, he guessed, "Your ex?" When I shook my head, he tried, "Tom?" Another shake of the head. "A therapist?"

"No."

"Who then?"

"Cookie Monster."

He digested my response for a few seconds before saying, "Ah. Well-qualified for listening and giving comfort, but not licensed to treat deep-rooted issues. I hope he doesn't charge much for sessions."

I smiled very slightly and said, "They're always free, and he's available twenty-four-seven."

"I may have to become better acquainted with Cookie Monster."

"Michael, you have to promise me that you won't use the skills you learned in your former profession to spy on me or dig into my background or have anyone else do it either. I would never do that to you. I think it's unethical and would be a relationship-ending breach of trust."

"Yes, ma'am." Kissing me on the temple, he changed the subject by saying, "There's only one thing left on your list of observations, the one you got completely wrong. You are not just okay-looking. You're beautiful."

"You're the one who's wrong."

"No, I'm not. Why do you think you're not beautiful?"

"There's nothing outstanding about my body."

Michael gathered some of my long, black hair in his hands and draped it across one shoulder. He ran his fingers through it and told me it was softer and thicker than any other woman's hair he'd ever touched. He then brought his hand to my face and reviewed the deep brown of my eye color, the shape of my bone structure, and my full lips.

Pulling my hair back behind me, Michael then slid his hands over my shoulders and then slipped them between my arms and body. He reached up and cupped both breasts before asking me how I could not think that those were perfection themselves. When his hands moved over my belly, I protested that it and my thighs were too soft.

"The feel of them under my hands and body is almost too much for me. I love them. I don't want hardness and tightness; I want to drown in the femininity that I associate with that softness." Wrapping his arms around my waist, he said, "I only wish we could have children together. Maybe it's thousands of years of genetic programming, but I want you to have *my* children."

"Perhaps something could be done to make it possible."

"There's nothing. Believe me, I've looked into it." He sighed then resumed with, "Now, back to you and your beautiful body. I love every bit of it and want you to love it, too. After all, it's your body." Sliding his hands along my hips, he remarked on the shapely curves before slipping his fingers between my thighs. "And this is beautiful, too," he said huskily. "But this isn't primarily what makes me want you. *All* of it is what makes me want you – your mind, your soul, and your body. Take away any of it, and you're not the same person. That's what makes Seneca Jones the most beautiful woman in the world to me."

I twisted around to face him, kissed him then took him inside of me. I felt the animal in him come forth. He managed to say that he loved me before surrendering to the wildness within him. I exploded with pleasure, and Michael soon followed.

Exhausted and sore but very happy, I sagged against him and savored the feel of *us*.

"Seneca?"

"Hm?"

"Are you okay?"

"I'm more than okay," I murmured. "At this moment, I feel beautiful."

Chapter Eight

"Seneca, look at this one!"

Adiba Saleh stood a few feet from me in the infant clothing area of Macy's. She was dressed in a long denim skirt, a long-sleeved black shirt, and a maroon hijab, a scarf-like piece of material that covered her head. She held up an adorable yellow infant dress that had flowers and butterflies on it. I looked down at Hadeel, who was asleep in my arms. The dress was way too large for her.

"I love it, but it's kind of big. Let's look for a smaller size."

It was a Saturday in mid-June, and Adiba had not been a client for over a week. Hadeel was now two months old, and the new mother was doing a great job. She'd picked up English at breakneck speed and had asked me to remain with her as her friend now that she was no longer a client of Hearts at Home. There was no way I could turn her down. I didn't want to. I really liked her and had known the baby almost from birth.

I got along fine with Rakeem, Adiba's husband, although his occasional flashes of male chauvinism irked me. When this happened, I told myself that male-female role boundaries in other countries were not always going to be to my liking. He was a nice man who'd had a different upbringing. Adiba was happy with their marriage, and she told me they were actually more liberal than many other couples from the Arab world.

"I am educated," she reminded me. "I drive and shop without my husband. I worked outside the home before I became a mother. I will work again someday. In my home, I dress as I please like many Muslim women do. In public, I dress modestly with long skirts and long sleeves but wear Western-style clothing with the addition of the hijab. This would be unheard of in certain places in the Arab world. I would be expected to wear a berka and maybe a veil over my face."

Michael and I had gone to dinner at the couple's home two nights previously. I had been nervous about the evening although I wasn't sure why. I'd had nothing to worry about. Both Rakeem and Adiba instantly took to Michael, who could talk with them about the area of the world in which they'd been born and raised. The fact that he also spoke Arabic was a huge mark in his favor.

"This one," Adiba was saying. "What about this?"

I glanced at the lime green dress with neon orange polka dots and tried to think of something positive to say.

My friend laughed and said, "I was knowing you would hate that one! You are too polite."

"Guilty as charged."

As Adiba wandered to one side of the department store's baby area, I moved towards the other. Hadeel stirred slightly in her sleep but then settled back into peaceful oblivion. I kissed her soft hair, then turned and froze.

The infant dress hanging in front of me had a pink cotton top with soft tulle-like material for the skirt. It looked like a little ballerina outfit and came with tiny ballet slippers for shoes. It was adorable, and I wanted to buy it.

I could get it for Hadeel, I thought. *She'd look precious in it.*

I realized I didn't want to buy it for Hadeel. I wanted to buy it for my own daughter, a daughter Michael and I would never have. I blinked back tears and felt tightness in my chest. For an instant, I was a teenager again running in a hot field surrounded by overgrowth and palms. I couldn't breathe, couldn't think, and couldn't run fast enough to get away.

"Seneca? Seneca!"

Adiba was shaking me ever-so-slightly. Tears slid down my cheeks, and I continued to feel as though I couldn't take in enough oxygen.

"Seneca, what is wrong?"

Forcing my throat muscles to relax, I decided to tell her part of the truth. I'd always been a terrible liar.

"If Michael and I get married someday, we can't have any children. He can't." I regretted the admission as soon as I'd uttered it and begged, "Please don't tell Rakeem or anyone else. I shouldn't have told you without discussing it with Michael first."

"I will not tell. Modern science has made impossible things possible," she offered. "Is he certain that he cannot make children?"

"He says he is. I don't know how he knows, but he does." I cried harder and said, "It makes him sad, but he's had time to adjust to the idea. I haven't."

"You have only known one another for several weeks, and Michael has been working many hours. That is not much time for adjustment to anything."

Adiba led me to a bench in the women's restroom. She lifted Hadeel from my arms and placed her in the stroller then got some tissues and sat next to me.

"How do I get over this?" I asked her. "I...I was married once and lost a baby, but it was pretty early on...and...and we were too young and I...I was relieved when I miscarried, which sounds horrible. I figured if I found the right man I'd have more children later when the timing was better."

"Medical treatment would allow you to have a baby by someone else even if you and Michael could not make one together."

"Maybe, but I want *his* baby."

"I understand, but if it is impossible then it is impossible. There is always...what is the word?" She thought for a moment before finishing, "Adoption."

"And I have nothing against adopting. I just want to have a baby with Michael, too."

Adiba passed me tissues then rested her hand on my wrist and said earnestly, "Some things were never meant to be. Your first baby, it did not survive because of some reason you were not meant to know. It was the same with my first baby, although he died during birth and not early like yours. Perhaps Allah sent Michael to you this way because you would die if you had a child or something would be wrong with your children because of some problem *you* have. We are not always meant to know everything."

What she was telling me made perfect sense, and it helped me to stop crying. She was right. Even if it wasn't what either of us wanted, there was obviously a reason Michael and I couldn't have children together. I felt a sense of calm descend upon me and wiped at my tears.

"Thank you. That was a great help."

She smiled and said, "I am glad."

I stood and announced, "I want to buy Hadeel the ballerina dress I like so much. I really do think she'd look so sweet in it."

"But if it would make you sad to see her in it, then I would not want that."

"No. It's okay. I'm all right with it now, thanks to you."

When we returned to the Saleh house, no one was home. Michael and Rakeem had gone fishing and were scheduled to return in about an hour. That gave us plenty of time to unload the car and to try the pink ballerina dress on Hadeel. She looked like a little doll, especially once we slipped on the tiny shoes.

Adiba and I were playing on the floor with the baby when the two men arrived home. They were talking in Arabic and were laughing as they came into the living room and saw us. It was evident that they'd been out for hours in the sun and were each in need of a shower.

Rakeem went immediately to his wife and daughter and said something that made Adiba smile. She answered him in Arabic and he looked at me and said, "Thank you for my daughter's gift."

"You're welcome," I replied with a smile of my own. "I couldn't resist. And the ballet slippers even came with the dress."

I glanced up at Michael and was planning to ask him if he liked Hadeel's outfit. His grave expression made the words catch in my throat. Perhaps he hadn't accepted his sterility as well as he'd imagined.

"What is it, my friend?" Rakeem asked seriously.

Michael went out the front door without a word to any of us. My heart sank, and I made to get up off the floor and go after him. Adiba reached out and touched my arm. When I looked at her, she merely shook her head. Rakeem excused himself and followed Michael outside.

I waited nervously for the men to return. The seconds turned into minutes then into a half hour. Hadeel began to whimper then cry, and Adiba fed her while I sat feeling anxious and sick to my stomach. When I heard the sound of Michael's SUV engine starting, I scrambled to my feet.

I had taken three steps when Rakeem opened the door and approached me. He appeared somber and said, "Let him be alone for a while. He is struggling with something and needs time."

I nodded resignedly and suggested that I go, too.

"No, you must stay," Rakeem insisted. "Michael and I caught many fish, and I wish for you to share a meal of them with us. I must scale the fish then bathe and change. Adiba will cook, and we can eat. It will help you to not worry so much."

I assented, knowing he was right. When I left two hours later, I was still worried but did feel better. I thanked Rakeem and Adiba, kissed Hadeel, and drove home. I was surprised to see Michael's SUV parked in my driveway. True, he had been spending almost every night at my place for the last month, and I'd given him a key. However, in light of whatever had happened at the Salehs I hadn't expected to see him at my house for at least the rest of the day.

Michael was sitting on the couch in the living room with the lights off. I could tell he'd showered and put on clean clothes, but I couldn't read his expression in the dim light of the room. I went to stand in front of him and said, "Rakeem told me you needed time alone. Yet, here you are."

"I had some time alone before you got home. I can't stay away from you for very long," he admitted. "Not even when I should."

"What's that supposed to mean?"

"It means you deserve to be with a man who can give you children, and that's not me."

"I lost my first baby. What if I can't actually have children either? How would you react if I told you that you deserved to be with someone who could give you children and that wasn't me? I know exactly what you'd say, so I want you to say it to yourself and get over it!"

"You want me to get over not being able to create life with the woman I love? I want to see you pregnant, to feel our baby kick while it's inside of you, to see it born, to see it grow up and become whatever it was meant to become! I thought I could deal with never having that, but it's pretty damn hard to accept when I watch how great you are with Hadeel and know how much I love you! You can't just dismiss this!"

Okay, so this is our first fight, I thought. *Probably not what most couples fight about their first time, but then we're not your typical couple, are we?*

"I'm not asking you to dismiss anything! I was in tears in the baby department at Macy's today because I wanted to buy that dress for the baby we'll never have! I understand that there has to be a

reason for this, and I accept it. I still wish it weren't true, but it is."
When he looked away, I continued, "So, we can't have children.
You think we're the only infertile couple in the world? We can
adopt or get a donor or be foster parents or –"

Michael stood so quickly that he was almost a blur. He grabbed
me by the shoulders and yelled, "You don't understand!"

"I won't unless you explain it to me!"

"I can't!"

"You mean you won't!"

"I mean I can't! The Navy –"

"Your sperm is classified?" I asked rather sarcastically. "Or did
the Navy force you to have a vasectomy before you started playing
spy games?"

I saw fury, hurt, and pleading in his eyes for a millisecond, then
he pulled me to him and kissed me hard. I responded to him
automatically. Even after such a short time of togetherness, it was
second nature for me.

When we were not touching, Michael was typically cool, calm,
in control. In the throes of passion, he was more like a sexual animal
who held a choke collar on himself in order to restrain his fervor and
keep it at an acceptable level. I found the physical power of him
amazingly arousing and always had multiple orgasms during our
lovemaking.

We ended up naked in my bed with our fingers entwined and
with him on top of me. He maneuvered my arms up, never slipping
his fingers from between mine. He covered my mouth with his then
pushed my thighs apart with his knee and drove into me.

During previous encounters, there had been foreplay before the
actual sex began. This time, my mind and body hadn't been
prepared for his quick and forceful entry. I was physically
uncomfortable for the first time since we'd begun having sex, but I
didn't want to tell him to stop. We'd been arguing about a sensitive
subject involving his manhood, and I wanted to show him that I
loved him and only wanted to be with him in any way he needed. I
wanted to show him that his inability to make a baby with me did not
impact my desire to be with him.

As the minutes passed and Michael continued to ride me hard
without coming, he deepened his kiss and quickened his rhythm.
My discomfort became pain. When I attempted to move under him,

I found it simply caused him to thrust more forcefully. My hands were pinned under his, and I was certain that he mistook my little cries of pain as cries of pleasure. When his breathing quickened and he came, I almost wept with relief.

Michael lifted his mouth from mine and kissed first my neck then my shoulder. He murmured apologies for being angry during our earlier conversation and talked of speaking to a therapist about how he felt regarding his sterility and asked if I wanted to attend some sessions with him.

"I think that would be good."

As I spoke those words, Michael stiffened and said, "Something's different in your voice. What is it?"

"Nothing," I insisted. "I just –"

At that point, he began to withdraw from me, and I gave a little yelp as I experienced searing pain deep within. Pausing, Michael released my hands and rested one elbow on the mattress on one side of my waist and placed his palm on the other for support. He looked down at me with such regret that it temporarily made me forget my own pain.

"I hurt you?

"A little."

Sighing deeply, he confided, "I can hear how much pain you're in by listening to your voice. You tried to stop me, didn't you?"

"Sort of."

He brushed his lips across mine before saying, "If I had known, I would've stopped right away. I was so blinded by my own goddamn sense of inadequacy. Jesus, this is like a nightmare."

My nightmares are worse than this, I wanted to tell him.

I knew that hurting me had been the furthest thing from his mind. What he'd done was succumbed and allowed the animal within free reign, and I'd inadvertently paid the price. It was an unfortunate event, but I knew he would blame himself regardless of his intentions.

"Forgive me," he said quietly. "That will *never* happen again."

"Of course I forgive you, because you didn't mean for this to happen. I don't want you to hold back all the time from now on because of –"

I yelped again as he tried to withdraw from me. He instantly paused and dropped his head to my chest then told me we should both stop talking and try to separate ourselves in such a way that it would cause me the least amount of pain.

It was easier said than done. Each time he made any movement, the pain was excruciating. I asked him to hold my hand and just pull out. He took my right hand in his left, and I squeezed it tightly and bit my lip hard while he eased out of me as carefully as he possibly could. I didn't let go of his hand even after he'd moved to kneel beside me.

"I'm okay," I assured him. "I'll be okay."

"You're not. I'm taking you to the hospital."

"Michael, no. I'll be fine. I am fine."

"You're bleeding. You could be hemorrhaging internally, too."

"I'm not."

"And you know this how?" he demanded angrily. "I'm taking you to the ER right now."

"No, I'm telling you I'm fine."

The look he gave me said, *Yeah, right.* His actual words were, "If you're okay then show me so I won't worry."

"How can I do that?"

He shrugged and suggested, "Get up. Go to the bathroom."

"I will," I declared firmly. "Why don't you go get in the shower, and I'll be right there?"

Leveling his gaze at me, he said, "I don't think so."

It felt as if I had butterflies in my stomach. I knew I was *not* okay and that any attempt to get up on my own was going to result in an increase in pain. I was determined to try and assuage his fears. I decided it couldn't be that bad and started to sit up but found myself unable to rise more than a few inches off the pillow. Michael hastened to stop me and forced me to lie back. He asked me what I wanted to wear to the hospital.

"I have to take a bath first," I protested.

"No way. I'm getting you dressed, putting on my clothes, then we're leaving."

Releasing my hand, he climbed off the bed and went to the drawer where I kept my pajamas. He pulled out my favorite ones that were patterned with brightly colored tea cups and coffee mugs. Then he paused, shook his head, and put them back.

"Michael, what are you doing?"

"Thinking about how pajamas wouldn't be the best thing for you to wear. They're just going to take off your clothes at the hospital, and a nightgown or something without bottoms would be easier and cause you less pain to put on or take off."

"I really don't want to go to the hospital."

"I know, but that's where we're going." Bringing a button-down shirt of his to the bed, he said grimly, "I'm going to have to help you sit up a little in order to dress you, and it's going to hurt you. Maybe I should just wrap you in a blanket and take you in like you are."

I told him I was not going to be taken naked into the emergency room even if I was wrapped in a blanket. He grimaced but nodded before placing the shirt next to me and sitting on the bed. My heart was pounding with the anticipation of more pain, but I refused to arrive at a hospital without any clothing.

Michael leaned across me and directed me to slip my arms under his armpits and up around his shoulders. He explained he was planning to lift me up so that he could slip the shirt under me. Then he would assist me in putting my arms into the sleeves and buttoning the front.

I was determined not to show any further signs of pain. My resolve lasted all of fifteen seconds. Once Michael had raised me up to about a forty-five degree angle, I had buried my face into the crook of his neck, was holding him as tightly as I could, and was repeating the word *ow* over and over. He urged me to hold on a little longer as he positioned the shirt beneath me, then he slowly lowered me back onto the mattress. I lay still and fought waves of nausea. Once they had subsided, Michael managed to get my arms in the shirtsleeves, rolling up the cuffs so that they came to my wrists. He buttoned the front of the shirt, then quickly gathered his own clothing, and dressed.

"I'll be right back," he told me before disappearing into the hallway and returning with the comforter from the twin bed in the guest room. He spread it next to me then gingerly moved me on top of it before kissing me lightly and assuring me that he would be back. He returned fully clothed five minutes later and sat beside me once more.

"Seneca –"

"Just pick me up," I said wearily. "I know it's going to hurt, so just do it."

He folded the comforter over the top of me before raising me from the bed. I repeated my "ow" mantra as he carried me through the house and to the SUV. The back of the front passenger seat had been reclined as far as possible. He placed me in the seat and fastened the seatbelt before shutting the door and returning to the house to lock up. I gritted my teeth and wished we were already at the hospital. The pain was consistently worse while I was in this position, and I could feel that the bleeding had worsened as well. I hoped our drive wouldn't last long, even as I dreaded what lay ahead.

Chapter Nine

When we arrived at the ER entrance, Michael parked the SUV then got out and came around to open my door. After unbuckling my seatbelt, he picked me up in my comforter cocoon and carried me towards the sliding doors. I cringed emotionally. I dreaded the questions, the explanations, the examination, and whatever treatment would be required. My eyes remained closed, and I tried to think of something else besides my physical discomfort and my embarrassment. I buried my face against Michael's chest.

I heard a receptionist ask what was wrong with me. Michael responded that I was bleeding, and she asked him where. He must have given her some sort of look that clued her in because she paused and asked if I was pregnant. His hold on me tightened ever-so-slightly before he told her that I was not.

"You'll have to fill out some paperwork," the woman said politely. "You can take this to the waiting room and –"

"And what?" Michael asked in a very controlled and very dangerous tone of voice. "You want me to put her on the floor while I fill out paperwork? Maybe I could call a local news channel so they can get some film of that while we wait."

I was soon lying on an exam table in a small room. I had expected to be stuck in some curtained-off area with patients on either side. It was a relief knowing that I would not have others hear my conversations with the hospital staff regarding my condition and how I'd ended up that way.

Michael was asked to leave so that a doctor could examine me. He refused.

"I'd prefer that you wait outside," I told him. "I'll be okay on my own."

He didn't look happy about this but merely nodded then stroked my hair and kissed me before telling the nurse he'd be in the waiting room and to call him back as soon as I was ready for him. Then he kissed me again and told me he loved me. I told him I loved him then watched him walk out.

My ER doctor was an older man with gray hair and a kindly smile. He asked me to tell him what had happened to cause my injuries. My face flushed, but I did. He listened patiently then asked if Michael had ever done this before, to which I responded that he hadn't.

"He didn't rape me," I insisted. "I would have told him to get out and called the police if he had."

"I'm glad to hear it. It's important that I ask. The police will ask him for his version of the story as well."

"The police?"

"Standard protocol when a woman is brought in with a sexually related injury."

"Will I have to talk to them?"

"Only if I suspect abuse. Let me check you out and make sure there's nothing seriously wrong with you before we do anything else."

A middle-aged nurse with a nice smile held my hand during the exam, which was agonizing at times. The doctor apologized for causing me more pain, and I told him honestly that I wasn't going to blame him for doing what he had to do in order to treat me.

"Most people in pain aren't so charitable," he confided. Once his initial examination was complete, he moved to stand at the head of the bed and said seriously, "I don't think you were raped; I think things got out of hand. My recommendation for that in the future is to develop some sort of non-verbal signal you can give your partner to let him know if he's inadvertently hurting you and you're unable to tell him to stop. Reviewing your injuries, I'm guessing that this man is…well-endowed. He can obviously hurt you without his being aware of it, so you have to let him know if he's being too rough. It's your body, and you have to make certain you protect yourself."

I meekly agreed. His advice about having a non-verbal cue was a wise suggestion, but I was more concerned with the doctor's diagnosis and treatment options at that moment.

"You have some pretty significant bruising and tearing of tissue. I plan to treat you and give you three prescription medications as well. Two will be oral and the other is topical. Stay in bed for a couple of days and take it easy for the next week. I'll write you an excuse for work. Definitely no sex for at least a month. See your regular GYN towards the end of the week, so he or she can make certain things are healing properly and then follow up with you again. If you start bleeding after this or develop more pain or a fever, then you must come back to the ER. Do you have questions?" When I answered no, he said reassuringly, "Don't look so scared. We're going to keep taking good care of you while you're here. Follow my orders when you leave, and you'll heal just fine."

I was given a shot and almost instantly drifted into unconsciousness. When I came to, I was back in the SUV. It was dark outside, and Michael was parking the vehicle somewhere under a streetlamp. Confused and still very much under the influence of the painkiller, I asked him where we were.

"The Walgreens that's open twenty-four hours. I have to get your prescriptions filled before I take you home. Will you be all right in the car by yourself?"

"If you don't leave me too long."

"I won't. If they tell me there's a wait, then I'll come and sit in the car with you and then go back in to get the prescriptions."

I nodded and started to cry. I had no idea why I was crying and apologized to Michael for not being able to stop. He unbuckled himself and leaned across until he was able to kiss my wet cheeks and stroke my hair.

"Never apologize to me or anyone else for crying about anything," Michael said softly. "It's one of the body's way of releasing tension, fear, anger, or sadness." Sighing, he went on, "I'm so sorry for hurting you, Seneca. I'm going to spend the rest of my life doing everything in my power to ensure that it will never happen again."

I tried to disentangle my limbs from the comforter so that I could touch his face, but the movement brought with it sharp pain. I lay still, crying, and I begged him not to torture himself for what had happened. He told me that was impossible. Then he said he would be back soon, kissed me, and got out of the SUV.

I must have fallen asleep again because the next thing I knew, I woke in my own bed. Although I continued to feel drugged, I could sense that it was still dark outside and glanced at the clock. It read 4:17. Michael was not in the room.

I listened for him, thinking through the veil of the painkiller that perhaps he'd gone to shower while I slept. I heard him talking in Italian in one of the other rooms. It also sounded as if he was crying.

I must be hallucinating, I thought. *I feel like Alice gone through the looking glass....*

I jerked awake and instantly regretted it. The terrible pain was back, and my involuntary movements heightened it to an almost unbearable level. I stifled a cry and knotted the sheet in my hand.

"Seneca, lie still," Diane said from beside me. "I'm going to help you eat some crackers so you can take your medications and rest again."

"Diane?" Looking up at her, I asked, "Where's Michael?"

"Talking on the beach with his grandfather. He called us this morning once he got you home from the hospital. Al's trying to get him to call the therapist who worked with him after his military service."

I glanced at the clock. It was 10:04.

"What about my Sunday lunch with Tom? He forgets his medications sometimes. I have to go."

Diane straightened and declared, "Under no circumstances are you going anywhere. Al is going to go to Tom's, take him his lunch, and explain what happened."

"He can't!" I insisted.

"He has to, Seneca. If he doesn't, then Michael will. But Michael really isn't in the proper shape to do that just yet. He respects Tom so much, and I know he feels like he's disappointed Al, Tom, and, most of all, you. I suspect all of this has triggered his PTSD, and so does Al. That's why he's pushing Michael to call the therapist."

"Good. I need a pain pill. I'll eat some crackers and take the pills, but I have to shower and go to the bathroom first."

"You can barely move. How do you propose to shower?"

Even though it made the pain worse, I began to laugh, and Diane looked taken aback and concerned.

"I need a Hearts at Home aide," I told her. "I can't call them, but that's what I need."

"You don't need anyone but me," Michael said from where he and Al stood in the doorway. "I'm going to take care of you."

"And abandon your business for a week?" The pain was making me agitated and highly irritable, and I didn't try to conceal my anger as I continued, "You'd let all those other people flounder to stay here and take care of me?"

"I'll work from home while you're asleep."

"Perhaps we could get a home health aide from another agency," Diane suggested.

"It's a close-knit group of people. We all know each other or of each other. Word would get out, and I don't want that." I added furiously in Spanish, "What I want is to go to the bathroom and take a shower and force myself to eat some crackers and take these stupid pills and not hurt for a while! And I want my mother here and for everyone else to go away and leave me alone!"

Michael lifted his chin and narrowed his eyes, and I knew he'd understood every word I'd uttered in both languages.

"You *lied* to me?" I continued in Spanish.

"I didn't lie," he replied, also in Spanish. "You knew a language I didn't, so I learned it. I'm good with languages, remember? I was planning to surprise you soon by telling you I could talk to you in Spanish. I thought it would make you happy."

"It would," I said in English. "It does." Wiping at the corners of my eyes, I admitted in Spanish, "I'm so worried about *you* and us."

"And I'm worried about you and us," he echoed. He took a deep breath, exhaled, then said in English, "How about this? Nonno's headed to Tom's to take him lunch. Diane's offered to stay here with you and me. You can eat something, take your medications, and I'll help you shower. Diane can change the sheets while we do that, then you can go back to sleep. While you sleep, I'm going to call my former therapist and talk to him or whoever's on call for him. When you wake up, we'll see how things stand."

I somehow managed to eat four crackers and didn't throw up afterwards. I then swallowed the painkiller and the antibiotic and kept those down, too. Michael pushed back the comforter and top sheet. I could tell he was purposely averting his eyes from the bloodstained bottom sheet as he bent down and lifted me from the bed. I whimpered with the pain but didn't cry out. He took me to the bathroom and stripped both of us naked then got into the shower with me so he could wash my flesh and shampoo my hair. That was the last thing I remembered before waking up at 3:00 p.m.

At first, I thought I was dreaming. Tom was sitting in a chair by the bed. He was loosely holding one of my hands in one of his and held a book in the other. When I stirred, he shut the book and put it on the nightstand before looking down at me and smiling rather sadly.

"That's my girl," he said softly. "How do you feel?"

"What are you doing here?"

"I had to make certain you were really all right and have a chat with Michael." When my eyes widened, he admonished, "Don't go getting yourself all worked up about it. You're like my very own daughter. If someone hurt you on purpose, I wouldn't hesitate to kill him with no qualms." I must have appeared shocked because he went on, "I've told you before I never believed in casually taking a life. That doesn't mean I never took a life."

"What did you tell him when you talked?" I asked nervously.

"That he needed help and to go back to therapy. I also said that if he ever did anything this goddamn foolhardy again that I'd make certain it would never happen in the future no matter what I had to do."

"You like him, but you'd have him killed?" I gasped.

"If I had to in order to protect you? Definitely."

Disbelieving, I exclaimed, "You can't!"

"My lovely Seneca, I'll do nothing of the sort because there's no need. Michael is an outstanding young man with enormous intelligence, skills, and a deep-rooted sense of honor. What he did to you will never happen again because he didn't mean for it to happen this time. He'll get help because he loves you and never wanted to hurt you."

I gave his hand a little squeeze and said, "I don't understand. Both of you are so gentle, but you could kill without a second thought about it?"

"If the circumstances warranted it, then, yes." He grinned and said, "You'd have to live it to understand the way we have to think. It's complicated."

"Where's Michael now?"

"In the other bedroom on that Skype computer thing talking to his doctor in Annapolis." Frowning, he asked, "Is it time for you to have another pain pill?"

"I want one. Where are Al and Diane? Diane will know when I took the last round of pills. I really need one, but I don't want to take them too close together and don't even know where the bottles are."

Tom rose painfully from the chair and limped towards the hallway. I waited until he was outside before giving in to a small moan. The phone rang, and I automatically twisted and reached for it. The terrible pain gripped me as I lifted the receiver, but I forced myself to offer a greeting.

"Seneca? What the hell is wrong with you? You sound awful."

"Glenda?"

In all the years I'd worked for her, my sixty-something, no-nonsense boss had never called me at home. I fought the nausea that accompanied the pain and asked her what was going on.

"I asked you first. You sound like shit. Are you all right?"

"Not really. I was going to call you in the morning to tell you I won't be in this week. I have an excuse from the doctor at the ER. I could scan it to you if you need it before I come back to work."

"As if I care about that. Do you need me to come to your house? Are you going to tell me what happened?"

"It's a female issue. The doctor says I'll be fine if I'm a compliant patient. I'm being well taken care of."

"I'll call you back," Glenda offered. "This can wait."

"No, it can't. You've never called me at home. It has to be super-important."

"Well, you'd probably find out anyway if you see the paper or watched the news. Sheila Hummel died last night."

My breath caught in my throat. I was used to dealing with the deaths of old and sick clients, but one could never be truly prepared. Sheila's condition had gotten progressively worse recently, but that had been no surprise to me. I knew what to expect.

"Thank you so much for letting me know. She was such a sweet woman."

"Seneca, that's not all there is to it. Her husband, Walt, shot her then shot himself. He died, too."

I was stunned into silence. My brain refused to accept what Glenda had just told me. Things had improved since Sheila's move to the other condo and Walt's attendance at the support group meetings. He *couldn't* have shot her and himself. He *couldn't*.

"Seneca? Hon, are you there?"

"I – I'm here."

"Our girl who was on duty said Mr. Hummel asked her to go up to his condo to get something. She was on her way back down when she heard the shots. There was a note. He said he couldn't stand to see his wife like that anymore and couldn't live without her. He –" She paused then said, "He said he wouldn't have made it this far without your help and that he regretted letting you down. He prayed you'd forgive him."

I was suddenly fourteen in the hot field on my knees and couldn't breathe. Spikes from a large cactus plant were scratching me, but I didn't notice. I was going to be sick and didn't care. Maybe if I ran a little farther....

"I – I have to go, Glenda."

"I understand. I'm so sorry to have to tell you this, especially when you're already not well. I'm going to call you to check on you, all right?"

I thanked her and hung up the phone with trembling hands. I then slowly got out of bed. I couldn't stand up straight, but I didn't care. I had to move or I would go insane. Nothing mattered except the certainty that I had to get away from the pain in my head and my heart. What difference was pain in my body?

I wandered through the dining room and into the living room. I had to *go* somewhere, but I had no place to go. I was lost in my own home.

"What are you doing out of bed?" Al asked from behind me. "It is not good for you to be up and about."

I turned and saw him shift instantly from kind-hearted grandfather to alarmed older man. He called out for the others to come quickly, as he came forward and took me by the shoulders.

"My angel," he breathed. "You are shaking and as white as a sheet."

I had no voice. I stared at him, wanting to talk and being unable to utter a sound. I was dimly aware that I was hot.

Michael, Diane, and Tom were suddenly in the room. Everyone was asking me what had happened, what was wrong, what did I need? All I could do was stand where I was feeling numb. All I could think of was Walt Hummel shooting his wife then blowing his brains out.

"Seneca, look at me," Michael ordered gently. "Did something happen?"

I nodded slightly.

"I heard the phone ring. Did you answer it?"

I nodded again.

"Who was it?"

"There was bad news," I managed to say.

"What kind of bad news?"

"Walt killed Sheila then himself."

"I saw that story on the television earlier," Diane said soberly. "So you knew them."

"Walt…Walt was better," I insisted. "Things were better. They were okay last week. He was going to talk at the next partner-support group meeting."

"No one can ever know what's going on in a person's head," Tom offered. "He probably was better overall, but that doesn't mean something couldn't have triggered some sort of emotional break."

I shook my head and tried not to think about Sheila's condo walls splattered with blood and brain matter.

"He asked for my forgiveness in his note," I said in a tremulous voice. "Why would he do that? It's not my job to forgive him. He doesn't need forgiving. He was overwhelmed. It wasn't his fault."

Michael lifted me and carried me to the couch. He held me while I sobbed against his chest. I couldn't stop shaking, and the pain from my earlier injuries was unrelenting. I was vaguely aware of the others discussing whether or not they should take me back to the hospital or call my doctor.

Michael said something to Tom in Arabic, and Cookie Monster was suddenly in my arms. My sobs gradually subsided as I held the doll against my chest. Eventually, I lay spent and gripped with pain, but I'd ceased crying.

I automatically ate the crackers Diane fed me and dutifully swallowed pills. Michael held me while I held Cookie Monster until my eyelids grew heavy and the pain receded. Al asked me if I wanted anything else before I was put back to bed.

"I want Tom to sing to me," I mumbled. "I want the song about the old lady who swallowed a fly."

He sang the children's song several times until I fell asleep, still holding my doll in my arms.

Chapter Ten

It was the evening of the Fourth of July, and Michael and I were waiting to watch the fireworks from my beach. It was something I loved to do each year. Boats around the area went far out into the water and shot off spectacular firework displays. I'd told Michael I didn't want to miss any of it. Unfortunately, I was still healing from the injury he'd inadvertently inflicted upon me and was uncomfortable sitting in the chair. Michael took my hand and asked if I wanted to lie on the blanket with him instead.

"Maybe in a while. It's so hot right now that I don't want to lie on a blanket or towel. I think I'll stand for a bit."

Michael stood as well and suggested we go into the water to cool off. I told him I didn't feel like putting on my swimsuit, and he asked me why I had to do that.

"It's your beach, and no one can see us. Just go in naked."

"I've never done that before."

"Why not? Have you ever gone skinny-dipping anywhere?" When I shook my head, he said, "It's a really freeing experience. Why don't you give it a try?"

"But there are things in the water."

"And the small amount of cloth you normally wear in there covers that much surface area? You'll be fine. It's been three weeks since…since I hurt you. I know you're still sore, but going in the water might actually help you to feel better."

We both stripped. Michael ran out, plunged into the surf, and began to swim. I loved watching his strong body as it moved so gracefully in the water.

"It's perfect!" he called back to me. "Come on!"

I waded out to where he stood. He was right; the temperature was not too warm but not too cool. It did feel freeing to be naked in the Gulf waters. I imagined a time when no one wore clothing and took such an experience for granted.

Michael wrapped his arms around me and kissed me as the waves gently lifted and lowered us. The feel of his wet, naked skin against mine was phenomenal, and I was aroused for the first time since he'd hurt me. I was relieved to discover that he was aroused as well and ached for him to ease into me even though I knew my body hadn't quite healed enough.

"Swim with me!" Michael urged, as he released me and swam out farther. He stopped about ten yards away and proceeded to tread water. When I didn't move towards him, he swam back to me and asked, "Is being in the water making you feel worse? No? Then what is it?" Taking my face in his hands, he said, "Don't be afraid to tell me."

"I'm not afraid. I'm embarrassed."

"About what?"

"I don't know how to swim."

"But you come out in the Gulf waters all the time."

"I stop when I can't touch bottom anymore."

"And what would you do if you got caught in a riptide?"

"I'm not that far from shore."

"Riptides aren't always in the depths of the water." He kissed me hard and held me tightly against him then murmured, "I thank God every day that I found you. I also wonder how in the hell you survived with the total lack of…of whatever it is that you needed to prepare you for…to…." He searched for the appropriate word and finally exclaimed, "I want to go back in time and save you from your childhood and everything bad that happened to you! Just when I think I've heard it all, I find out there's more."

"I'm glad I keep you on your toes," I remarked tartly. "Why are you so upset?"

"Where should I start? Your parents loved you but raised you in a terrible place with constant arguing, poor living conditions, uncertain circumstances, not enough food, and a substandard education for someone with your intelligence level. You worked in the groves or fields when you should have been playing or learning or dancing! They didn't even take you to a pool to teach you to swim."

"You think there was a swimming pool in our run-down trailer park in central Florida? There wasn't even a pool at the run-down high school I attended! I'd never been to the coast until I moved to this area after college, and I'd lived in Florida my entire life!"

He was speechless. I was furious.

"You think I *liked* my life? I was a *child!* I had no say in any of it!"

I was practically shouting by this time and was near tears. Michael shushed me and pulled me to him. I pressed my cheek against his chest as we drifted in the water, and he stroked my skin and hair. Eventually, he said gently, "I could teach you to swim."

"I'd like that," I said in a small voice.

Michael was an excellent teacher. By the time the sun set, I'd learned the basics of swimming, although I remained very much a beginner. As the sky darkened, I started towards the shoreline.

"Where are you going?" Michael asked.

"It's getting dark."

"Stay in the water with me a little longer," he suggested. "We won't go deep."

"But I can't see what's around me in the water."

"It'll be okay. I won't let anything happen to you."

I was slightly anxious but agreed to try it for a few minutes. I discovered that the dark water wasn't as scary as I'd anticipated, at least not with Michael there beside me.

We returned to the beach when the fireworks began. We lay on the oversized blanket and enjoyed the colorful displays. I never ceased to be awed by the variety of fireworks and the beauty of the reflections on the water's surface. I knew from past experience that this local production would last for at least an hour, and I was prepared to drink in every moment of it.

Michael began to speak to me in Spanish. When I made an effort to turn my head towards him, he asked me not to and said he wanted to tell me things he couldn't yet say while looking into my eyes. As I stared at the stunning explosions of light, he talked in general terms of specialized training with the Navy, of traveling the world and facing challenge after challenge on covert operations, of having to kill and watch others die, and of constantly struggling to balance what was right and what was wrong. He described how he'd come to the conclusion that it was his personal mission to help veterans and had dedicated his post-Navy life to making their lives better. He told me of his love for his family and his country and of his desire to find the woman he would love, marry, and have children with. His dream of having a family of his own had been ended with the discovery of his sterility. He'd come to terms with the harsh reality and had resigned himself to the truth of it – until he'd met me.

I knew he wasn't telling me everything. He couldn't. I truly did understand the need for extreme security measures when it came to many military operations. I was grateful that he was sharing with me what he felt he could. I was thankful he was confiding in me and greatly appreciated his exposure of his vulnerabilities. That, combined with his continued declarations of love for me and his actions over the last three weeks, cemented what I'd hoped from the first time I'd met him. He *was* the man from my lovely dream.

As the brilliant fireworks display continued, Michael propped himself up on one elbow, looked down at me, and declared, "I love you, Seneca."

"And I love you, Michael."

"I want you to marry me. I know it sounds crazy after everything that's happened in the short time we've known each other and with the interesting dynamics of our relationship –"

"I want to marry you," I interrupted. "Our relationship has definitely been atypical, but we're sort of odd compared with other people anyway, don't you think?" He laughed but sobered when I continued, "I only have one condition. I don't want to leave my house. This is my home forever. I was meant to be here."

"Then I was meant to be here forever, too."

While we lay holding each other as the fireworks display wound down, I blurted out, "I think I'm going to quit my job after I leave the reading of the wills of Walt and Sheila Hummel tomorrow. I still don't understand why I've been summoned for that, but I'll go."

"I could go with you."

"You have meetings all day. I'm a big girl. I can handle it."

"You hurt when you get in and out of the car."

"But I can do it. It'll be one trip to the lawyer's office and then to Hearts at Home. I'll manage."

"And if you quit? What then?"

"I want to work with you and the veterans at John's Place."

"Because you're running away from dealing with what happened to your client and her husband or because you really want to help the vets?"

"Both. I have a lot to give, but I'm done with the home health coordination job. I need a change."

"It's not going to be easier. In some ways, I think it'll probably be harder. Vets have a lot of baggage."

"I know. It's a different kind of baggage from dementia, Alzheimer's, end-stage cancer, and the like."

"Yeah, it's PTSD, lost limbs, damaged minds, and the like. It's stressful." He sighed and said, "See how it goes tomorrow. If you still feel the same way, then I'd love to have you on staff. We can use a social worker since we only have one psychologist and one consulting psychiatrist at this point. I don't think it'd be good for us to work together every minute though."

"Definitely not. Being in the same building would be nice, but too much togetherness isn't healthy."

He gave me a small smile and said, "Neither of us is truly emotionally healthy at this time. Speaking of that, my therapist wants to meet you. Are you up for Skyping with him? I wouldn't be in the room, at least not at the beginning. He thinks bringing you in will help me to work through some of the issues I'm trying to sort out."

"Sure. I've never been involved with virtual therapy before. It should be interesting to see how it works between the therapist and his patient."

"Spoken like a true M.S.W."

I dozed in his arms, waking in the middle of the night to find him sleeping beside me. The instant I stirred, he was wide-awake. I apologized.

"It's not your fault. It's years of training that's ingrained in me. It kept me alive more than once."

"So, you never sleep deeply?"

"A part of me does. The other part is always ready."

"For what?"

"Whatever."

I sat up stiffly and looked at the sky. I had never slept outdoors in the nude before, and I was enjoying it. There was a constant breeze from the Gulf that was cooling us, and no bugs were biting or buzzing around.

We went into the house, showered, then crawled into bed. As I nuzzled against him, Michael said, "We never discussed what we'd use as a non-verbal cue if you needed to stop me during sex and couldn't talk. I think you should just bite me."

"What?"

"If I'm kissing you and have you pinned and you're in pain, then bite my tongue as hard as you need to get my attention."

I couldn't think of any other plausible option when I reviewed the previous mishap and told him I agreed to his proposal.

"Good. Speaking of proposals, I have an idea about the ring I'd like to give you. Are you okay with being surprised? What did you do for your first marriage?"

"I trust you. As for my first marriage, we were eighteen year-old college students with a baby on the way. We had no money for rings."

Michael was silent, and I knew he was once again thinking about how deprived my earlier life had been and how much he wished he could have been there to somehow spare me.

When the alarm rang at 8:00 a.m., I woke alone in the bed. There was a note on the pillow beside me. It read:

Seneca, I'm going for my usual run and work-out at the gym. If you need me at all today, don't hesitate to call. I know I have meetings from 8:00 until 5:00, but that doesn't matter. I'm always available to you 24/7. Text me anytime, and I'll call you back as soon as I can. Love, Michael

I smiled and put the note on the nightstand beside me. Then I got up, fed Doc, ate breakfast, and puttered around the house for a while before slipping into a black dress and black pumps. Since I was going to the reading of the wills, I figured the outfit was apropos, especially since I'd been physically unable to attend the memorial service and wouldn't have been able to handle it emotionally even if I had.

I'd never been to a will reading before in my life. Both of my parents had died intestate and had nothing of real value to leave me anyway. The trailer was rented, and most of what we'd had in it was not worth keeping. The only articles I possessed that had belonged to my father were his favorite shirt and hat. Out of my mother's things, I'd held onto her hair stylist tools and the rosary left with her when she'd been abandoned by her birth mother at the church the day she was born.

I went to the closet in the guest room and got down the box that held their things. Once I'd placed it on the bed, I lifted the lid. I took my time and pulled out my father's green, white, and blue plaid shirt and the straw hat he'd always worn in the fields. I didn't open the stylist kit but held up the rosary, which was quite beautiful with its rose quartz beads and dainty silver cross. I cried for a little while before putting everything back in the box, returning it to the shelf, and then leaving for the lawyer's office.

The conference room was large and full. Everyone gathered snapped to attention once the attorney started his review of the dispersal of Walt and Sheila's assets. Their estate had been valued at over fifty million dollars. A significant amount of monies had been left to what few living relatives the couple had. More money and property had been left to the church the Hummels had attended for the last several years. Another large amount was designated to a foundation that researched treatments for Alzheimer's and dementia patients.

The attorney concluded by stating that I was to receive five million dollars from the Hummel estate for all of the assistance and caring I'd shown to both the husband and wife during the final year of their lives. I was literally stunned and felt as though I was going to pass out. My shock must have shown on my face because someone brought me a glass of water while another person asked me if I wanted to lie down. I shook my head and sipped the water until my heart rate slowed to an acceptable pace.

I left the lawyer's office an hour later and sat in my car with the air-conditioning running for fifteen minutes before texting Michael. Another ten minutes passed before he called me. When my iPhone rang, I answered but couldn't find my voice.

"Seneca? Seneca, are you okay?"

"I don't know."

"What happened at the lawyer's office?"

"They left me five million dollars for helping them." Blinking back tears, I declared desperately, "I don't' know what to do."

"Stop and take a deep breath."

"I could donate it to John's Place or another charity."

"Nothing has to happen today. You don't sound like yourself. Maybe I should cancel the rest of my meetings and –"

"No, I'll be fine. It was just such a shock. I'm going to Hearts at Home then to Tom's. I need to talk to Tom. I'll see you tonight when you get back from work."

"Don't cook," he ordered. "I'll pick up dinner for us on my way home."

"It sounds so nice to hear you say that."

"What?"

"Home. I'm glad you think of it as *home* now."

"I better think of it as home since we're never moving, right? I love you very much, Seneca. Call me back every five minutes if you need to."

I told him that I loved him, and I promised I'd be all right and would see him later at the house. Then I drove to Hearts at Home, had a difficult conversation with Glenda, turned in my resignation letter, and said my goodbyes to my co-workers. Normally, I would have given two weeks' notice, but I was in no shape to work at that time, and Glenda and I both knew it. I cleaned out my desk and loaded up my car.

Krystal and I went to lunch at Cracker Barrel, and I told her about the visit to the lawyer's office. She, like Michael, urged me not to make any rash decisions. I agreed that both of them were right but wanted to be rid of the money as soon as possible.

"The lawyer said Walt's will was prepared six months ago and that Walt was definitely in his right mind when he made the arrangements. I'm still creeped out about it. It's not like –"

I had been about to say, "It's not like when my father died, and I was finally 'compensated for my loss' by those responsible for covering it up."

I drank some water and continued instead by saying, "I know you're going to say that I shouldn't, but I feel responsible for what happened with Walt and Sheila. I feel like I should have known somehow, that I should have sensed it."

"You couldn't," Krystal insisted. "You can't blame yourself."

"I know, but I do. Maybe I'll talk to Michael's therapist about it. He wants me to Skype with him to help Michael."

"That sounds like a great idea. How was your Fourth of July?"

My mood immediately improved, and I smiled and said, "We swam and watched the fireworks over the water." Barely able to contain myself, I paused dramatically before adding casually, "Oh, and Michael proposed."

Krystal was out of her seat and on my side of the table in seconds. She hugged me and told me she was so excited for me and wanted to know all the details.

"There are none, yet. We have no rings, no date, no nothing. We just agreed to get married." I hesitated before asking, "Do you think we're rushing things? I love Michael and can't imagine life without him, but we really haven't known each other long and have our problems and –"

Krystal interrupted me by saying, "You two belong together. Anyone who's met both of you can see it right away. This is so great! I can't wait to tell Greg! Maybe it will plant a seed in his mind for me and him."

"He and Michael got along wonderfully when we all had lunch for the first time last week. Perhaps I could drop a hint to Michael. The two of you seem like you were made for each other, too."

"I love Greg, and he says he loves me. We still haven't had sex, but we both want to wait a little longer for that. We've each had bad experiences in the past with people using us in different ways, so it's making us cautious. I do hope we end up together. I'd be happy to be his wife."

"And I hope someday you will be. I'm glad you're taking it slowly. You need time *without* sex. Greg really seems to love you, and I'm sure you'll end up together."

Her face suddenly clouded and she asked, "Will you and I still be seeing each other? You're not going to stop going with us to Less of You each week now that you're not working at Hearts at Home any longer?"

"Of course not! Krystal, you and I are friends forever. Just because we won't be working at the same place doesn't mean I'm not your friend anymore."

We hugged again, and Krystal went back to her side of the table. Once she'd taken her seat, I said, "I want you to be my Maid of Honor."

"Oh, Seneca! I'd be honored, but I can't!"

"Why not?"

"Because I'm still too big! I've only lost nineteen pounds! I'd be a large blob and mess up all your wedding photos."

"You would not," I assured her. "And nineteen pounds is fabulous! Krystal, I don't even know when we're getting married. It might be a year from now or tomorrow. No clue. Whenever we do, I want you as my Maid of Honor. I don't care what size you are. You're my best friend."

All traces of doubt vanished from her expression, and she beamed and immediately moved on to, "Where do you want to get married? What kind of a dress will you wear? What kind of a dress will I wear? What are your colors going to be?"

I laughed and told her I hadn't thought much about it but would appreciate having her input and would share any updates with her. We parted ways after paying our bills, and I drove to Tom's. After our customary greeting hug, we went to sit in our usual spots in the living room and discussed his lunch and medications. Then I reviewed everything that had happened in the last twenty-four hours. Tom listened without interruption then said, "You've had quite a day. How are you handling all of this, my girl?"

"I'm thrilled about the engagement, but this thing involving the will is making me really...stressed."

"Michael and your friend, Krystal, are right. Talk with Al and Diane and their financial people, then make an informed decision. Don't act rashly because you're afraid." Rising painfully, Tom limped over to where he'd placed the framed pictures Michael had taken the night we'd visited him before going to the opera and declared, "I love these photos of you and me. You bring out the best in me, my lovely Seneca."

"I could say the same about you, Tom."

"I'm only an old fool who did the best he could with his life. I want to see you marry and be happy before I die, but none of us can know when our last day will be. I'm not planning on going anywhere anytime soon, mind you. I'm just saying that I know I won't live forever. When I do go, I don't want you to dwell on it. Just keep me in your heart, and I'll continue to live on in you."

"I will," I promised in a subdued tone of voice.

"Good. Now, on to something practical."

He left the room and returned with a small fireproof box that had a combination lock on it. He informed me that his birthdate was the combination and that I was to open the box and make use of what was inside if anything ever happened to him.

"The envelope is in case you're in real trouble," he said. "Don't hesitate to use what's in there if you're in danger."

Wondering if his mind was deteriorating more rapidly than I'd thought, I asked, "Why would I be in danger?"

"Michael is a man who will love and protect you until his dying breath. You can't forget he has a past like mine and that he worked in extremely dangerous environments for years. One never knows when one's past may come back to haunt him."

"Has someone tried to hurt you?"

"Not in the last decade or so, but there were three instances before that. Most retired operatives go on to lead relatively normal lives, but Michael and I are a little different from most operatives. I can't explain it. I think everything will be fine, but I want you protected just in case. Understand? Hide the box. Keep it safe."

"Break glass in case of emergency?" I said in an attempt at humor.

"Exactly." Patting my hands, he said, "You are more precious to me than any other living creature in this world. I want you safe at all costs."

I nodded and tried not to cry. The day had been a whirlwind of ups and downs, and I was tired and sore. As if he could read my mind, Tom asked if I needed to go home to rest. I answered yes but told him that I had something I needed to ask before I left.

"I want you to walk me down the aisle when I get married," I announced. "I want you to give me away."

"I'd be honored to walk you down the aisle, but I will never give you away. I want you always for my very own."

When I got home, I unloaded the car with my things from Hearts at Home and the fireproof box Tom had given me. I dumped everything on the coffee table then went to the built-in wall unit and opened one of the cabinet doors at the bottom. After removing the oversized books on the lowest shelf, I reached towards the back and pushed at one spot on the wall. A panel opened outward, and I stared at the empty space.

Before I'd moved in, the previous owner had shown me the secret compartment he'd had installed as a hidey-hole for valuables. I'd never had the need to use it but was happy to have it available to me now. I turned the fireproof box on one end and awkwardly inserted it into the hole then closed the panel. After replacing the oversized books and shutting the cabinet door, I sat on the floor and wondered how I was going to get up. All of the bending, reaching, lifting, and twisting had not helped my abdominal soreness.

Michael walked in at that moment and looked down at me. He was holding a bag filled with something that smelled like Chinese food. I knew he was wondering what I was doing on the floor, and I sensed for some reason that I shouldn't tell him about the box.

The best defense is a good offense, I thought.

"What are you doing home early?" I asked with a hint of curiosity in my voice.

"I'm not early. It's six-thirty."

"Really? I had no idea I was at Tom's that long. No wonder I'm so tired."

Michael put the bag on the end table then crouched beside me before asking, "You unloaded this stuff from the car and carried it in?"

"It wasn't so bad."

"Yeah, right. That's why you're sitting on the living room floor looking like you're about to faint." Slipping one arm under my knees and the other behind my back, he picked me up and carried me to the dining area. After depositing me in a chair, he removed the cartons from the bag and placed them on the table.

"Did you eat lunch?" he asked. "Did you take your Advil?"

"This must be how Tom feels when I ask him that kind of stuff all the time," I grumbled. "And yes, Krystal and I ate at Cracker Barrel." When he joined me at the table, I asked, "Did *you* eat lunch?"

"No time." When I made a disapproving noise, he said, "I've gone for days without food, Seneca. Skipping lunch once in a while won't kill me."

It was wonderful to be at home with the man I loved eating good food. All I wanted to do was stay in that moment and not deal with the stress that had accompanied the reading of the wills, the resignation, and Tom's talk of danger and dying.

"Are you up to Skyping with my therapist for a few minutes tonight?" Michael asked, as he cleared the table after our meal. "It doesn't have to be a long talk this first time. I just really want you two to meet so we can go forward."

An hour later I was sitting in front of Michael's laptop meeting Dr. Kent Forrester. He was an African-American man of perhaps thirty-five. He had a great smile and friendly manner that instantly put me at ease.

"So, I finally get to meet the smart, beautiful woman Michael's been telling me about for the last several weeks."

"And I finally get to meet the wonderful psychiatrist who's been working with him."

The man grinned and said, "I guess we know where we stand when it comes to Michael's views of us."

"What's your view of Michael?"

"That might take a while. I don't want to keep you long tonight because Michael says you've had a really rough day. I just wanted to meet you and see if you'd be up for scheduling sessions involving you, Michael, and me in the future so that he can work through some of his issues."

"Of course."

"Great. Dealing with psychological issues is often more challenging for genius super-achievers. It may take a while."

"I'm really glad he has you as his psychiatrist."

"And I'm really glad he has you as his partner. Because of his personality type, he'll stick with therapy until he works through his issues, even if it takes the rest of his life. He knows his limits but is always testing them." When I nodded slightly, the psychiatrist said, "You look like you're ready to drop. We'll pick this up again very soon. Perhaps the three of us can all get on Skype together and work out a schedule."

"I'd like that. Thank you again."

"Thanks to you, and congratulations on your engagement."

Once Forrester and I had ended the video call, I went to find Michael. He was sitting on the couch reading a book I'd finished over a month ago during my lunch hour at work but had forgotten to bring home before that day. I sat beside him and leaned my head against his shoulder then closed my eyes.

"What did you think about this book?" Michael asked. "Did you like it?"

"I thought it was probably the most thorough study of String Theory I'd ever read. I find String Theory an interesting hypothesis in physics and am intrigued by the speculations of scientists when it comes to how many dimensions there really are. I personally think there are four, but I know there are arguments for everything from one dimension to nine."

"My physics teacher in high school was set on three," Michael told me. "My project for the year involved proving that there were four. I changed his mind and got an A." He closed the book and kissed the top of my head before asking, "Was it your physics teacher who inspired you to keep investigating the possibilities?"

"My high school only had biology and chemistry, which I enjoyed. I checked out a book in the library about physics and got hooked. I started studying it on my own."

"Seneca, this book is written for professional physicists."

"Is it?" I asked sleepily. "No wonder it was on the sale rack at Books-A-Million."

He shifted his position and put an arm around my shoulders before saying, "You have no idea what you really are."

"I'm Seneca Jones, the daughter of Robert and Christina Jones and the future wife of Michael Benedetto."

"No. You're *Seneca*. Your identity isn't tied to your parents, me, or anyone else. You're a wonder all by yourself."

"That's very sweet."

"It's the truth. Tell me what else intrigues you besides social work, art, history, and physics."

"Sleep," I murmured. "We have the rest of our lives to talk about everything."

He helped me to stand, and we walked towards the bathroom. While we got ready for bed, Michael asked me what I thought of his therapist. I explained that I really liked him and that we had agreed to have a meeting with all three of us to discuss scheduling. Michael seemed pleased by this and thanked me for participating.

"I'd do anything for you," I told him. "And you'd do anything for me."

"You've got that right." Kissing me, he said, "God, but I love you."

Sighing, I told him, "I'll be so glad when we can have sex again. This is so frustrating! I want you in me."

He laughed and assured me there was no other place he'd rather be. We went to bed, and I quickly fell asleep in the comfort of Michael's protective embrace.

Chapter Eleven

I felt horror, revulsion, and an all-encompassing sense of impotence. I could hear Michael frantically saying my name from somewhere in the distance but couldn't quite find my way out of the hot field. I was screaming and crying and wanted to get away, but something was holding me back. I attempted to break free, but it felt as though I was struggling to disengage myself from a vise grip.

"Seneca! *Seneca!* It's Michael. Stop twisting! You're going to hurt yourself!"

My eyes flew open, and I struggled to breathe. Michael was holding me against him, and I continued to hear myself screaming and tried to stop without success. I was crying uncontrollably and battled to contain my emotions, even though I knew it was pointless. My lips and throat were parched, and my heart was racing so fast that I was lightheaded.

Gradually, I ceased my struggling and the screaming, but the shaking and crying continued. Reminding myself that this was part of the normal post-nightmare progression, I sagged against Michael and wept. He loosened his hold on me and held me tenderly as I sobbed. He spoke to me in Spanish, telling me that he was there, that I was safe, that it would be all right, and asking me what else he could do to help. I couldn't utter a word in response.

"What happened to you?" he muttered in English. "Tell me, Seneca. Did you hit someone with your car? Did you use drugs and overdose? Were you raped?"

I covered my ears with my hands and cried, "No! No! No! No!"

Michael covered my hands with his, eased them down, and told me not to worry about anything. He stroked my hair and skin and talked of how much he loved me and would always be there for me. He asked me again what he could do to help, and I managed to convey to him that I needed my Cookie Monster doll.

He extricated himself from the embrace and promised to be back in seconds. Cookie Monster was soon in my arms, and my crying lessened, then stopped. Michael left the room once more and returned with a glass of water, which he urged me to drink before wiping my face and nose and lying beside me again.

When I was able to speak, I said in a quavering voice, "You have to go to work."

"It's 4:00 a.m. on a Saturday. Quit worrying about me and worry about yourself. Whatever just happened –"

"Don't! I told you no!"

"Okay," he said quickly. "I won't press you anymore right now. Just tell me how I can make it better."

"You can't."

"But –"

" Krystal," I groaned. "I have to call her and tell her I won't be at our weekly meeting. And Tom –"

"I'll take care of it," he said firmly. "Rest."

"But you can't tell them!" I insisted. "Nobody knows."

That gave him pause. Finally, he asked, "How often does this happen?"

"Usually once every few years."

"You said usually. What about this time?"

"I had the last one right before I met you. The preceding one was two and a half years before that."

"And what will today be like?"

I started to cry again and told him I would sleep for most of the day and be back to normal by Sunday. He kissed my forehead and told me he wasn't leaving the house and to go back to sleep before spooning his body next to mine. I was asleep not long afterwards.

I woke to find myself alone in the room at 6:30 p.m. I put on my robe and walked through my house. Michael was sitting on the floor of the living room with books, CDs, and DVDs spread all around him. Almost every bookshelf in the enormous built-in wall unit was empty.

Still exhausted and slightly dazed, I asked him what he was doing.

He looked up and said, "I'm learning."

"Learning what?"

"You. I couldn't concentrate on work, so I thought I'd find something to read in your collection here." Scanning the room and the piles of books, he added, "I had no idea."

Sitting on the couch, I asked, "No idea about what?"

"How angry it would make me to realize exactly what you were denied."

Rubbing tiredly at my eyes, I said, "You're not making sense."

"I'm making perfect sense." Gesturing towards the books, he said, "Look at your library! You've got biographies, books on statistics, biology, psychology, political science, history, art, fiction, non-fiction, and then physics and astrophysics, some of which I don't even understand." Lifting one book and scanning the title, he went on, "And this is just your present personal collection. I can only imagine what you've read at college or through the public library."

"So?"

He groaned with frustration before asking, "Where did you go to college?"

"I got my undergraduate degree from University of Central Florida and my graduate degree from the University of South Florida."

"Why'd you pick those schools?"

"Because I had grants and scholarships to each that allowed me to go for free as long as I completed my degrees within a certain time period. Everything was paid for, except my meals and living expenses."

"What did you do for those?"

"I got jobs washing dishes and cooking at local Spanish restaurants."

"How many hours did you have to take each semester when you were an undergraduate in order to finish in this allotted time you were talking about?"

"Sometimes eighteen. Usually twenty-one."

"They don't typically let people take that many hours per semester without special permission."

"They let me."

"I'm sure they did." He paused then asked, "Why'd you pick social work as a field?"

"Because I wanted to help people who couldn't help themselves."

"I understand." Allowing his eyes to roam across the living room floor, he asked, "What's the furthest you've ever traveled?"

"From where to where?"

"Let me rephrase the question. Where have you traveled during your lifetime?"

"When I was thirteen I went to Texas with my dance teacher for the audition with the Houston Ballet Junior Company. It took us two days to get there because we went halfway and spent the night then finished the drive the following day. We spent a few days in Houston; then it took us two days again to drive back. That's the only time I've ever been out of Florida."

I was so tired and so oblivious as to where he was going with all of these questions. I understood his wanting to know me as well as he could. After all, we were engaged to be married. But he seemed deeply affected by what he was seeing and hearing about my past, and I didn't know what to say to give him what I sensed he wanted.

"Have you ever been to Disney World?" he asked suddenly. When I answered no, he prompted, "Universal? Discovery Cove? Sea World?" Again, my answer was no. "Yet, you lived in Orlando while you got your undergraduate degree."

"And took the maximum amount of credits each semester, worked, and studied when I wasn't in class or at my job. I didn't have the time or extra money for theme parks." Rubbing at my temples, I asked, "Is there a point to this?"

"The point is that your I.Q. is probably equal to or higher than mine, and you could have gone to any college, including any Ivy League school."

"You think it was easy for me to get into college, period? My little backwoods high school wasn't exactly known for its academic reputation. It was probably only because of my ACT and SAT scores and my poverty status that I was able to go at all, and that was because I managed to do it myself without a computer or a home phone! My mother certainly didn't know how to fill out the forms for scholarships and grants, and the school counselor barely had more brains than my 4-H pig, Hamlet!"

I put my hand to my mouth and instantly regretted saying such an unkind thing about the well-meaning but clueless counselor. I silently prayed that God would forgive me for being uncharitable.

"You didn't have a home phone and no computer, not even at school?"

"No home phone. One computer in the school library that everyone had to share. That was how I got the info on UCF and printed out the forms."

"What were your ACT and SAT scores?"

"I...I made perfect scores. I got an award for that."

He flashed me a rueful smile and said, "Me, too. That's pretty unusual for people to get perfect scores on one of those tests, much less both. What are the odds that you and I would each do that?" He gave a bitter laugh and proposed, "Maybe that's why we can't have children. If we did, they'd be socially inept because they'd be so damn smart."

"Maybe."

"If you wanted to, you could go back to school, you know?"

I got to my feet and said fiercely, "I like helping people and don't need more degrees to do that! Just because I'm interested in things like String Theory and Statistics doesn't mean I want to work on them all day in a lab or office! Stop trying to fix me! If you think I'm that damaged, then move on to someone else! I'm not going to be with you so you can work on me like I'm your pet project!" As he scrambled to his feet, I yelled, "And if you do fix me, then does that mean you'll leave me and move on to another woman you feel equally sorry for?"

"I told you I fell in love with you the moment I saw you, and I didn't know a damn thing about you then! It makes me furious to know how your beauty and intelligence were so grossly overlooked your entire fucking life! That doesn't mean you're my pet project! I love you and want you to be happy is all! You need to go to theme parks and other places in other states and other countries to have some fun and stimulate your brain! You need to live, not because I want you to but because you've always wanted to and were denied and denied and denied again!" Taking me by the elbows, he ordered, "I dare you to tell me you don't want to explore everything you can in this world! Tell me you don't want to share it with me!"

"I can't! I do!"

He slanted his mouth over mine, and I melted against him. I wanted so badly to take him in me. When he picked me up and carried me to the bed, I thought he might actually do it. I should have known better. He wasn't going to take any chances before the doctors okayed me for sex again.

That night, I dreamed of an older woman I hadn't thought about in years. Her name was Esmeralda, and she'd moved to central Florida from Mexico to live with her son, who worked on the farms with my father. She was known for having the gift of being able to see people's pasts and futures. My parents had told me to be respectful of her but had made it clear that they didn't believe in her gift.

When I was thirteen, I'd met Esmeralda on the road when I'd been walking home from school. She had long, black hair and wore an embroidered red dress. We were only together for a few minutes and chatted in Spanish about the heat and the need for rain. Before we separated, she turned towards me and declared, "You will be a great woman. I have something for you. Bring it to me when you are older, and we will talk."

Esmeralda had held out her hand, and I'd extended mine and accepted what she put into it. Then she'd walked down a side road and was gone. I'd looked down at my hand. The woman had given me a polished stone shaped like a heart. It was dark in color and lovely in its simplicity. I'd hastened to pocket it before my mother saw it. Something told me she'd disapprove of my acceptance of this gift.

I woke with a small start. Michael was instantly awake and asked me what was wrong. I glanced at the clock: 6:14 a.m.

"I just remembered there's something I have to do today."

"Are you sure you're up to it? After yesterday –"

"I told you yesterday that I'd be back to myself by today. I am. I'm fine."

He kissed my throat and said, "You are so far from fine that you couldn't find it with a map, but I won't argue about it with you this morning."

"Good." I slipped my fingers into his hair and asked, "You want me to make you some breakfast while you run? I'll be heading out after that. You can get your work done today while I'm gone."

"Will you tell me where you're going?"

"I have to visit an old friend. I'll stop by Tom's for dinner on the way back. If you're free, then you could join us. I can call you with a time."

"I'll plan on it."

"That'd be nice. Did I tell you I asked Tom to walk me down the aisle when we get married and asked Krystal to be my Maid of Honor?"

"No, but I think those are great choices. What about Adiba?"

"Since she's Muslim and I'm not, can she be in my wedding?"

"What kind of wedding are we even having?" he asked. "We haven't talked about any of it."

"What do you want?"

"To marry you in whatever way you like. The only thing I care about is having my family there to share in it. I've been away from them for so long. I need to reconnect with my aunts, uncles, and cousins. You haven't even met any of them."

"So, why don't we get married when they all come down here next month? Al said almost all of them would be here on vacation."

"Do you really want to do that? You're going to be assailed for the first time by the relatives at our wedding."

"They haven't seen you in years. I think you'll be an equal target."

While Michael went for his morning run, I showered and slipped into a peach sundress and sandals. I went to my jewelry box and put on my diamond studs and hoop earrings. I also fished in the bottom of the box and removed the dark polished stone Esmeralda had given me over half a lifetime ago. I put it in one pocket and went to make breakfast.

Two and a half hours later, I arrived in the middle of nowhere. It was where I'd grown up, and I was very familiar with the area, even though I hadn't been there in almost a decade. Not much changed over time in that part of Florida, and it was easy for me to find my way back to the trailer park, the now-closed hair salon, the liquor store where my uncle had worked, the gas station and convenience store, and the local grocery store. The only additions I could see were a McDonald's and another gas station.

I went directly to the grocery store and bought a box of freshly made almond cookies and a bottle of water. While I was checking out, I asked the middle-aged clerk if Esmeralda lived close by. As I suspected, the woman knew her and was eager to give me directions.

Esmeralda lived in a small, neat wooden house that was near the highway. It was unremarkable and looked similar to many other older homes in central Florida, save for its bright blue paint. A statue of the Virgin Mary welcomed me at the front door.

I didn't even get a chance to knock. Esmeralda opened the door and said enthusiastically in Spanish, "Come in! I have been waiting for you a long time. I was beginning to wonder if you had forgotten about me."

I handed her the box of cookies and admitted, "I sort of did forget about you for a while. I dreamed about you last night."

"And I dreamed about you. That is how I knew you were coming." Ushering me into her home, she said, "Thank you for the gift. Please, come and sit in the kitchen. We should talk."

I glanced around as we walked through the living room. It was filled with an odd assortment of Catholic paraphernalia and what looked like strange folk religious accoutrements to me. I was leery but also knew I had to be there. I'd had that dream for a reason.

"Sit at the little table in the corner," she directed. "Would you like coffee?"

"I have water. Thank you though."

"Do you have the stone I gave you?"

I withdrew it from my pocket and placed it on the table between us. Esmeralda stretched out her hands with the palms up and encouraged me to place mine in hers. The heart-shaped stone lay between our clasped hands.

"Close your eyes," she instructed. "Trust me. I have been doing this since I was a child. My grandmother taught me. Relax and be still."

I wasn't certain how long we sat like that at the table. When the old woman said my name, I jerked and felt as though I'd been awakened from a deep sleep. I started to apologize for nodding off, but she stopped me and said, "You were not asleep. You were simply elsewhere."

I began to question my decision to come out to this place to speak with a woman I'd met once over a dozen years before. I didn't even know if I thought what she possessed was real or if she was a fraud.

"You are questioning yourself," She told me. "Do not do that, child. You made the right choice by coming here for guidance."

Is that why I'm here? I thought. *Why did I really come?*

"What I see and say is the truth," Esmeralda went on. "I will now give you proof that you can trust me." She smiled and said, "Not long after I saw you, your parents divorced. Your father died several months after that, and your mother died before you went away to school. I needed no special powers to learn any of that, and it proves nothing. However, it is what I will tell you regarding what came after that will hopefully convince you I am no charlatan. Keep your mind open."

"I'll try."

"Once your mother was buried, you left and never spoke to anyone here or came back. You were sad and lonely and found a boy who was also sad and lonely and gave yourself to him. There was a child, a child who died before it could have a chance to live. You and this boy eventually parted ways, but you did not give yourself to another for many years, not until recently. You were so alone for so long," the elderly woman continued. "But you did such good work and helped so many others. The problem was that you forgot about yourself. Ever the brilliant gem that refused to shine in the presence of others.

"You found a father and a friend in an old man and are extremely close to him. He recognized you for what you were and treated you as you should have been treated all along."

"Tom," I said quietly.

"He is a very smart man with a very tangled past," she proclaimed. "He loves you very much." When I began to cry, she said, "It will be quick. He will not suffer."

I was grateful for her words but cried harder. Esmeralda moved her chair and sat beside me then put an arm around my shoulders and offered me a tissue.

"As for the man you love, he is another male who is smart, handsome, loyal, and loving. However, his past is also tangled like a skein of yarn that cannot be unwound. He will love you until his dying day and you him. You will have many happy memories. There will also be some seemingly insurmountable challenges."

"What kinds of challenges?"

"*That* I cannot see. All I can say is that he will be gone from you for a time but not by his choice, and it will be up to you to find him. There will be danger there although I do not understand what kind or why. You will do what you have to in order to save the man you love, just as he will do with you."

"Will Michael and I have children?"

"The man you love can never father a child. You will have a family, but you should never try to carry a baby yourself again. You are not able to carry one to term. Each of your babies would die, and you would not be relieved as you were the first time. So, it is fortunate that things worked out this way." She gave me a knowing smile and said, "There are children in need, and the two of you have much to give."

I smiled back and wiped away my tears. So, Michael and I weren't meant to have biological children. It wasn't the end of the world. This was an opportunity.

"You have recently received a large amount of money and are troubled by its source. You want to get rid of it, but you should not give it away. The tragedy that brought it to you was unavoidable and should not taint what was meant to be a gesture of thanks."

"What should I do with it?"

"Invest it and let it allow you and your lover to do good work in your business and in your family. Remember the goodness of the people who gave you this money and not the circumstances of their deaths."

"Do you see how they died?"

"No. I only sense that it was a tragedy and that you blame yourself. It was not your fault."

"I'll try to accept that. What else?"

"You need help, a professional person to talk with about your past. You run away from this, but you can't run forever." When I stared at the tissue in my hands, she added, "Most importantly, you must tell this man you love about what torments you, or else your future together is in jeopardy and nothing I have foreseen will come to pass."

Neither of us spoke for a long while. Finally, I asked, "Will I ever know where I came from? Did you see anything about my ancestors?"

She nodded distractedly and said, "Your father was a simple farmworker whose father was a simple farmworker married to a farmer's daughter. His father was a brilliant but reckless man. One of those he seduced was a young woman from a wealthy family. She was shamed by your grandfather's birth, and he was marked for life as a bastard child."

"Could you see his real name or that of my great-grandparents?"

"The gift does not work like that. I do not "see" names, sweet girl."

"And my mother?"

"Her mother was very young and gave birth terrified and alone under a tree, poor child. The father never knew about the baby. Your mother was left at a church with her mother's most prized possession. The girl never recovered physically or mentally from delivering and abandoning her daughter and died not long afterwards. It is very sad, although your mother was raised by loving people. Because of her own abandonment, she always felt as though she was lacking somehow. She was a giving person." Picking up the stone from the table, she said, "Your brilliance comes from your great-grandfather, and your heart comes from your mother. The combination is a beautiful one, and you should never deny or waste either gift. Trust your heart, and all things are possible."

She handed me back the stone heart and folded my fingers around it.

"What can I do for you?" I asked her. "You revealed things about me and my family that no one else alive could ever know. You spoke of so many private details regarding my life that helped me to believe you. I trust what you've said that filled in some of the blanks, even though there are a lot of blanks left."

"That is the beauty of life. If we knew and understood all, then why would we go on?"

"Surely there's something I can do for you," I tried again.

"There is."

Esmeralda disappeared into the back of the house and returned five minutes later carrying a large box that had once been white but had yellowed with age. When I went to lift the lid, she stopped me and told me to wait until I got home and until no one else was around to view the contents. I agreed and thanked her for sharing with me whatever was inside.

"Such a good girl," Esmeralda remarked. "I told you that you would become a great woman, and I was right. Take care of yourself. Have a beautiful life."

Placing the box in my trunk, I got into my car and dialed Tom's number. I was surprised when Michael answered the phone and said, "I decided to work over here this afternoon."

I could hear the strain in his voice and asked, "Tom's not well?"

"No."

"How are his sugar levels?"

He hesitated, and I knew Tom must be nearby and was listening to Michael's side of the conversation.

"I've played this game with relatives of clients before and have learned a few tricks over the years," I told Michael before instructing, "Just answer yes, no, or I don't know. Are his sugar levels high?"

"Yes."

"How high?"

"I don't know."

"Has he taken his meds today?"

"I don't know."

"He won't talk to you about it?"

"No."

I sighed and told Michael, "You're going to have to convince him to tell you or go to the hospital. I'm over two hours away from his house, and he needs to get his levels down before then."

"You're a couple of hours away?"

Now it was my turn to answer in monosyllables.

"Yes."

"You went home," he stated matter-of-factly.

"Yes and no." As I started the engine of my car, I said, "Let me speak to Tom. Don't worry. I won't let your senior officer know you've been ratting him out."

Michael laughed, and I relaxed slightly. I hadn't realized how tense I'd become during our talk until then.

"My lovely Seneca," Tom said, as he came on the phone. "Did I hear Michael say you were two hours away?"

"You did. I won't have time to cook, so I was going to pick up some food for our dinner. What do you want?"

"Pasta would be good."

"What's your blood sugar level this afternoon?"

When he told me, I took a deep breath and asked, "Did you take your medications this morning?"

He couldn't remember, and tears stung my eyes.

"Tom, I'm going to ask Michael to help you with your meds, so do what he tells you, okay? Pretend like it's me."

"But he's not," Tom insisted. "I'm glad for the company, but I can't for the life of me remember why he came over."

I could hear the confusion in his voice. I asked to talk to Michael again and told him I would be at Tom's house as soon as I could with something that would *not* be pasta. I had to work hard to keep my voice level as I said, "Michael, his blood sugar is dangerously high. You're going to have to help him."

"How do I do it? How much medication do I give him?"

"I'll review it with you. How did you end up at his house today?"

"I'll explain later. Tell me what I have to do now."

I directed Michael to test Tom's blood sugar levels again and reviewed how the machine and test strips worked. Once he verified the high number, I explained the treatment and how best to get Tom to cooperate.

"Seneca, you know what I was. I'll get the job done."

"Tom was what you were, too. He may be old and a bit confused right now, but I suspect he could instinctively react if he got mixed-up and thought you were trying to kill him. I don't want either of you hurt, okay?"

"I'll be careful and do what you said."

Relieved, I asked Michael to test Tom's sugar levels again after he'd given the medication time to take effect. He promised to call me with an update. By the time I made it to Tom's house Michael had updated me several times, and Tom's sugar levels were only slightly elevated.

"I'm too goddamn tired to eat," Tom grumbled after I'd hugged him tightly and told him I'd brought steak and salad for dinner. "I feel like crap. Michael wouldn't let me go to bed."

"That's because I told him not to. You have to put something in your stomach before you sleep tonight. Michael said you weren't sure what you ate for breakfast or lunch or if you took your pills, even though you promised me you would."

"Well, I didn't feel like eating cardboard today," he said grumpily. "I didn't want to get a lecture on how I had to eat and take my damn meds!"

"If you had taken them, then none of this would've happened," I countered. "You really need to think about moving into a retirement community or having a full-time companion. I told you that a long time ago."

"Absolutely not," he said indignantly. "I refuse to move in with a bunch of old coots!"

"Tom, it was very fortunate Michael was here today. You could've died."

"This isn't living; this is existing." He looked away and said, "I'm ready to go."

It took every ounce of willpower I possessed not to break down and cry, but I wasn't about to do that in front of Tom. If I did, then I knew I wouldn't be able to get the reaction I needed from him in order to keep him fighting.

"You're not going anywhere," I informed him. "You said you were going to walk me down the aisle at my wedding, and I dare you to renege on your promise!"

He straightened in his chair and said, "I did promise you that, didn't I? I do want to be there when you and Michael tie the knot." Settling back in his recliner, he added, "It'd be nice to see you have babies. You're going to make a great mother, and Michael will be a great father."

I touched his cheek and said, "You know, we've been talking about that. I think adoption might be the way to go for us. There are so many children out there who need homes. Look at my mother. She was adopted."

While Tom ruminated on my idea, I went to the kitchen to take the food out of the boxes and prepare our plates.

"Were you serious about the adoption thing?" Michael asked as he came up behind me and slipped his strong arms around my waist.

"Yes." I leaned back against his chest and said, "We're not even married, yet. We have lots of time to discuss it."

"I have to talk about this now. It's bothering me."

"Are you against adoption?"

"Not at all. Even if we had our own kids, I wouldn't mind adopting. I just want to have babies of our own, too. We can't, and it's my fault. It's so damn frustrating!"

"It's not your fault."

"It is," he argued.

I sighed and asked him if we could talk about it later in private since I could hear Tom making his way into the kitchen. Michael agreed and released me, and we all sat down to steak and salad. The mood at the table was tense for the first time since I'd eaten a meal at Tom's house.

We sat with Tom for an hour after he ate, and I checked his sugar levels again before admitting he was stable enough to be left alone. Michael and I said our goodbyes to him, and he thanked us for helping him while he'd been confused and for his dinner.

"I need to go to Nonno's," Michael told me as he walked me to my car. "I've got a staff meeting tomorrow and all my paperwork relating to it is at his place. I'll probably spend the night there and go straight in to work from his house in the morning."

I knew this was avoidance on his part but merely kissed him and told him I'd miss him that night and would talk with him tomorrow. Then I drove home, went to the laptop Michael kept next to mine in the guest bedroom, logged on, got on Skype and called Dr. Forrester. We had a long discussion about Michael, his sterility, my suggestion of adoption, and his reaction. The psychiatrist suggested a few ways I could help Michael but basically told me to be patient.

"I'm Michael's therapist. I work with extraordinary men and women like him who've served our country in Special Forces and ended up damaged in various ways." Leaning forward, he said, "You may not fit into the military category, but you are definitely extraordinary and definitely damaged. When you're ready, I'd like to help you, too."

If I'm ever ready, I thought.

After we'd ended the video chat, I went to my bedroom and stared at the box Esmeralda had given me. I was tired and sad and didn't really feel like opening it, but my curiosity wouldn't let me wait. I lifted the lid of the box and saw blue tissue paper. I carefully unfolded it and saw white tissue paper underneath. Reaching into the pile, I gingerly pulled out the contents of the box and reminded myself to breathe as I stared at the handmade wedding dress.

I stripped off my clothing where I stood and took great care in slipping on the garment. Considering that Esmeralda was probably seventy, I estimated that her wedding gown was at least fifty years old. The bodice was fitted, and the skirt was full and had definitely been made to be worn with a petticoat. Handmade lace covered the entire dress. The same lace had been fashioned into long sleeves. A matching lace shawl was folded beneath the dress. A lace veil lay under the shawl.

The dress fit me perfectly. It was beautiful, flattering, and would be exactly the right length once I had a petticoat underneath the skirt. I had a false sense of belonging, of having older female relatives creating this gown specifically for my wedding day.

I returned the gown and the other articles to the box. The only things I lacked were shoes and the petticoat, and those would be easy enough to find. I was thankful that the tissue paper or whatever the elderly woman had done to preserve the dress had protected it and stopped it from yellowing. It was certainly antique and looked it, but it was in near-mint condition.

After tucking the box in the closet, I poured myself a glass of red wine and took a long, hot bath then got ready to go to sleep. I felt lonely without Michael lying beside me, and I hoped he would only be gone for one night.

Chapter Twelve

At the end of July, I was given permission by my doctor to resume all normal activity, so I started working at John's Place. I was quickly caught up in my interactions with the veterans and their families and got along extremely well with my co-workers. I was also busy planning a wedding that would take place at the beginning of August. Tom had been hospitalized again with pleurisy. Krystal and I continued to attend our weekly Less of You meetings, and I'd introduced her to Adiba. The three of us and little Hadeel were spending time together each week either eating, shopping, or cooking, and Michael, Greg, and Rakeem had formed an equally diverse but close friendship. Al and Diane had gone to Sicily for a week and had returned with exciting stories of their trip and of Al's visit to the area where he'd lived as a boy.

Michael and I had resumed our Friday night attendance at Ceviche with The Gang for dinner and dancing, but we'd decided to wait to make love again until after we were married. *That* had been a challenge, and Michael had been sleeping at his grandfather's house every night. When he was at my place, we'd spent a considerable time in the Gulf waters where he'd taught me how to swim well. I had taught him the basics of cooking. We'd also read, watched DVDs and television, discussed a variety of interesting topics and events, and talked about the upcoming wedding. In other words, we'd pretty much done everything except have sex.

Michael was receiving individual therapy from Dr. Forrester, and both of us were participating in virtual sessions with the psychiatrist regarding Michael's struggle with accepting his sterility. I still refused to discuss my nightmare with anyone. I tried, but I found that I couldn't even begin to talk about it. Neither of them pushed me, but I knew they were both concerned.

The Benedetto relatives began to arrive on August first. For the next week, Michael and I spent each day at John's Place and every evening with the family. There were so many aunts, uncles, and

140

cousins that it was going to take me years to put faces with names and remember the relationships between everyone. Al and Michael were eager for me to accept them all and to be accepted, and things went well. For the most part, the relatives were happy, friendly men, women, and children who seemed to genuinely like spending time together. I was looking forward to getting to know them over the course of the rest of my life.

On the night of the rehearsal, a Wednesday, the principals in our wedding party arrived in the atrium courtyard next to Michael's on East Restaurant in Sarasota. We'd decided to marry there since it provided an unusual setting and a huge reception room. The courtyard was long and rather narrow but had a fountain in the center, murals on the wall, and live plantings in various locations throughout the space. The place would be packed, but we were confident it would fit the number of people attending.

Tom was escorting me from outside the gates to the designated spot where the ceremony would take place. Krystal was my Maid of Honor, and Michael had asked Al to be his Best Man, which had pleased Al enormously. Although Rakeem and Adiba had been asked to be part of the wedding party, both had declined for religious reasons but had been completely supportive of our marriage and were, therefore, invited to the rehearsal. Greg was there as well. Diane had emerged as the consummate last-minute wedding planner and was in her element telling everyone where to stand and what to do.

One of Michael's uncles was a priest who lived in northern Florida and had readily agreed to marry us even though I wasn't Catholic and the ceremony was not to involve a traditional Roman Catholic Mass. We had been in close contact with him via e-mail regarding our wishes, and he'd worked with us to refine our ceremony. I was thankful for his guidance.

The practice run didn't take long, and all of us went into the restaurant for the rehearsal dinner. Adiba was worried about Hadeel, whom she had left with a babysitter for the first time. I had recommended the woman from Hearts at Home and reassured her that her daughter would be fine. I was glad to see her relax.

We all had a wonderful meal and a nice evening together before saying our goodbyes. Michael kissed me deeply before wishing me sweet dreams and telling me how much he was looking forward to our wedding. I told him how much I loved him and made him promise not to stay up all night working.

We were taking two weeks off from John's Place to go on a honeymoon. I'd told Michael we could wait, that his business was too new, and my time there too short for both of us to leave for that length of time. He had been insistent that we have a proper honeymoon but wouldn't tell me where we were going. Frankly, it made me slightly nervous not to know our destination, but it was exciting as well.

Krystal was spending the night at my house to help me pack and get ready the following day for my 6:00 p.m. wedding. She was as excited as I was. I prayed that Greg would ask her to marry him soon.

"So, are you dying to see your ring?" Krystal asked for the umpteenth time before we went to bed. "I think it's really cool that neither of you has seen your wedding rings before the ceremony, although what if you don't like it?"

"I guess I'll have to fake it if it's not to my taste. It's a ring, Krystal. It's the symbolism that means something to me."

"You are so different," Krystal said with a grin. "That's what makes you so special."

"You're special," I protested. "You're a great friend."

"Thanks. You, too." She stretched and asked, "Does it feel weird to be getting married on a Thursday?"

"It was the only date we could have it at Michael's on East with such short notice and have the facility and catering in the hall. I think it's kind of sweet that we're doing it differently from most people. The Benedetto relatives are all here anyway, so we're not putting anyone out by asking them to take off during the week to congregate here. Since it's after work, it won't affect anyone else locally except you since you'll be taking off tomorrow."

"I'm happy to do it. Your wedding is going to be perfect, Seneca. I just know it will."

If I dreamed that night, I didn't recall anything. I was fine with that. I woke at 7:00 and found Krystal having coffee on the lanai. I joined her, and we talked of the day to come before going inside to feed Doc and eat a light breakfast. Then Krystal helped me pack my suitcase and carry-on bag for my honeymoon.

We met Diane for lunch, then we went to the salon, where we were all treated by Diane to the usual round of pampering that she adored so much. Krystal was in awe and loved every moment of it. By the time we left, we were completely ready for the wedding save for our special attire.

Everything was waiting for us at Diane's. The two women fussed over me and carefully helped me to don the antique dress. They were the only persons who'd seen the gown, and Diane had helped me find the perfect low-heeled white shoes to match. Krystal was the one who had gone with me to buy the petticoat.

I sat patiently as Diane put on a light green satin dress that had a short jacket and a skirt that went to her calves. I'd told Krystal to buy whatever gown made her feel the most comfortable physically and emotionally, and she'd chosen a deep pink taffeta gown that had a simple neckline and cap sleeves. Although she'd lost almost thirty pounds, she was still a large woman. The way the dress was cut was very flattering for someone her size.

"You both look great," I said enthusiastically. "This all feels so surreal."

"Well, you do like those Surrealist painters," Diane pointed out. She smiled gently and said, "You look like a Spanish princess, Seneca. I'm so glad you had the stylist leave your hair down with the loose curls. It's going to be perfect with the veil." Glancing around the dressing room, she asked, "Now, where are your earrings? Oh, there they are."

She handed me the pearl earrings that hung from French hooks, and I slipped them into the holes below my little diamond studs. Then she and Krystal painstakingly placed the band across the top of my head that would secure the veil. It looked like a narrow crown adorned with tiny pearls and was exactly what was needed in order to keep the waist-length veil in place.

Barely able to contain her excitement, Krystal asked, "Are you ready to see how gorgeous you look?"

I steeled myself and stepped in front of the full-length mirror. I *did* look beautiful, and I so wanted my mother standing in the room with us to see me dressed up like a princess. I wanted my father waiting nearby to tell me how pretty I was. I swallowed the lump in my throat.

"You want your parents here," commented Diane. "I had the same feeling on my wedding day. The shame of it was that they were still alive and could have come but chose not to. Yours may be gone, but I'm sure they can see you from wherever it is they are now. They'll be with you for your wedding. Remember that."

Krystal, Diane, and I arrived at Michael's on East in a limo at quarter to six. The following fifteen minutes went quickly, and I was soon standing outside the gate to the courtyard. Krystal gave me a quick once-over while we waited, and we fiddled with our bouquets. Mine was composed completely of white roses, while hers was assembled with white roses and tiny pink rosebuds. Al and Tom looked distinguished in their black tuxedos. Al beamed at me and said he was forcing himself not to hug me so that he wouldn't mess up my clothing, make-up, and hair. Tom became emotional the instant he saw me and told me how lovely I looked and how proud he was of me. We took our positions, and I placed my hand on his arm.

I peered around the corner. Dozens of chairs had been arranged in rows facing the area of the courtyard where we would take our wedding vows. The place was packed with Benedettos, co-workers from John's Place, some of Michael's Navy buddies, our friends from the Ceviche group, some of my former co-workers and my former boss from Hearts at Home, and Greg, Adiba, Rakeem, and Hadeel. We had quite an audience.

The string quartet began to play, and Krystal lowered the veil over my face before stepping beside Al and taking his arm. The two of them walked towards the fountain where Michael and his uncle were waiting. Tom and I moved forward. Our progress was slow since he couldn't walk quickly regardless. I was relieved that we didn't have too far to go.

When we reached Michael, Tom lifted my veil and lightly kissed me on the cheek before carefully making his way to his seat in the front row next to Diane. Everyone was extremely quiet, even the small children. It was an odd feeling to have all of those eyes focused on us.

I turned towards Michael, who looked amazing in a black tuxedo. I'd originally wondered if he would wear a U.S. Naval dress uniform, but he'd told me that wasn't his intention and hadn't elucidated. He'd decided to wear a black tux specially purchased for the occasion. What he'd chosen was not dramatically different, but it did seem to highlight his powerful body even more than usual, although that may have been my imagination.

My heart swelled with love and pride as I stared up at him. I saw that his blue eyes were shining with tears. He seemed awed by the sight of me, and I blushed.

Michael's uncle opened the ceremony with a prayer then gave an eloquent sermon about Michael and me, our love, and our marriage. The vows we'd written promised that we would love, honor, trust, and protect one another and use our bond and gifts in order to make the world a better place.

"And now the rings," Michael's uncle announced.

Al handed his grandson my wedding ring, and I held my breath with anticipation. I hadn't realized how curious I'd been about the ring until then. Michael lifted my hand, slipped the ring on my finger, and proclaimed, "With this ring, I thee wed."

The platinum ring had a filigree Art Deco appearance and held a half-carat single cut diamond with smaller diamonds on either side. It looked antique, and I wanted to take it off on the spot so I could examine it more closely. Instead, I smiled up at Michael and reached back to Krystal for his ring.

I'd selected a gold bullion Mexican peso ring for Michael. It was definitely not the traditional wedding band, but I'd been drawn to it the moment I'd seen it. The jeweler had explained to me that the reverse side of the coin faced out. It displayed the image of an eagle holding a serpent in its beak, was made of the purest gold produced in the oldest mint in North America, and was almost one hundred years old. The ring was beautiful, solid, and pure with an image that reminded me of something strong and noble overpowering what was sly and evil. It reminded me of Michael himself.

Michael smiled broadly when he saw it, so I took that to mean he liked the ring. I slipped it on his finger and said, "With this ring, I thee wed."

Michael's uncle concluded the ceremony with, "By the power vested in me by the State of Florida, I now pronounce you husband and wife. May God bless you all the days of your lives. Michael, kiss your bride. Seneca, kiss your husband!"

We kissed, and those gathered clapped and cheered. Michael's uncle announced us as Mr. Michael Benedetto and Mrs. Seneca Benedetto, and we got a standing ovation. The string quartet began to play again, and Michael escorted me towards the banquet hall section of the restaurant. Round tables with balloon centerpieces filled the room. A deejay had been hired to play music of varying types such as jazz, rock, blues, and pop but not at top volume since none of us wanted to have to shout to be heard.

Waiters came around with trays of appetizers as the buffet tables were being readied. For the next three hours, those in the hall talked, ate, drank, danced, and laughed. The photographers and videographers were kept busy with our lively group.

Eventually, things began to wind down. Michael glanced at his watch and nodded to me, as I excused myself and went to change clothes. Krystal and Diane assisted me as I removed my gown and accoutrements. Since Michael had requested in advance that I dress comfortably for the trip ahead, I donned a long, full, black cotton skirt, some backless sandals, and a dark purple shirt that buttoned down the front. I put on my silver hoop earrings in place of the pearls.

I thanked Krystal and Diane for all of their help then hugged each woman. Krystal threw herself into the sisterly embrace, but Diane was more reserved. I wasn't offended and was actually pleased that she'd hugged me, period. Normally, the only person she showed physical affection for was Al.

When I returned to the reception, Michael was waiting for me in dark blue jeans, a long-sleeved black shirt, and casual black shoes. Everyone gravitated towards us as we headed for the exit, and we were showered with birdseed and well wishes.

"Wow," Michael muttered tiredly. "That was the best wedding and reception I've ever attended."

"Me, too. I'm glad we agree since it was ours."

He suddenly turned towards me, slipped one hand behind my neck and the other into my hair, and slammed is mouth down on mine. The electrical charge between us was instantaneous, and my fingers were soon woven into his hair and my body was pressed firmly against his. I felt his fingers trail from my neck to one breast then one leg. He pushed up the hem of my skirt and slid his hand underneath the material. His palm glided along the outside of my knee and the back of my thigh before moving to my hip. I wasn't wearing any underwear, and he groaned slightly.

"Have you ever had sex in a limo?" When I told him no, he said, "Me neither. On our way home from the honeymoon, we'll have to try it."

We were soon walking through the Sarasota Bradenton International Airport with our bags. It was 10:30 p.m., and the airport was fairly deserted. This was when Michael told me we were heading to Washington, D.C. and its surrounding areas for our trip. I was thrilled but nervous. I was completely clueless when it came to air travel and followed Michael closely as we went through Security.

I'd expected us to take a commercial flight, but I was informed by Michael that a friend of his from the master's program at Harvard had his own plane and had agreed to fly us up to D.C., where he was already headed for business. I was then introduced to the friend, an ordinary-looking man with extraordinary business savvy. He apologized for having to miss our wedding due to prior commitments. Michael assured him that we understood.

I hadn't known that Michael's friend was also the pilot of the plane until we boarded. He introduced us to his co-pilot, who happened to be his personal assistant. She was a brunette who seemed to be highly intelligent. She had enormous breasts, and I wondered what her salary was and if she was simply his assistant or if she was an "assistant with benefits." It didn't matter to me as long as the two of them were satisfied with the arrangement.

Michael and I took our seats and buckled ourselves in. The night was clear, the moon was full, and I had an excellent view of the sky and the twinkling lights below as we began our flight northward. I found the experience of flying exhilarating and couldn't stop looking out of the window no matter where we were. Michael seemed tickled by my delighted reaction but also seemed sad. I asked him about the kinds of vehicles in which he'd been a passenger and got a long list that included different types of cars, planes, trains, tanks, and helicopters.

Suddenly, Michael got out of his seat and knelt in front of me. When I asked him what he was doing, he grinned wickedly and said he was getting ready to make love to me. I thought he was joking and told him to stop teasing. When I saw the animal look in his eyes, I knew he wasn't.

"We can't!"

"Why not?"

"There are two people at the front of the plane, remember? What if they come back here? Even if they don't, they'll hear us!"

"They won't, and they can't."

"How do you know that?"

"Because men talk, and my friend flying up there has told me about some of his exploits back here when he's had other people piloting the plane. You and I got married a few hours ago, and he's a really bright guy and will know what we want to do. His assistant's got a lot of brains as well as breasts. They'll stay up front and give us plenty of notice over the intercom when we need to prepare to land."

Michael unbuttoned my blouse and undid the hook on the front of my bra. He slid both hands under my skirt and pushed the material up towards my waist. At that point, he stopped and sat back on his heels.

"What is it?" I asked breathlessly. "What's wrong?"

"Nothing and everything. Any other night, I'd take you right here, right now, right like this. But tonight's our wedding night, and I want it to be right."

He stood and offered me his hand. Confused, I took it, rose, and allowed him to guide me towards the back of the plane. At the end was a door. Behind that door was a room with a bed. Michael removed my blouse, bra, and skirt after I'd stepped out of my sandals. I unbuttoned his shirt and unzipped his jeans then helped him off with his clothing once he'd kicked off his shoes. The brown silk sheets felt cool on my hot flesh, as I stretched out on top of them.

I knew he was afraid of hurting me again, but I was healed and more than ready. I wanted him immediately all the way inside of me but gave him time to be certain I was all right. As he finished his careful entry, I tilted my hips back and forth and thrilled at the growl of passion I got in response. He cradled the bend of my knees in the crook of his arms and moved so that my legs were spread wide. I was tight and pulsing around him and gave in to my first orgasm of the evening. Within minutes, I had another and then another as clouds passed by our window. The fourth and final one came when Michael lost himself in the most intense climax I'd ever seen him experience. He seemed more affected emotionally as he stilled above me and spilled inside me.

We lay exhausted and comfortable in someone else's bed in a plane that was thousands of miles above the earth. Michael lifted my left hand, brought it to his mouth, and kissed my ring finger.

"You really like the ring?" he asked.

"I love it. I think it might distract me too much since it's so beautiful and unique. Where did you find such a thing?"

"It belonged to Nonno's mother. His father gave it to her in 1929."

"Oh, Michael. That…that makes it even more amazing. Do you really like your ring?"

"I do. It…fits."

I knew he was talking about more than how the ring fit on his finger and explained why I'd chosen it. He kissed and caressed my skin while I spoke, which was deliciously distracting. After I'd finished my explanation, he told me how my perception of him gave him more strength and validation than anything else in the world.

"You can't know how I felt when I saw you in your wedding dress for the first time. It was almost too much for my heart to hold. I love you more than anything, Seneca. I only pray that I don't disappoint you in the end."

I was preparing to tell him he could never disappoint me when the pilot's voice announced over the intercom that we would be landing in forty minutes. I kissed my husband and prepared to rise from the bed, but he stopped me.

"Promise me that you'll always love me no matter what," he said soberly.

"You know I will. I want the same promise from you."

He nodded then kissed me again. We hastened to shower – yes there was actually a shower on the plane – and dress before returning to our seats. When we landed, Michael's friend and his well-endowed assistant asked me how I'd enjoyed my first flight.

"I'll never forget it," I told them truthfully. "It was a once-in-a-lifetime experience that I never expected to have."

"Unexpected experiences can be the best ones," Michael proclaimed. "You never know what's in store for us. That's part of the thrill of life."

Chapter Thirteen

"Seneca, it's time to eat."

"Five more minutes," I said as I read the plaque on a case that held an ancient artifact. "Look at this!"

Michael came up behind me and slipped his arms around my waist. We were both wearing khaki shorts, and I had on a light cotton embroidered top while he wore a brown shirt that hugged his muscles and flat belly. He pressed against me from behind, and I could feel his hardness through our clothing.

"We can come back after lunch and look around more." Kissing my neck, he murmured enticingly, "We can go to the restaurant in the National Museum of the American Indian."

"You're not playing fair," I told him. "You know I won't say no to that ever."

The food at the museum was representative of authentic Native American cuisine, and I'd quickly become addicted to it. The restaurant had emerged as "my" place to eat lunch. Michael was thrilled, since he loved it, too. The one day when we'd been too far away to eat lunch there, we had eaten chicken strips and fries at a stand. We'd both been sorely disappointed.

We left the Smithsonian Institution National Museum of Natural History and walked through the oppressive heat towards our lunch destination. We were halfway there when we heard someone call out, "Michael!"

Michael tightened his grip on my hand and moved closer to me as he quickly looked in the direction from which the voice had emanated. When his fingers loosened, I knew he must recognize whoever had called out to him. He smiled as a brown-haired man in tan pants and a blue shirt approached us. The man had what I'd come to think of as "The Look." He was tall, well-muscled, confident, and with no extra weight or fat on his frame. Another current or former operative for the government....

The men warmly greeted each other then Michael said, "Seneca, this is my friend, Rob Kilmer. Rob, this is my wife, Seneca. We got married last week. I would have sent you an invitation, but I literally didn't know where in the world you were."

Rob grinned and congratulated both of us before telling me what a pleasure it was for him to meet me. I told him the pleasure was mine and that he shared the same name as my father, Robert. I also informed him that we were going to lunch and asked if he wanted to join us. He readily accepted, admitting that he and Michael hadn't seen one another in several years and that he'd appreciate being able to spend a little time with him.

"How long have you been in D.C.?" he asked, as we walked towards the museum for our lunch.

"A week," I answered excitedly. "We've been to all the major museums, the Jefferson Memorial, the Washington Monument, and the Bureau of Engraving and Printing, plus the Library of Congress."

"Seneca's never been to D.C. before," Michael told his friend.

"I've never really been anywhere before," I corrected. "I'm loving it! I think I'd live in the Museum of Natural History if they'd let me."

Both men laughed, and Michael gave me a quick kiss before telling Rob, "Don't believe for a minute that she's joking."

Rob grinned and asked Michael something in what sounded like Greek. Michael nodded and responded in the same language, and Rob suddenly clapped him on the back and said something that made Michael chuckle and shake his head.

"Okay, so I don't speak Greek," I said with mock irritation. "English or Spanish, please."

"Guy talk," Michael told me. "Don't worry. What I said was very flattering."

Realizing they must have been talking about sex, I blushed and turned my head. As we stepped into the lobby of the museum, I excused myself to use the restroom. I took my time freshening up in order to give the men an opportunity to talk for a while.

I found them sitting on a bench deeply engrossed in a conversation in Greek. When Rob looked up at me, there was a new respect and admiration in his eyes. I deduced that Michael must have told him more about me and wondered what he'd said.

151

As we ate our lunch together, we learned that Rob was currently employed by NASA and was temporarily at the Museum of Science, coordinating a special exhibit opening in September. He and I got into a discussion about the Large Hadron Collider and the scientific questions that could be answered by the research being performed using its resultant data. During this conversation, it was Michael who sat quietly and merely listened to our debate, which lasted a considerable length of time.

"Holy shit," Rob said when we'd concluded our discussion. "You're a social worker? What's your I.Q.?"

"Okay, I know I'm guilty of asking the same question of Michael, but I'm so over the I.Q. thing. Why is everyone so hung up on that? It's a number, and I'm a person."

"She's smarter than me," Michael put in. "She refuses to be tested."

"You could be working for NASA," Rob offered. "Hell, you could be working for *anyone*. Why didn't you go into science as a career?"

"I prefer helping people face-to-face. Studying science is one of my personal passions, but I didn't want to do it as a profession. The same could be said for history or various other subjects."

Shaking his head, Rob muttered, "Unbelievable." He reached into his pocket and pulled out a business card then handed it to me with the words, "If you ever change your mind, call me."

I smiled and thanked him before handing him my business card and slipping his into my wallet. I knew I would never call him for a job, but his contact information might be useful if I was in the mood for scientific debate.

"So, what are your plans for the rest of your honeymoon?" Rob asked.

"Tonight we're going out for a very special dinner experience," Michael told him. "Seneca's been after me to tell her where we're eating, but it's a surprise."

"Surprises can be good," Rob agreed. "And tomorrow?"

"Tomorrow we'll go to the Lincoln Memorial and all the war memorials before we head to Mount Vernon, Monticello, and the Blue Ridge Mountains. We'll come back here for one last day next week then fly home early the following morning."

We parted ways, agreeing to meet for dinner on our last night in D.C. Michael and I returned to the National Museum of Natural History, stayed until closing time, and then took a cab back to our hotel. We showered, and he donned a dark suit with a dress shirt, silk tie, and dress shoes. I slipped into a sophisticated, sexy red dress and black pumps.

I could see his reflection in the mirror as I put on my make-up. He had the animal look in his eyes, and I wondered if we were going to make it to dinner after all. I would have been satisfied either way. In the end, Michael busied himself by checking his e-mail while I arranged my hair and put on my jewelry. When I was ready, we left the room, took the elevator down, and hailed a taxi. Michael gave the driver an address, and I settled back into his arms as our cab wound its way through the evening traffic.

"You can't imagine how happy I am to reconnect with Rob," Michael told me during our ride to the mystery destination. "You really impressed him" he continued, as he fingered one of my curls. "It takes a lot to impress him."

"He impressed me, too. He seems so nice, and he certainly knows his science."

"Among other things."

"How long did you work together?"

"About six years off and on." As he ran his hand along my leg and up to my waist, he added, "He's a good man and great at what he did."

"Which was?"

Michael slid his hand higher up, and I felt my face flush as he caressed my breast then lifted my chin so that he could kiss me. By the time we broke apart, the cab had stopped in front of a building that looked more like a grand old mansion than a restaurant. We entered through the front door and were greeted by a congenial elderly man dressed in formal attire.

"Good evening, Mister and Missus Benedetto," he said in greeting. "Welcome."

We both thanked him, even though I was mystified as to where exactly we were and what was in store for us. Michael put one arm around my waist and tucked me close to him in that age-old wordless male declaration that said "mine" as we walked past a couple in the hallway who were obviously on their way out. I noticed that the man, who oozed an aura of power, and the woman, who seemed well-heeled, appeared totally relaxed but looked a bit disheveled. I said nothing as we followed the elderly man to a door at the end of the hallway.

"Your room is the first one on your right. Have a pleasant evening."

A man who was also attired in formalwear asked us to take a seat at the small dining table so that dinner could begin. Since we were still not alone, I scanned the room and was left speechless by the luxurious setting. Everything around us seemed to be made of marble, crystal, silk, fur, or gold leaf. Normally, such opulence did not impress me. I was still a poor girl at heart and preferred simple elegance to lavishness. Yet, this sumptuous feast for the eyes was not off-putting; it was breathtaking.

Candles in faceted crystal holders flickered in various locations. I saw a piece of furniture that resembled an old-fashioned settee, two ornate end tables, a small dining table with two chairs, a sideboard, and a large gold-leaf bed with large matching nightstands on either side. A huge crystal chandelier hung from the ceiling.

Michael led me to the table set for two that was situated in one corner of the large room. The china, stemware, and flatware were elegant and obviously very costly. Beautiful flowers had been artfully arranged in the center of the table around a glowing candle in a crystal holder. The well-dressed man pulled out my chair for me, and I took my seat. Michael sat across from me, as a woman in an elegant black dress appeared with a bottle of wine.

Once our glasses had been filled, another woman who was similarly dressed brought in two plates dotted with something that looked sinfully delicious. She explained that it was lump crabmeat in their signature sauce complemented by two tablespoons of a special paella then excused herself from the room so that we could start our meal.

Before I could begin to ask the first of my long list of questions, Michael said, "Trust me and just enjoy yourself. This is a place where people come for amazing food, amazing drink, and an amazing time together. A friend told me about it a while back. I swore if I ever got married I'd bring my wife here at least once to experience all that this is."

The food brought to us throughout the next hour was divine, and the alternating wines and champagne were outstanding. Although the portions were small, I knew I was probably going to gain ten pounds after the meal but had to admit that it would be worth it. Following dessert, a man came and cleared the table then left us alone. Michael and I moved to sit on the settee, which turned out to be surprisingly comfortable. He held me in his arms, and we talked of the things we'd seen and done on our trip and of the places we would be heading to next. I was truly happy. When I shared this with Michael, he smiled at me and told me that I'd made him happier than I could ever know.

"I love to hear you say that," I murmured. "Let's never stop saying these things to each other."

"Never."

We kissed for what seemed like forever. By the time we came up for air, my pantyhose and underwear lay on the floor, and Michael's fly was unzipped. His suit jacket, tie, and shirt were draped over the back of the settee, and his hands had found their way up under my skirt and were holding me firmly on the hips. His fingers were quickly inside me, and I climaxed immediately.

"I love the way you come so often when I'm with you," he confided. "To know that I can make you feel that way over and over provides me with indescribable pleasure."

"I never did that before I met you," I reminded him.

Michael stood and deftly removed his shoes, socks, pants, and boxers. He unzipped the back of my dress and lifted it up over my head then removed my bra. Staring down at me, he shook his head as if in wonderment before walking across the room and lifting a large, thick, dark, fur coverlet that was draped across the foot of the bed and spreading it out on top.

"Michael, if someone has to clean that –"

He pulled me to my feet and told me not to worry about anything except us. Then he led me to the bed and guided me until I was stretched out on my back. Simply experiencing the sensation of lying on top of the thick fur was arousing, and I trembled slightly as Michael climbed onto the bed and knelt beside me.

I looked up into those blue eyes of his and knew he was waiting for something. He began to caress me with his palms and stroked my entire body in this way from my head to my feet, all the while

155

allowing that beautiful hardness to rub against my flesh. He suddenly lay beside me and slipped his arms around me then effortlessly lifted me until I was on top of him. He closed his eyes and moaned as I drove him into me and undulated my hips.

"Tell me you love me," he said, his voice barely recognizable.

"I love you."

"Tell me you want me."

"I want you."

"Tell me you forgive me."

"I forgive you."

He shuddered beneath me, and I felt wetness on my thighs. I had the distinct impression that he hadn't been asking for my forgiveness regarding the injury he'd inflicted upon me earlier that summer. I sensed that he wanted forgiveness for what he considered to be transgressions against others, mankind, God, or himself, and that he somehow felt I could absolve him of his guilt and pain. Obviously, somehow I could.

I lay beside my husband and rested my head on his chest as he wrapped his arms around me. Exhausted, I slept deeply and woke some time later to find myself bundled in the fur throw. I was overly warm but also extremely comfortable in this cocoon of fur and didn't want to get up. The chandelier had been turned off, but the candles still flickered around the room. Michael was not in the bed with me, and I wondered idly where he'd gone.

I finally determined that I had no choice but to rise and go to the bathroom. I sat up in bed and let the fur fall away from me before standing and stretching. I went to the bathroom half-expecting to find Michael there, but he was not. So, I showered and washed my hair then toweled dry and went back to the main room to dress.

Michael was sitting on the settee. He was fully dressed, and I could tell as I approached that he'd already showered. He watched me walk naked across the room towards him and pulled me into his lap once I got close enough. He then buried his face against my neck and said, "I dreamed I got you pregnant."

"We'll have our babies, just not like that."

He was silent, and I simply held him, although I was getting cold sitting in the open with no clothes on. I lowered my hand and began to rub my palm across the front of his pants. His clothing was soon removed once again, and we pushed away the fur and pillows and ended up between the cool silk sheets. Although he didn't hurt me, Michael was like some wild beast that had been unleashed and had but one purpose, which was to bring us both to climax after climax.

I had anticipated being worn out by dawn, but Michael and I seemed almost intoxicated and invigorated by our night of ceaseless passion. We were brought a fabulous breakfast, which we quickly devoured. When we left the house, whatever it was called, the doorman thanked us for coming. I swore there was a mischievous twinkle in his eyes when he said it.

We returned to our hotel. Since we'd both showered once during the night then again at dawn, we simply brushed our teeth, changed, and packed up our things. We checked out of the hotel and checked our bags at the desk, declaring that we'd return for them and the rental car later in the day. Then we took a cab to the Lincoln Memorial.

I was fascinated by the sheer size of the statue of Abraham Lincoln. It was all I could do to tear myself away from his kindly yet imperious presence, but I knew I couldn't linger forever. We had other places we needed to be.

The National World War II Memorial was nicely done but wasn't emotionally affecting for me. This was unexpected since I'd always been fascinated by World War II history and impacted by events and stories of those who'd fought and died during the war. Michael shared with me that he'd had the same reaction, which made me feel better.

The Vietnam Veterans Memorial Wall brought tears to my eyes the moment I saw it. Some people were crying, and some were merely observing. There was talking, but it was a quiet sort of talk that showed respect for those whose names appeared on the monument. As Michael and I walked slowly past name after name, I saw little tributes left by others. There were tiny flags, flowers, toy tanks and planes, teddy bears, and a myriad of other trinkets along the ground. People were taking pictures of particular names and touching the wall when they found friends or family members listed. Michael and I walked slowly and solemnly through the memorial but didn't stop.

The Korean War Veterans Memorial had an immediate and deep impact on me. A triangle of granite walls depicted military action on land, sea, and air. As we wandered inside the area along the perimeter of the "field" of larger-than-life realistic-looking soldiers made of steel, I began to cry. The "men" brought home to me more than any other war memorial the personal loss of life, limb, and innocence as well as the dedication to the ideals of their country. I removed a tissue from my bag and wiped at my eyes before looking across to where Michael stood near one of the statues. Tears were streaming down his cheeks.

I went over to him and put my arms around his neck. He held me tightly against him and cried. I wondered what thoughts regarding his own service as a soldier were racing through his mind, what battles were being replayed, and what losses he was re-living. Reflecting upon my own reaction to the memorial, I could only imagine how this was affecting him and hoped that it would help to heal old wounds and not re-open them.

"I need to go," Michael said quietly. "Let's go."

We went back to the hotel and retrieved our bags then loaded them into the rental car and drove out of D.C. Even though we were both sitting in the front seat of the car, Michael was a million miles away. I left him alone in his thoughts and watched the changing landscapes as we headed towards Shenandoah National Park.

I was fascinated by the beauty of the Blue Ridge Mountains, the trees, and the wildlife. Our room was located in the main lodge of the park, and we ate dinner that night in the lodge restaurant after watching a beautiful sunset over the mountains.

The following morning we drove to Mount Vernon and toured the house of George and Martha Washington. I loved the house and the river behind it and even our long walk around the property that left us drenched in sweat.

"The history!" I exclaimed, as we left the gift shop with a beautiful porcelain Christmas ornament that looked like something straight out of the 1700s and several books on the first President and his legacy. "I can't believe they've preserved all this so well with everyone traipsing through it on a daily basis."

Michael smiled at me and kissed me before starting the car. I was worried about him. Our visit to the war memorials had left him slightly detached from me and the rest of the world. It was as if he was going through the motions of our activities without actually participating.

I tried to dismiss my perception as nonsense. Michael had been to the Blue Ridge Mountains, Mount Vernon, and Monticello before and was probably just humoring me by escorting me through these places.

He'd been to everything we saw in D.C. already and was having a great time until we got to what he hadn't seen before, I thought with some anxiety. *Maybe I should try to reach Dr. Forrester. But how? When? Michael and I are together all the time, and there's no reliable Internet reception up in the mountains.*

We ate another delicious meal at the lodge that night and went to Monticello the next morning. I was like a little girl wandering in Thomas Jefferson's house and on his property. Again, I found the experience of going back through history an inspiring and memorable event. But once again, Michael seemed somehow removed from his surroundings.

After another delectable dinner at the lodge, we went to sit on the back patio behind our quarters. We had such a majestic view, and I wished we could somehow transport a few of these mountains and surroundings to Florida. When we finally went inside, I put on my nightgown and climbed into bed with a book I'd purchased earlier that day about Thomas Jefferson's inventions and aspirations. Michael sat in a chair and went back to reading one of the books we'd bought at Mount Vernon the previous day. We read for about an hour before I marked and closed my book then placed it on the nightstand.

"Come to bed," I urged. "I want to touch you."

He shut his book and smiled at me then stood and stripped off all of his clothes. He came over to the bed and lay down beside me. We began to kiss and caress, but I didn't come quickly as I usually did when we were together. The lingering concern was interfering with my mind and body, and I couldn't relax enough to let myself go.

I knew that Michael sensed the change in my reaction to our lovemaking. Being Michael, he would want to fix whatever was wrong. He intensified his efforts, and I did become aroused but still didn't climax.

Michael wrapped one hand around my wrists and lifted them over my head then used the other hand to finger me while he drew his tongue along the flesh of my breasts and nipples. Normally, I would have had at least one orgasm by now and probably more, but this time nothing happened.

Withdrawing his fingers, Michael brought his mouth up to mine and began to ease into me. I tried to position myself so that I was more open to him, but his weight on top of me was preventing me from succeeding. When he started thrusting, there was instant pain. I didn't hesitate this time to do what I had to in order to stop him. I bit his tongue. Hard.

Michael was instantly off me and standing beside the bed. He looked rather dazed and totally conflicted. He asked me if I was all right, and I said I would be fine, that he hadn't had time to hurt me like before. He nodded curtly, quickly dressed, and left.

I lay on the bed and waited for two hours for Michael to come back. When he didn't, I got up, dressed, and then went outside and walked to the front desk. Michael hadn't been there, and the rental car was still in the parking lot. I returned to our room and undressed again then got into bed. When another hour passed and he remained gone, I rose, went onto the patio, and called Tom.

My cell phone reception was good at the lodge, but I knew my battery would drain more quickly than normal because of my location. I briefly explained to Tom about Michael's remoteness, that Michael had almost hurt me again, and what had happened afterwards. I asked Tom what to do.

"Leave him be," Tom said firmly. "He's most likely reliving all that goddamn crap that floats around in our minds once we've lived that kind of life. It pushes you to your limits physically and mentally, and you have to shut down a part of your brain in order to function like a normal human being. What he went through walking around in those war memorials probably triggered a butt load of memories he's locked away deep in his head."

"But what if he hurts himself?"

"He won't. He's a good soldier who was taught to fight to live and has a woman he loves to care for and a mission in his business helping other vets. He's a survival expert. He can survive indefinitely in the mountains. Just be patient. He'll come back to you. When he does, you comfort him. You were right not to let him hurt you though, and don't you ever let him do that no matter what." Sighing, he said, "I really think this will be the last time he lets that happen."

"How do you know?"

"Because I have some experience with everything he's going through. Trust this old man. Keep taking care of yourself and him."

"Don't tell Al or Diane," I hastened to say.

"Not a word. You and Michael talked to them a few days ago, so they've got no reason to worry. I won't give them one."

"Thank you for everything."

"Anytime. Good night, my lovely Seneca."

"Good night. Sleep well."

"You, too."

Tom?"

"Yes?"

My eyes filling with tears, I said, "I love you."

"I love you, too," he replied, his voice thick with emotion. "You can't know how much you mean to me."

"I feel the same way about you. I hope you know that."

"I do," he answered. "I thank my lucky stars you and I met and became friends. You're a phenomenal woman, and don't you ever forget that."

I was about to tell him he was an amazing man, but my phone battery picked that moment to die. Feeling anxious, sad, and tired, I went to bed and hoped to wake with Michael beside me. Unfortunately, I woke to find myself alone.

Chapter Fourteen

I showered, dressed, ate a late breakfast at the lodge, and decided to go for a walk in an attempt to distract myself from my worry. I braided my hair then put on suntan lotion. I threw a bag of wheat crackers, a small container of bug spray, and a few bottles of water into my small backpack and left the room. I took a trail that led me eastward away from the lodge. The woods were peaceful, and I unconsciously relaxed as I climbed up and down hills and took in the grandeur of the mountains. I watched with fascination as deer passed me only a few feet away. I simply enjoyed *being* with nature and forgot about everything else.

When I had one full water bottle left, I turned around and headed back towards the lodge. Glancing at my watch, I was shocked to see that it was after five p.m. I'd completely lost track of time and hadn't realized it was so late in the day and that I'd been hiking for over five hours. I was never going to make it back to the lodge before dark. Plus, I was hungry and tired and would soon be out of water. My wheat crackers had been eaten hours earlier, and I had no flashlight or skills of any kind that would help me find my way back in the dark.

I dug in my backpack for my iPhone and realized with horror that I'd left it charging on the nightstand in our room after my conversation with Tom. I experienced a brief surge of panic. I was stranded with no way to call 911, the lodge, Michael, or anyone else.

I may have to spend the night out here, I thought fearfully. *I'll hike as far back as I can then stop and spend the night along the trail. Tomorrow morning, I'll get up and hike back the rest of the way. Everything will be fine. I'm a grown woman, and I'm not disoriented or injured. One night in the woods won't kill me. I can do this. I've lived through worse.*

The sun began to set at 8:00. I looked around for some sort of shelter and saw none. Bugs were everywhere, so I sprayed on more insect repellant and sipped a little of my remaining water. I was hot, miserable, hungry, thirsty, and scared.

I tried to bolster my spirits by considering starting a fire. I had never done such a thing without matches but had watched survival shows on television and decided to try. When multiple attempts resulted in complete failure and a particularly nasty scrape on my left arm, I sat near a tree and wrapped my arms around my legs.

With the setting of the sun, the temperature began to drop dramatically. The high had been near ninety during the daytime, but it was soon in the lower sixties. The shorts and tank top that had been appropriate for a daytime hike were totally inadequate for a night in the mountain woodlands. I shivered and wished I hadn't been so stupid.

High I.Q. my butt, I thought. *If I'm so smart then how'd I end up alone in the middle of nowhere without any supplies or shelter or fire?*

After a while, I told myself to stop being such a big baby and suck it up. It was one night. Many people were lost in the woods for days and managed to survive. I wasn't even lost; I was still on the trail. I just couldn't trust myself to stay on it in the dark.

The forest was pitch-black and noisy with all of the creatures that were alive and moving within it. I thought I heard something larger roaming in the brush and trees and scooted closer to the tree. I was shivering from cold and fear and knew it was going to be a long, long night.

Sometime later, I had an irrational notion that Michael was going to magically stumble across me in the middle of the wilderness and save me. He would build a fire, find water and food of some sort, and hold me until morning. That did not happen, and I suffered throughout the night alone.

When dawn came, I got stiffly to my feet and began my walk back up the trail. I was so happy to see the lodge and hoped I'd find Michael in our room. But he wasn't there, and it was obvious that he hadn't returned during my absence. There were no new voicemails or missed calls on my iPhone.

After drinking two bottles of water, I forced myself to shower, dress and go to the lodge restaurant to eat. My eyelids were heavy; my injured arm hurt; and my entire body ached. After my meal and some delicious hot tea and more water, I went to our still-empty room, removed my clothing, crawled into bed, and slept.

I woke to the sound of Michael softly saying my name and the feel of him stroking my hair. I opened my eyes and saw that he was sitting beside me on the bed. It was evident he'd recently showered and put on clean clothing. He looked tired and worried.

"Where've you been?" I asked groggily. "What time is it?"

"2:00 p.m. Where've you been? How'd you get the gash on your arm? It looks infected."

"I went out for a walk yesterday and lost track of time. I'd left my iPhone charging in the room. When I realized I wouldn't make it back before dark, I got as far as I could then spent the night where I was on the trail. I hurt my arm trying to make a fire."

"You spent the night in the woods with no fire."

"Yes."

"Wearing…?"

"Shorts and a tank top."

"Did you have any food or water?"

"I had one bottle of water left before sundown. I ate the crackers I had with me earlier in the day and had drunk all my other water while I was hiking."

He sighed heavily and asked, "Had you ever built a fire before?"

"No, but I've watched people do it on television and in movies. I couldn't get it going myself. One of the times a branch slipped, and that's how I cut my arm. It was a terrible night, and I hated it. Plus, I was so worried about you and where you'd gone and wondered if you'd ever come back."

"I'll never willingly leave you for any length of time, Seneca. Let me make sure you're okay; then I want to talk. I need to talk."

The way he said it made me understand that he wanted to talk about what was going on in his head. I got out of the bed and almost fell. Michael caught me easily and helped me to sit back on the mattress.

"Have you had anything like Gatorade?" he asked me.

"No, just the water all day yesterday and then more when I got back here plus some tea. I ate an egg and a piece of toast for breakfast."

"Your electrolytes are probably out of whack. Stay in the room, and I'll go get you something that will help."

He left and returned with two bottles of Gatorade. I obediently drank one and did start to feel better, although my arm was throbbing and the torn flesh did look like it was getting infected. After eating a pre-packaged peanut butter and jelly sandwich he'd also purchased from the small snack area in the lodge, I allowed him to spread some antibiotic ointment over the injured area on my arm and loosely bandage it. I had no idea where he'd procured either item and didn't ask.

"You never did answer my question," I said as he sat beside me in the bed. "Where have you been?"

"I went out into the woods to think. I needed to be away from everyone and everything."

"But you didn't have anything," I protested. "You fussed at me for not taking Gatorade and food and things, but you didn't."

"I did. I bought them and some other necessities like a first aid kit at the store up the road before I set off. That was the only rational thing I managed to do." Sitting in the chair, he said, "I'm sorry I left the way I did, but I'm really proud and impressed that you kept your head in a bad and completely unfamiliar survival situation and made it back in relatively good shape. I'm thinking maybe I'll have to teach you some basic survival skills though." As I rested my cheek and the palm of my injured arm against his chest, he put an arm around me and continued, "You know that I was in Intelligence for our government. That kind of existence is physically demanding, exciting, draining, intellectually stimulating, and all-consuming. There are certain people you know you can and do trust with your life, but most are giant question marks. It's a tricky business."

I snuggled closer to him but dared not speak. I wanted him to keep talking and sharing and wasn't about to interrupt.

"It's past time I told you about John. I'm sure you've been wondering who John was ever since you found out my business was called John's Place." After I nodded, he went on, "I met him when we both started the special program. We were kindred spirits. There is a connection between soldiers, but this was a true brotherly link. We trained together and worked closely together for years. There's so much...." His voice trailed off, and he tightened his hold on me. "I *will* tell you everything I can about him, but I can't do it all at once. It'll probably take the rest of our lives." Bringing his other arm around me, he continued, "John was an amazing friend. We were a great team for a long time."

After a prolonged period of silence, I said, "I'm sure he was the one you mentioned who sent the Frida Kahlo print for your birthday. You said he died before he was able to explain why he sent it, but you seemed to understand once I described her creativity, her broken body, and her nourishing of the earth."

"Early on in our friendship, John told me he had the ability to know things others couldn't. He said it was a part of his gypsy family heritage. His special ability proved invaluable during missions. He was the first one who told me I'd never be able to father a child. When I pressed the Navy doctors, they confirmed that I was sterile."

Thinking back to my conversation with Esmeralda, I asked, "What else did he tell you?"

"That I'd find the love of my life someday and would know her the instant I saw her. My wife would be beautiful and smarter than I was. I'd die a happy, old man with loving family and friends around me. John said a lot of other things."

"So, what about the Frida Kahlo print?"

"We were on a mission in Afghanistan. John hadn't been acting like himself for a few days, but he assured me he was just feeling out of sorts. He told me he'd ordered a birthday present for me that represented everything he'd told me about myself and my future. He'd had it shipped to my apartment. I said he'd have to review his predictions with me after I opened the present. He looked somber, and I knew something was wrong but wasn't sure what."

"You think he foresaw his own death?"

"I didn't realize it at the time, only in hindsight." Kissing my forehead, Michael said, "Once you talked to me about the Kahlo print, then I saw everything John said. You, the woman I knew I was destined to be with forever, look remarkably like Kahlo does in the print. The rocky and barren landscape is the unpleasantness of the world around us, but life and hope would grow from us and spread to others. Kahlo couldn't have children, and I knew we wouldn't be able to have children of our own either. Yet, she saw the difference she made in others' lives through her efforts. *Roots* represents reality – good and bad – and the promise of life itself."

"I would've liked your friend, John. Did he have eidetic memory like you?"

"No, but the Navy was well aware of his unusual talent for sensing things and his talent for knowing information about others and their pasts and futures. They studied him extensively."

There was another extremely long period of silence, and I knew that Michael was trying to bring himself to the point where he could discuss his friend's death.

"That last day started out well," he finally said. "We were in the market of the town and –"

His voice caught in his throat. My ear still lay against his chest, and I could hear his heart rate increase dramatically. His breathing also became slightly erratic. He was struggling to maintain his control.

"An IED detonated close to where John and I were standing."

"Is that how you got the scars on your side?" I asked, as I looked up at his face. His jaw was clenched, and he was blinking back tears. He nodded.

"And John?"

Michael began to cry and said in a heart-wrenching tone of voice, "John was blown apart in front of my eyes. I knew he was dead before either of us hit the ground, but I had to go to him. I crawled to where he was and when I saw him –"

He began to sob then, and I pushed myself away from his chest and knelt on the bed beside him then took him in my arms. I urged him to turn so that I was sitting with my back against the headboard of the bed. He leaned against me. He cried hard and held onto me tightly for quite some time. I kissed him and told him I was so sorry that he'd lost his friend and that he'd had to watch it happen. I told him I loved him and that he'd been lucky to have such a special friend so close to him for so long.

After quite some time, the sobs lessened and became streams of tears then stopped altogether. Michael lay with his head against my chest and his arms around my waist. Without warning, he slept.

I sat holding my husband against me as if he were a child and breathed a sigh of relief. He had done it. He'd told me about the most horrifying event he had ever experienced.

I knew his struggles regarding John's death and his inability to prevent it in some way were not over, but I sensed that things would be better for him now that he'd shared it with me. If only I could share my own personal nightmare with him, then maybe it would be better for me, too.

I shuddered involuntarily. I obviously wasn't ready, yet. I truly doubted I could ever talk about it with anyone but remembered Esmeralda's warning that if I didn't, my happy future with Michael was in jeopardy.

Be thankful for tonight and worry about that later, I told myself. *John saw good things in store for us. His other predictions were accurate. Maybe Esmeralda's aren't as good.*

I sensed that wasn't true, but I couldn't think about it at that moment. I cradled my husband against me and counted my blessings. I was married to the man of my dreams, and we shared a great passion, an intellectual connection, and a deep love for one another. We had Tom, Al, Diane, Krystal, Greg, Adiba, Rakeem, and Hadeel in our lives, as well as our other friends and the Benedetto family. Our common goal of helping others was making a difference in the world through John's Place and every person we met. My house had become our home. We were fortunate. Deciding not to dwell on all of our hardships and tragedies, I lightly kissed my husband on the top of the head and prayed that everything would go smoothly for us from that moment on.

Chapter Fifteen

Our commercial flight back to Florida was not so memorable as the flight up to D.C., but I still enjoyed it. It was exciting to be able to see outside the plane window in the daytime and observe the changes in rural and urban areas thousands of feet below. As before, Michael seemed delighted and saddened by my almost childlike enthusiasm.

"I want to do this again soon! I want to fly over the Grand Canyon or an ocean or something."

He smiled and said, "We can fly wherever you want. I've traveled around most of the world. You lead for now."

When we arrived at the Tampa International Airport, we deplaned, made a stop at the restrooms, retrieved our bags, and walked to a waiting limousine. The driver, who was perhaps my age, was an amiable, handsome guy who looked like he'd been a football player in college. He loaded our luggage in the trunk then held the door open as we got into the vehicle. I sat facing Michael. Once we were seated in the back and the chauffeur had taken his seat in front, the man informed us that there'd been an accident on the Sunshine Skyway Bridge that was causing traffic delays and asked if we needed anything before he raised the glass that separated the front seat from the back of the limo. When we told him no but thank you, the glass went up and the limo began its journey to our house.

Our house. It was legal now. That knowledge made me feel even more secure.

Michael reached in the little refrigerator and got out a bottle of water. He drank some then offered me the bottle, but I shook my head. He placed the water in a holder, leaned back, and spread his arms along the top of the seat. He was wearing black jeans and a fitted black knit shirt. The way he looked and reclined made me think of him as an Italian lion relaxing in his den. I knew the look in his eyes all too well.

"Michael, we can't," I protested.

"Why not? We talked about it on our wedding night. Here we are in a limo, and there's a delay on the road. What would normally be an hour ride will take us longer. We have room back here to do what we want. The covering on the windows makes it so that we can see out but no one else can see in."

"What about the driver?"

"What about him?"

"He'll hear us."

"The barrier's supposed to be soundproof."

"What if it's not?"

"Would it bother you if a stranger we'll never see again heard us?"

I thought about this and was startled to realize that the possibility of the handsome driver hearing me have multiple orgasms turned me on. Like sex in the plane on our wedding night, I knew we weren't going to be having sex in a limo on a regular basis. That afternoon might be the only time in our lives when we would experiment with the experience.

"I want to, but wouldn't it be kind of gross for someone to have to clean up after us?"

"I wouldn't be crass enough to do that. They keep blankets in here in case someone wants to cover up and sleep. We'll put them under us then take them with us and pay for them. It'll be worth it."

I smiled invitingly at him and reached for the top button on my blouse. He watched as I slowly undid all of the buttons and removed my shirt. I lifted the camisole I'd worn underneath over my head. I wasn't wearing a bra.

Michael spread a blanket across his seat and gestured for me to move to that side of the limo then knelt in front of me and slipped his fingers around the elastic waistband of my skirt. He pulled it down along with my panties. My sandals were already on the floor.

I reached for the hem of his shirt and lifted it up. I slowly pulled the shirt over his head. When I asked him to take off his shoes, jeans, and boxers, he didn't waste a second. He was quickly naked.

There was soon a blanket on the floor, and I found myself on top of Michael and watched him revel in the movements of my hips that rubbed him around deep inside me. My breasts rose and fell with my efforts, and he groaned. I happened to look up and out of the limo window directly in front of me. I saw a businessman in a Lexus glance over towards the limo. I knew he couldn't see me, but it appeared that he was looking straight at me. I imagined he was watching me, seeing me naked and straddling Michael. I climaxed hard.

"How can you do that?" I panted, once I had somewhat recovered myself. "How can you hold off like that when I come?"

"I told you it pleases me to know I can make you feel like that so easily and so frequently. I love to feel it. I want to feel it as many times as I can before I decide I can't wait any longer." Sitting up with me still on top of him, he said in a low voice, "What do you want right now, Seneca?"

I told him I wanted him to do whatever he wanted with me for the rest of the drive home. He was to be totally dominant without hurting me. I put myself completely at his mercy.

The feral expression appeared on his face, and he reached for a button in the side console. The glass that separated the front and back seat areas went down an inch. I hadn't expected him to lower the glass but found I didn't care. He was touching me with his mouth and hands in all the right ways and places. I knew he wouldn't be able to hold off much longer and was soon on my back.

I was momentarily afraid. He seemed consumed by that passion of his that tended to overwhelm his reason, and I worried he was about to savage me. He shook his head and told me in Spanish never to worry about his hurting me ever again. I smiled with relief and lifted my hips slightly in a silent offering. There was no discomfort in what followed, only ecstasy.

I felt the vibration of the floor underneath me and reached for Michael. I screamed as I held onto his biceps and urged him deeper. His breathing ragged now, he obliged and growled my name as he climaxed. He collapsed on top of me once we'd both finished, and I wrapped my arms and legs around him. Neither of us moved or spoke. I was worn out.

We separated and helped each other to dress before the limo turned onto the long driveway to our house. We neatly folded the blankets we'd used and stacked them, then carried them out of the limo with us when the driver opened the door. The man looked slightly stunned, and I blushed and turned to hide my smile. Michael gave him a generous tip before he drove away.

We went into the empty house, deposited our bags and the blankets on the floor, and stood in the darkened living room. Michael came over to me, took me in his arms, and said, "That's the most intense sexual experience we've ever had. I don't think we should attempt to recreate it and don't want to taint the memory of what we just did."

"I agree, although I wouldn't mind experimenting with other things. We've had sex in a plane and in a limo. I wonder what it'd be like in a boat?"

He laughed and kissed me before telling me we could experiment all I wanted. All he wanted when we made love was to hear me scream with pleasure before he gave in to his own release.

"What an ego boost for any man to know that he makes a woman feel that way," he murmured. "You amaze me, Seneca."

"And you amaze me," I responded. "As a matter of fact, I'm so amazed that I think I'll go say "hello" to Doc then shower and take a nap."

"I'll join you. We're not supposed to meet Nonno, Diane, and Tom for dinner until seven. We have plenty of time."

Doc was swimming happily in his bowl. Krystal had left a note letting me know he'd been a good fish and that she'd hoped we'd had a wonderful trip. She also indicated that all of our wedding presents had been deposited in the guest room.

"Oh, my gosh!" I exclaimed when I opened the door to that bedroom. "Michael, come look at this. Where will we put it all?"

Coming up behind me, he said, "Wow. I guess we'll have to get started on the expansion earlier than I'd thought."

"Expansion?"

"Of the house. We'll need another bathroom and at least one more bedroom if we're going to adopt a kid or two, right?"

I forgot how tired I was in an instant and asked, "What sort of expansion were you thinking about?"

"I'm not sure. This was your house before it was ours, so it's up to you. I don't think we can put on a second story easily, and I doubt if that would be what you'd want. I was thinking of knocking out the lanai and adding on there." Before I could voice my objections, he hastened to say, "I know you love the back porch. So do I. What we could do is expand the house in that direction then build a new lanai that runs along the entire back of the new part of the structure."

I nodded slowly and said, "That would work. I just want to maintain the look and feel of the original house. It's what makes it my home."

He grinned and said, "*Our* home. Our family's home."

"How many kids do you want to have?" I asked on the spur of the moment. Shaking my head, I said, "I'm sorry. I'm so getting ahead of myself. We just got married and –"

His mouth covered mine and silenced me. When we broke apart, he said, "Don't be sorry. Whatever happened to me when we were in the mountains made it okay. I've made my peace as best I can with not being able to have any biological children of our own. Are you all right with it?"

"You know neither of us will ever be truly all right with it, but we have to live with the reality of our situation. I want us to have a family, but it won't be a biological family. Maybe that makes it even better for the children, since they'll know how much we really wanted them."

We showered, took a nap then dressed. Michael slipped into shorts and a Navy t-shirt, while I opted for a comfortable black sundress. We went to Target to have the photos from our trip "instantly" developed on the self-service machine. Instantly for us took about an hour since we debated about which pictures to develop and which ones needed editing. The printing machine spat out our pictures, and we paid for them. Then went to the photo album aisle and selected one we liked that would hold our combination one hundred and ninety-one pictures and postcards.

I sat in the backseat of the SUV and proceeded to begin slipping the pictures into the album. It was not difficult, just time-consuming. When we arrived at Tom's house fifteen minutes later, Michael suggested that I pass him the album and remaining postcards and photos and go on ahead of him into Tom's. I knew it would only take him about five more minutes to complete the project, and so did he. He was thoughtfully giving me time to see Tom face-to-face first before he went in and before Al and Diane showed up for dinner.

I had phoned Tom the morning after Michael's return from his woodland escape while Michael had been out for his morning run. Of course, I neglected to tell Tom about my own misadventure in the mountains. Tom had advised me to encourage Michael not to stop his therapy and suggested that he and Michael have lunch when we got back. I'd told him that was a great idea and thanked him for his guidance.

The next time I'd talked with Tom was when Michael and I were in the taxi on our way to the airport earlier that morning. He'd promised me that he'd eaten breakfast and taken his morning medications. He'd sounded excited and said he would be waiting for us, Al, and Diane that night.

"I already spoke to Al, and he and Diane are going to bring pasta," I told Tom. "After all, it's a celebration, and we should live dangerously once in a while."

"That's the ticket!" he said enthusiastically. "My lovely girl and pasta. What more could an old man like me ask for?"

I smiled as I remembered his comment and walked towards the side of his house. I opened the door with my key and announced, "Tom! We're here!"

There was no response. Although the light was on next to the recliner, Tom was not sitting there. A book and a glass of water rested on the end table beside it.

He's probably in the bathroom, I told myself. *Everything's fine.*

I didn't really believe it. I could sense the unnatural quiet in the house that came with the inevitable. I knew immediately that he was dead. Working with elderly clients, I'd been the one to discover several who had passed away while alone. It was to be expected, but this was different. This was Tom.

I put my purse down on the floor. The living room was deserted. I wandered through the bedrooms and bathrooms, but they were empty. So, I walked slowly towards the kitchen and dining area.

Tom was lying on the floor near the table. I stared at him and considered the notion that he was merely unconscious. I knew better, but I knelt and felt for a pulse anyway. His skin was cool, and there was no heartbeat.

Michael called out for me and Tom as he came into the house. I wanted to answer him, but I couldn't find my voice. I heard him call out our names again, this time with concern.

"Here," I managed to say.

Michael came directly to the kitchen but stopped when he saw us. Analyzing the situation in approximately two seconds, he placed the photo album he'd been carrying on the dining room table and crouched beside us. He felt for Tom's pulse, and then said something in Arabic that sounded like a prayer or a tribute of some sort.

I was transported back to the hot field. I was running, perspiring, and having trouble breathing. I had to get away. I had to keep running to get away. If I could just run far enough –

"Seneca!" Michael barked. "Seneca, look at me!"

His hands were on my shoulders, and he appeared almost panicked. I still couldn't breathe and was beginning to feel dizzy. I reached for him and fought to make my lungs work. He seemed to understand instinctively. He grew calm and ordered me to inhale. When I didn't comply, he shook me slightly and said more loudly, "Seneca, breathe through your nose!"

I did, and my lungs gratefully expanded. The spell was broken, and I was able to inhale and exhale once more. I was shaking but breathing, which was a great relief to me.

"What happens when you have these flashbacks?" Michael asked. "What do you see?"

I shook my head and looked at Tom.

"We should call someone," I said distractedly. "There's a non-emergency number."

"Fuck the non-emergency number!" he snapped. "We're calling 911."

"But he's gone. He's obviously been gone for at least an hour."

I couldn't bring myself to say "dead," yet. Maybe I never would when it came to Tom.

"We've found someone we care about dead on the floor," Michael said quietly. "We don't know what killed him, and we need police and paramedics."

"Whatever it was, it was quick. He didn't suffer."

Eying me suspiciously, Michael asked, "How do you know that?"

"An old woman who has gifts like your friend John told me last month. She said when Tom went, it would be quick and that he wouldn't suffer."

He stared at me for a long moment before asking, "What else did she say?"

"That I should keep the money left to me by the Hummels and use it to take care of us, the business, and our children. That you couldn't father children and I shouldn't try to have any more anyway because all my babies would die. Other things she couldn't possibly have known without some unearthly power. It was her wedding dress I wore when we got married."

"Good God, Seneca. Why didn't you tell me all this when you first heard it?"

"Why didn't you tell me about John?" I countered. "I didn't think you'd believe me. How was I to know your best friend was a fucking gypsy!"

I covered my mouth with my right hand and shut my eyes. I never said the F word or the G word or the S word. My mother had raised me not to swear, and I'd just uttered the mother-of-all swear words. I began to cry and thought, *I'm sorry, Mommy.*

Michael took me in his arms and stroked my hair. When I was all cried out for the time being and sagged against him, he withdrew his iPhone from his pocket and speed dialed his grandfather. He spoke to him in Italian, and I knew he was telling him about Tom and not to come to the house with Diane and the food. His next call was to 911.

The authorities determined in a relatively short amount of time that Tom had experienced a natural death, but they would have the coroner do an investigation as was routine with any death that occurred in a home. They took statements from me and from Michael and told us we'd have to leave the house once Tom's body had been removed. I told them I'd left a few things around the house and needed to get them before we departed. They knew from their interviews with us that I'd been Tom's caregiver, so they agreed, even though it was against protocol. I offered a silent prayer of thanks for their leniency.

There were three items I wanted from Tom's house, things I didn't want his disinterested children to have. When the coroner's people arrived with their stretcher on wheels and a body bag, I excused myself from the living room and went to Tom's bedroom while Michael continued to talk with the policemen. I walked over to the closet and slid the door open. I reached to the right and pushed several hangers aside until I found Tom's tie that had abstract designs emblazoned upon it. I removed it from the tie rack and rolled it up before stuffing it in the pocket of my sundress.

Next, I went to the guest room and lifted a worn teddy bear from its place of honor on the double bed. Tom had told me his beloved grandmother had given it to him when he'd been born, and it had provided him with comfort and refuge when he'd been a child. Although he had never elaborated on the childhood abuse he'd mentioned during our conversation regarding why he'd become a spy, I'd come to think of his teddy bear as the equivalent of my Cookie Monster. I would place it on my bookcase where its significance would never be forgotten as long as I was alive to remember.

I walked to the third bedroom, which Tom had always used as an office and storage area. I headed directly for the shelf above his computer. On it rested what he'd told me once was his most prized possession. It was a small, curving, oddly shaped piece of art made of blue glass. He'd shared the story about it with me many times and had insisted that I take it and cherish it if anything happened to him since none of his children would care about anything except getting rid of his art pieces by selling them to the highest bidder.

I carefully slipped the piece of art into my other pocket then returned to the living room. The policemen gave me an odd look when they saw that all I had in my arms was a faded teddy bear. I lied and told them the bear was all I'd located of my things. Silently apologizing to my mother for lying, I prayed they wouldn't want to search the pockets of my sundress. Luckily, the folds and material helped to conceal the items tucked inside.

Michael, who was holding our honeymoon photo album in one arm, handed me my purse then thanked the officers before leading me outside to the SUV. He opened the passenger door for me. I was mindful of the glass in my pocket and eased myself into the seat before buckling the seatbelt.

Michael got into the driver's seat, put the album in the back, then turned to me and said, "You are a terrible liar, Seneca. I'm surprised they didn't pat you down before they let us leave. What else did you take?"

"Just drive before they decide they should have checked my pockets," I urged. "I'll explain when we get to the house."

We didn't speak during the ride home. Al's BMW was parked in the driveway, and lights were on inside the house. I wanted to see

Al and Diane, and I didn't want to see them. I was torn and beyond devastated and didn't know what to do next.

Michael got out of the SUV with the album then came around to open my door. When I didn't move or look at him, he put a hand behind my head and kissed my temple before encouraging me to come inside with him. I unfastened the seatbelt and climbed out holding the teddy bear and my purse and being careful not to bump into anything on the side where the artwork was tucked in my pocket.

When we entered the house, Al and Diane came into the living room from the kitchen looking somber and worried. Diane's eyes were red from crying, and this surprised me. Both of them offered me their condolences and asked if there was anything they could do. I shook my head.

Michael placed the photo album on the coffee table and suggested I sit on the couch. I handed him the teddy bear and asked that he put it on one of the high shelves of the built-in bookcase so it would be safe.

"Teddy was Tom's Cookie Monster," I said in explanation. "He's as old as Tom." Looking up at the stuffed bear, I said, "Older now."

"What else did you take?" Michael asked again.

I put my purse on the coffee table then withdrew the tie from one pocket. I held it up so that the others could see it and said, "This was Tom's favorite tie to wear when he was a college professor. His first semester teaching art history in college a student gave it to him and told him he'd changed her outlook on art and the world forever. He said he wore the tie at least twice a week after that for the next couple of decades until he retired from university life."

Al nodded with understanding, and Diane wiped at the corners of her eyes with a tissue. Michael asked me what else I'd removed from Tom's home. I gently withdrew the glass artwork from my pocket and held it out for the others to see.

"What is it?" Al asked.

"It's art," I replied, as if the answer should be obvious to anyone who saw what I was holding in my palm. "Salvador Dali made it and gave it to Tom. Tom made me promise to cherish it if anything ever happened to him since I knew its intrinsic value. He said his children would only want to sell his collection for the money and would never appreciate the truth about any of it, especially not this piece."

"What is the truth?" Michael asked.

"Many years ago, Tom was having dinner in a restaurant where he met Dali and his wife. He and Dali became deeply engrossed in a conversation about art as a conduit for the artist's creativity and need for expression outside the normal mores of society. Dali was working with glass at the time, and he invited Tom back to his studio to see his latest efforts. Tom was ecstatic, of course.

"When they entered the studio, Tom immediately walked over to this piece and declared it represented the potential for balancing the material and immaterial in the universe. Dali handed it to Tom with the words, "For you, my dear friend." Tom never saw him again but never forgot that night or what Dali said."

"Do Tom's children know that story?" Michael asked seriously. "If so, they would be very interested in getting their hands on that piece of glass."

"Tom said he never told anyone except me about it. He said when he died, it should reside with me."

"None of us should ever speak of that story with anyone else," Diane remarked.

"I concur," said Al.

"As do I," Michael agreed. "However, I do think we should have it put in some sort of protective case so it doesn't get damaged."

I stared at the piece of glass and remembered how animated Tom had been when he'd told me the story. I asked Al and Diane if they knew someone who could take care of making a case for such a piece that would protect it and yet properly display it. Al said he'd have it taken care of immediately. I gave him the piece and stood staring at the floor.

"You should eat," Al announced. "When is the last time the two of you ate?"

"We've only had granola bars for breakfast," Michael volunteered. "We were too…preoccupied earlier to eat lunch."

"I'm not hungry," I said flatly.

"Seneca, you must eat," Al prodded. "Diane, talk to her."

Diane took my hand and led me to the kitchen. She sat me at the table and went to the refrigerator. She put some of the pasta they'd gotten to take to Tom's for dinner on a plate and heated it in the microwave. Then she brought the plate and a glass of water over to where I sat and put them in front of me. I made no attempt to drink from the glass or lift a utensil.

"Try to eat," she ordered gently.

My hands remained in my lap, and my eyes fixed on the rim of the plate. Michael moved an empty chair next to mine and said, "You have to take in some food. It'll help."

"Help what? Will it bring Tom back?"

"No, of course not." Tucking some hair behind one of my ears, he proposed, "How about if I help you?"

When I didn't outright object, he scooped what appeared to be ziti in a creamy cheese sauce up with the spoon and brought it to my mouth. I parted my lips and accepted the food. I felt like I was a toddler, but I knew that my husband wouldn't give up until I'd eaten at least a portion of what was on the plate. Once a quarter of it was gone, I told him I'd had enough. I could tell he wasn't happy about it, but he didn't press me to eat any more. He sat back and ate the remainder of what Diane had prepared for me then drank some of my water before coaxing me to drink the rest.

"Do you want us to sleep here tonight?" Al offered. "Perhaps it would be a good idea."

"I won't be sleeping tonight," I declared. "Maybe you and Diane could take our bed, and we could clear the guest bed for Michael. I'll read in the living room."

"You have to sleep eventually," Diane pointed out.

"Not tonight," I insisted. "I'm not sleepy."

"It's only 9:00, and you have had a great shock," Al said kindly. "Later, you will probably want to sleep."

I could feel the heat of the field taunting me from somewhere nearby and got to my feet. After telling the others I was going outside, I went through the house and out onto the lanai. I sat in one of the rocking chairs and looked out at the waves as they ebbed and flowed at the edge of the beach. After a while, Al came out and sat in the rocker beside me. We rocked for a long time without speaking.

"I'm sorry I'm not very good company tonight," I told him.

"Ah, my angel. You should never apologize for grieving the loss of someone you loved. Diane and I did not know Tom long, but we considered him a good friend. Michael and he had become very close, and I know that Michael respected him immensely. You *loved* him. There is a difference, and you will grieve more deeply than we will."

"Where are Michael and Diane?"

"Diane is eating some dinner in the kitchen. Michael is on the computer with his therapist."

"He's talking about me, isn't he?"

"What he says to his doctor is not my business. I know that I would be talking about you to the man if I were Michael." Taking my hand in his, he said, "Perhaps you should go in and talk to the therapist as well."

"I can't tonight. I feel as if I'm too numb to do anything. Michael and I have to go to work in the morning, and I don't know how I'm going to function."

"You are definitely *not* going to work tomorrow. I do not even know if Michael will go in at all under the circumstances."

"But we've been on vacation for two weeks!" I exclaimed. "We need to get back to work!"

"Seneca, the man you thought of as a father has just died, and you were the one who found him. You would do no one any good were you to go in to work."

I didn't argue. I was in no shape to perform my job in any productive manner. All I wanted to do was stay in my house, lock the doors, shutter the windows, and avoid ever going to Tom's again. I couldn't bear the thought of his children callously going through his treasured things and disposing of them without any consideration for their father and his life.

At least I wouldn't have to deal with any legal proceedings. I knew I wasn't in Tom's will. He and I had discussed it the previous year when he'd been hospitalized for one of his bouts with pleurisy. He'd declared that he wanted to leave everything he owned to me because I'd been more like a daughter to him than his own children. However, he knew them well and said they'd hire attorneys and take me to court in order to get what they felt was rightly theirs. He said he didn't want to torment me with "that goddamn crap" and asked what I wanted. I'd told him that I wanted to be his friend and didn't care about material objects. He agreed not to change his will as long as I promised to make certain I took the Dali piece and anything else

181

I wanted from his house before the children descended. I had promised.

Michael came out on to the lanai and asked how I was doing.

"I'm doing."

"I called Krystal and Greg as well as Rakeem and Adiba and let them know we were back. I also told them about Tom. They offered their sympathies. Krystal and Adiba said to call them when you are ready to talk."

"Diane helped me to move the wedding presents off the bed. She volunteered to sleep there, and Nonno's going to sleep on the fold-out couch, so you and I can sleep in our bed."

"I told you I'm not sleeping tonight."

"You don't have to sleep," he assured me. "If you want to stay up and read all night, then that's fine. I just don't think you should be alone tonight. If you refuse to sit in the bed I'll stay up and read all night with you in the living room."

"I don't want to make you do that," I said. "I…I guess I can read in the bedroom while you sleep. The light won't bother you?"

He kissed my forehead and said, "I've slept in so many different places and conditions over the years. No, the light won't bother me."

Al squeezed my hand and released it before we rose from the rocking chairs. I felt badly that Al and Diane had no nightclothes with them. Diane wouldn't fit in any of my pajamas or nightgowns, so Michael gave her one of his loose, casual t-shirts and I gave her my robe. Michael lent his grandfather a pair of pajamas, which were too large but would serve the purpose for one night.

After Al and Diane had gone to sleep, Michael donned pajama bottoms and a t-shirt, and I slipped on a nightgown. Then we finished getting ready for bed and went to our room. Michael read a book about international finance for a couple of hours, while I tried to concentrate on a book reviewing statistical probabilities and their impact on culture in America. Finally, Michael shut his book, kissed me, then switched off the lamp on his side of the bed and rolled over to sleep. I kept reading. This was one night I refused to sleep.

Chapter Sixteen

The heat in the field was overwhelmingly oppressive, but I couldn't stop running. I was fighting for breath, scratched and scraped by plants and rocks, yet somehow I had enough air in my lungs to keep screaming. I had to get away, no matter what it took. If I could run hard enough and fast enough, then maybe I wouldn't remember anything.

I ran blindly through the field, my heart pounding and my leg muscles burning. I was crying and screaming, but I kept running. Slamming into something, I fell. Moments later, the something fell on top of me, and I was pinned beneath it. I fought to free myself. I had to get whatever it was off me, so I could keep running. Daggers of some sort drove into me in various places all over my body, and I screamed with this new pain.

"Fuck!" I heard Michael shout. "Nonno! Diane! I need you *now*! Put on some shoes and get in here!"

There came the sound of hurrying feet then exclamations of distress from Al and Diane.

"We have to get it off her," Michael said urgently.

"Maybe we should wait until –" his grandfather began.

"There's no time!" Michael shouted. "No telling what kind of damage it's done. Diane, call 911!"

I became dimly aware I was lying on my back on the floor of our bedroom. The large mirror I kept propped against the wall had fallen on top of me and somehow shattered in the process. I could barely breathe although I wasn't certain if this was totally a result of the weight of the mirror or if I was also hyperventilating from the terror I'd experienced in my nightmare.

"All I did was go to the bathroom for sixty seconds!" Michael said angrily. "Sixty fucking seconds and this happens! Damn it!"

I sensed the two men moving to stand near the top end of the heavy mirror. Michael told Al he would do the brunt of the lifting but needed someone to help push or turn the broken mirror one way or another. They counted to three in Italian and began to lift the enormous weight off me.

I howled as pieces of glass twisted further into me or, alternately, were eased out as the mirror was raised. After I heard it crash somewhere away from me, Al said hoarsely, "Holy Mary, Mother of God!"

I saw blood hit the ceiling and thought that odd. Wasn't I lying on the floor?

"Shit!" Michael exclaimed. "She's got an arterial bleed. I hope to God there's just one."

I wanted to tell him he shouldn't swear so much but was beginning to feel woozy. True, I had stopped screaming, but it was only because I couldn't seem to make my vocal cords cooperate with my brain.

"Oh, Seneca!" I heard Diane cry, as I felt an almost unbearable pressure on the upper part of my left leg.

"Be careful!" Al ordered as she came closer. "There is glass everywhere. Michael's feet and knees have already paid for it, and I have a cut on my arm."

"Sorry," I murmured. "So sorry."

"Don't be sorry, sweetheart," Michael told me. "Nonno, I know she's cut all over, but I'm worried about her neck. See the blood? Move her hair so I can get a clearer view of the wound."

"My neck is wet," I said drowsily.

I felt the hair being moved from my face and neck and heard Michael swear again. Then there was pressure on my neck although it wasn't as much as on my leg. I was getting light-headed.

"Call 911 again and see how close the paramedics are!" Michael ordered Diane. "Tell them she'll need to be airlifted to Bayfront Medical Center's trauma unit and that she's got at least one and maybe two arterial bleeds!"

"Everything feels wet," I said, my words barely audible. "Michael?"

"I'm here."

"I'm cold."

"No, you're not," he insisted. "Don't you *dare* leave me, Seneca. This isn't how it ends, remember?"

"I'm so sorry."

"There is nothing to be sorry for," Al said thickly. "No reason in the world."

"Si, hay una razon," I mumbled in Spanish. It meant, "Yes, there is a reason."

I was lying in the sun in the middle of the hot, dusty field. Mommy was calling out for me, but I couldn't answer her. All I could do was silently scream for my Poppy.

"Michael?"

I wasn't even certain I'd said his name aloud. I worked hard at focusing my eyes on him, and he was looking at me and speaking but I couldn't hear a word he said. He was covered in blood – my blood – and there was fear in his eyes. I wanted to remind him of what he'd said to me when we'd first become involved, that he wasn't afraid of anything.

"My Poppy," I said, or at least I think I said. "He died."

Michael mouthed the words, "I know." I was certain he'd spoken them, but I could only read his lips.

"Esmeralda told me I had to tell or nothing would be right," I struggled to say. "My Poppy died, and it was my fault."

I felt a palm rest on the top of my head and knew it must be Al's free hand. It comforted me. I wanted to tell him I appreciated it, but there wasn't any time.

"My fault," I repeated. "He died because of me."

Michael shook his head and said no. Tears were streaming down his cheeks, and I knew he wanted to hold me but couldn't move his hands away from the wound on my leg. I watched as he looked to his grandfather and said something I couldn't understand. Then I felt Al's lips on my temple.

Others were suddenly in the room. There were men and women in nice, clean paramedic uniforms that were soon smudged and spattered with blood. Al's hands were removed from me, and I wanted them back. Someone else was pressing on the wound on my neck, and the awful pressure on my leg momentarily eased then returned. Michael appeared directly in front of my face and kissed me lightly on the lips before telling me he loved me. I realized I'd heard his voice and wondered if I was hallucinating.

Everything was a blur. There was a flurry of activity as the EMS team fought to stabilize my condition enough to move me. Well, that was what I supposed they were doing. All I knew was that I was on the verge of death. I lost consciousness for a while and woke in a helicopter that I knew must be heading for the trauma center in St. Petersburg. I'd never ridden in a helicopter before and wished I could see outside as it flew through the night sky. I imagined that it afforded a spectacular view of the coast and the Gulf.

I lost consciousness again and came to in a room filled with doctors, nurses, and agony. I screamed and twisted on the gurney but was quickly restrained by several sets of strong hands. Men and women were trying to convince me that everything was going to be all right, but I was in too much pain to believe them. I cried out Michael's name, but he wasn't there. I watched as a nurse injected something into an I.V. tube that must have been inserted somewhere like my hand or arm. Whatever drug they gave me began to take effect, and I stopped screaming and writhing and lay still. My eyelids felt weighted down, and I was soon unconscious again.

I half-woke several times after that but couldn't identify my surroundings or recognize anyone. Although I knew I was heavily medicated, the terrible pain that extended over most of my body refused to be quelled. Each time I would cry out, and each time someone would give me more medication and things would go dark.

Eventually, I woke to the terrible pain. I was able to refrain from screaming. I wanted to know where I was and where Michael was before someone drugged me again. It was tremendously difficult to concentrate, but I was determined to get some answers before I had to ask for more drugs. I tried to turn my head without success. Something was preventing me from moving it, and I experienced a few moments of panic. When I heard someone moving nearby, I said, "Hello? Who's there?"

In truth, what I actually said didn't sound anything like that. The words were unintelligible. Still, it got the attention of the person, and he came into my line of sight and smiled down at me although worry was evident in his expression.

Michael looked terrible. It was clear to me that he hadn't slept much in some time and hadn't been able to shave for days. I wondered how long ago I'd been injured and struggled to ask. "Michael, where am I? Why can't I talk normally? Why can't I move my head? Come to think of it, why can't I move much of anything?"

"You're at Bayfront Medical Center in the Critical Care Unit. You can't speak normally because you had a breathing tube and haven't used your vocal cords for a few days. You can't move your head because they have it resting on a special pillow that won't allow you to turn it. The same goes for your left leg. The rest of your body is stiff because of your injuries. Do you remember what happened?"

"The big mirror fell on me."

"It did. You must have run into it in your sleep, and it hit the nightstand on its way down. It shattered on top of you. It also crushed you. No more big mirrors in our bedroom, okay?"

"How bad?" I asked nervously. "The truth, Michael."

"Glass from head to foot, although most of the cuts were clean, superficial wounds. Three more serious punctures did the worst of the damage, plus the weight of the mirror falling on you caused hairline cracks in all of your ribs and bruised just about everything."

"The three," I whispered. "How bad?"

"One nicked your jugular vein; one came within a few millimeters of your right lung but miraculously didn't tear it or anything else important in the vicinity. The third one lacerated the femoral artery in your left leg." He narrowed his eyes and said, "If I hadn't been there with the medical training I'd been given in the military, you would have died within minutes." Shaking his head, he went on, "I won't sugarcoat it. You should have died regardless. The force of the mirror falling on you would have been enough to kill many people. You were in severe shock by the time you arrived here and lost an enormous amount of blood. They almost couldn't change the bags fast enough during surgery because you were bleeding out so quickly. No one was certain you'd make it for the first seventy-two hours."

"You were actually scared," I stated in my dry, raspy voice. "I saw the fear in your eyes at the house."

"I've never been so scared in all my life. I thought I was going to lose you. I've seen so much injury and death in war-torn areas. I knew how serious it was the moment I saw you lying on the floor under the mirror."

"Your feet and knees," I mumbled. "Al said you hurt them."

187

"I wasn't wearing shoes, and I had to kneel to treat you. There was a helluva lot of glass. They took care of my feet and my knees when I got here while you were in surgery. They're better."

"I'm sorry," I told him then groaned with the pain. "So, so sorry."

He stroked my hair while telling me not to apologize and that all I needed to do was focus on healing and following doctor's orders. Then he pressed a button and someone appeared with more drugs. I experienced blessed relief as the painkiller hit my bloodstream. Thankfully, I succumbed to unconsciousness once more. I hoped that when I woke the next time, the pain would be manageable.

Thankfully, I woke and didn't feel as though I was going to scream. The doctors examined me and determined that the foam pillow that had kept my head immobile could be removed. My neck was horribly stiff, but they said that was good and would deter me from moving it too much as it continued to heal.

"What about my leg?" I prompted. "Can that foam pillow be taken away, too?"

"Not a chance," the doctor told me. "We'll see how you do over the next few days then make that determination. I am going to have you moved to a regular room though, but you have to do as you're told or else you'll end up back in C.C.U. Twelve days is long enough in here."

"I've been in the unit for twelve days?" I asked in disbelief.

He nodded and said, "Twelve days for you is miraculously short."

"What about my long-term prognosis?"

"Provided there are no unforeseen complications, it's good if you rest, rest, and rest some more. You have to literally be still and allow your body to knit itself back together."

"How long?"

He shrugged and said, "We'll be continuing contact with your internist, and he'll be the one to release you for normal physical activity and then work. I'd estimate one to three months before the first release and four to six months for the second, but that will depend on you and your rate of recovery."

I was stunned. I'd heard what Michael had said about the fact that I shouldn't even be alive, but it never occurred to me that my recovery time would be so long. Considering the extent of my injuries, I decided I shouldn't be shocked.

"You may not feel truly well for a much longer period," the doctor warned. "Conversely, you might feel great and overdo. The main thing is to be careful. You've cheated death once. I don't think you can do it twice."

I was moved to a regular hospital room. Michael was waiting there for me. His face lit up like a Christmas tree when he saw me, but he waited until the staff had left the room to come over to the bed and bend down to kiss me gently.

"I want to hug you, but I can't lift my arms," I confided. "It hurts too much to move anything."

"The doctors say you have to be still while you're in here unless a physical therapist is directing you," he told me. "You think you can do it?"

"I have to. I'm not happy about it, but what choice do I have?"

"None."

"Where are Al and Diane?"

"They're at John's Place. They've been running it for me while I stayed here with you, which worked out fine since they were running it while we were on our honeymoon. You know they're great at taking care of things. They've been in to see you every evening, but you were out cold each time." He kissed me again and said, "The others have come to sit with me, even though they couldn't go in to see you. Krystal and Greg have been here every night for at least an hour, and Adiba's come with Hadeel and brought me lunch every day. Rakeem's been working overtime and so has only been able to come every other evening. All the staff and clients at John's Place have been asking about you. Nonno says there've been lots of voicemails on the home phone from our Ceviche crowd, and Krystal says the people you used to work with from Hearts at Home have been pumping her for information every day."

"I wish I could thank them all."

"You'll have plenty of time to e-mail and talk on the phone between naps once we get you home."

"I missed Tom's funeral," I said quietly. "You missed it, too."

"There was no funeral."

"What?"

"His kids came and had some private burial at a local cemetery. They didn't invite anyone. They didn't even put an obituary in the paper." He saw my eyes filling with tears and softly commanded, "Don't cry. It'll hurt you."

"But Michael —"

"Once you're well, then we'll go to his gravesite and have our own memorial service. He'll be honored as he deserves to be honored."

I'd planned on nodding but found even that simple movement impossible.

"Michael, what do I look like? I want to see."

"No. You can't get up, so how would you see anyway?"

"Is it that bad? The truth."

"I hate it when you say that, you know? It's pretty bad right now. It's going to take time for everything to heal. As I said before, you have a ton of superficial cuts as well as the three more serious ones. You look like someone's beaten you up from your shoulders to your shinbones. Don't panic, okay? The doctors say all the bruising will gradually fade and the lines left by the cuts will all fade away except for a few. You'll definitely have a noticeable scar on your leg, but even that will fade to a thin line. You had phenomenal surgeons, and there's all this new stuff that makes scars fade faster. I knew you'd ask once you were cognizant, so I already talked to them about it once I wasn't so fucking worried you were going to die."

"You shouldn't swear so much," I said tiredly. "If my Mommy was alive, she'd chide you for that. She'd do it nicely, of course. She was always so sweet."

"I'm sure she was," he said rather sadly. Taking one of my hands in his, he asked, "Are you ready to talk about what you said regarding your father the night the mirror fell on you?"

Beginning to cry, I begged, "Please, don't make me talk about it now."

As Michael reassured me he'd wait as long as it took, I tried to stem the flow of tears. He'd been right; the act of crying hurt me terribly both inside and out. When I couldn't stop, I began to shake with the pain. Michael buzzed for the nurse, and I was soon drifting off again into medicated oblivion.

Even though I'd been moved to a regular room, the doctors had declared that I was to have no visitors except Michael until I was transferred to a hospital closer to my home or released. I protested, but Michael refused to dispute the doctors' decision and said I needed to rest undisturbed. Even more tears from me didn't cause him to change his mind, so I gave up trying to dissuade him.

Three weeks after my accident, I was released from the hospital with a long list of restrictions and requirements. I was to have round-the-clock nursing care and minimal visitors and was to remain on complete bed rest. Although none of this made me particularly enthusiastic, I was glad to be going home and thankful to be alive to do so.

I was transported by ambulance from St. Petersburg south to my home on the coast. Michael rode with me but made certain to stay out of the way of the paramedics as they rolled me into the vehicle and monitored my vital signs. When we pulled up to the front of the house, I expected to find some strange nurse waiting for me. Instead, the first person I saw was Krystal. She beamed at me and took my hand and squeezed it as soon as the EMS people had rolled me to the front door.

"I don't understand," I told her. "I'm so happy to see you, but what are you doing here? Did you arrange for the nurse?"

"*I am* the nurse," she answered. "I was an LPN before I got my Associate Degree in Business and started working for the office of Hearts at Home last year. I'll be with you from eight to four, then someone else will come from four to midnight, then the last person will come from midnight to eight."

"But what about your job at Hearts at Home?"

"Glenda suggested I make the switch indefinitely until you didn't need me anymore. She's paying me my salary. I'm just doing different work."

Bless you, Glenda, I thought. *You're going to be one of the first people I call.*

It felt so good to be home. I breathed a sigh of relief, even though it hurt to do so. As we entered the house, I gasped, which also hurt. I couldn't help myself. There were flower arrangements, balloon bouquets, and wrapped presents all over the living room. Michael promised me that he'd bring each item into the bedroom one by one, so I could see what was there and find out whom it was from.

"Everyone waited until they knew you were coming home," Krystal said. "They wanted you to have time to enjoy all of it. You still haven't even gotten to open your wedding presents!"

"Well, time is definitely what I have lots of right now."

I was soon in my bed, lying propped on a pillow that raised my torso at a slight angle. I definitely wasn't sitting up, but I also wasn't lying flat on my back. It was uncomfortable, but I was willing to put up with some discomfort for a while in order to avoid staring at the ceiling.

"Did you have someone paint the ceiling?" I asked Michael. "I don't see any blood."

"The whole room's been repainted," he said grimly. "The ceiling wasn't the only surface that had blood on it."

"Are you ready to look at some of your gifts?" Krystal asked a little too perkily.

"Maybe. I'm kind of tired."

Krystal smiled sweetly at me and said, "How about if we show you a few and then let you sleep?"

I saw a beautiful flower arrangement accompanied by a lovely card signed by every member of the staff at John's Place. Then I was brought a huge cluster of balloons held by a realistic-looking stuffed bear sent collectively by our Friday night Ceviche friends. Krystal and Greg had put together a basket filled with all sorts of Less of You products I always said I planned to buy and snacks I loved. Adiba and Rakeem had given me a soft, gorgeous blanket that had intricate Arabic patterns woven throughout.

I was so comforted by the warm wishes, but I was starting to hurt worse and was feeling exhausted. Krystal handed me a twelve-inch square box that was wrapped in shiny purple paper and had a large silver bow on top.

"The card says *All our love, Al and Diane*," she read.

I opened the box and almost dropped it. Inside was another box made of something like Plexiglas. There was a stand in the center that held the Dali artwork I'd taken from Tom's house. Michael showed me a switch at the base, and an LED light came on and illuminated the piece. The effect was stunning.

"I have to call them," I murmured. "This is…perfect."

"They'll be by this evening," Michael told me. "You can tell them yourself. They would have been here when you got home, but they didn't want to overwhelm you right away."

I nodded very slightly and asked if I could have a painkiller and lie down. Michael and Krystal helped me to take a pill and drink some water. After some time had passed, they removed the slanted pillow. I fell quickly to sleep but woke to find Al and Diane sitting at the foot of the bed talking to Michael. I wasn't sure where Krystal was and automatically tried to turn my head in order to look at the clock. There was instant pain across my neck, and I sucked in my breath, which caused shooting pains in my chest, ribs, and belly. Frustrated, I started to cry, which made things worse.

The others immediately surrounded me and offered me words of comfort and assistance. I was so relieved to see Al and Diane after such a long separation that I quickly ceased crying. I thanked them profusely for my gift and for taking care of John's Place and my personal business while I'd been in the hospital. They assured me it had been no trouble and were happy to help.

"What time is it?" I asked Michael.

"9:00 p.m. You want to meet the nurse on duty?"

"In a minute. First, I want –"

"No," he said firmly.

"You don't even know what I'm going to say," I protested.

"You're going to say you want the bathroom and to take a shower or bath. Absolutely not. The doctors said you aren't even supposed to sit up straight for at least another week."

"But that's too long! I can do it."

"No, you can't," he said coolly.

"I can," I retorted.

Michael crossed his arms over his chest and said casually, "Try it."

Surprisingly, neither Diane nor Al interjected anything during this conversation. Older and wiser than the two of us, they probably surmised that we needed to figure out on our own where we stood when it came to my condition and terms of recovery.

I did try to get up. Nothing worked. I couldn't raise myself off the pillow or turn to either side. Even the slightest movement caused pain. Eventually, I gave up.

"I hate this!" I cried.

"At least you are alive to hate it," Al put in. "I do not know how you survived, my angel."

"She obviously has a guardian angel watching over her," Diane said in a no-nonsense tone. It was an unusual thing for her to say, and the three of us looked at her with curiosity.

"Well, it's true," she declared. "There's no way Seneca could have survived what happened without some sort of Divine intervention. She was meant to live."

I thought of what Esmeralda had told me during my visit to her about Michael saving me and my saving Michael. I hadn't thought of it in a literal sense. I'd figured she meant that we would save one another emotionally by being there for each other like I'd been there for him when he'd told me about John. I supposed I had been wrong and wondered if Michael was destined for a near-death experience.

I remembered the old woman saying Michael would go away from me for a while but not by choice. What had she meant by that? Would his work take him to other places while I was homebound? Or had it meant something more sinister?

I pushed those thoughts from my head and met my new nurse, ate some soup, took some pills, then went back to sleep. Resigned to my current fate, I decided that worrying about the future was unproductive. I couldn't even get out of bed, so how was I going to save my husband? Whatever was destined to happen wasn't going to take place anytime soon. I had to get better so I could be ready.

Chapter Seventeen

A week after my return home, I was taken by medical transport to my internist's office for examination. He was impressed by my progress, commended me on following doctors' orders, and gave me permission to sit up straight, walk short distances, and shower as long as someone was assisting me. I was thrilled and ready to try everything. He discouraged me from attempting to tackle more than one new freedom each day. I dismissed his cautious approach and was determined to accomplish all three things before Krystal went home at 4:00 p.m.

"Michael would *kill* me," was Krystal's response when I told her of my plan.

"He doesn't have to know. He's been back at work for four days now. He won't get home until 6:00 at the earliest. Come on, Krystal. I'm so done with lying around all day, and I feel so much better than I have since the accident. How about if we do all three things at once? I can sit up, walk to the bathroom, shower, and walk back. You'll be right there with me."

Looking doubtful, Krystal pulled her blonde hair up into a ponytail and agreed that we could try as long as I did what she said and sat on the plastic stool in the shower while she helped me to wash and to shampoo my hair. I breathed a mental sigh of relief. I had an ulterior motive for wanting to achieve all of my goals for the afternoon.

No one had let me see myself in a mirror or without clothing since I'd been injured. Although Michael had described my condition in detail, I hadn't been left alone for a moment and wasn't able to attempt to take a peek under my nightclothes or the sheets and blanket. My doctor had somehow managed to examine me without letting me see any skin. Even if I could simply make it to the bathroom, then I could try to catch a glimpse of myself in the full-length mirror that hung behind the door.

I'd counted on the fact that both of us had training in moving sick and injured persons to make moving myself not quite so difficult. I'd underestimated how challenging such a simple thing as standing would be regardless of whether or not I had help. It gave me a better appreciation of how my clients must have felt when they were in similar situations. At least I was supposed to get better. Many of them never would.

I was trembling by the time we made it to the bathroom and was more than ready to sit on the plastic stool in the shower. Krystal told me she was going to sit me down then remove my nightgown and help me wash my body before cleaning my hair. Unable to conceal my discomfort as she aided me into the tub, I merely nodded and gratefully allowed her to lower me onto the seat. Then she stopped and frowned.

"Please don't tell me I can't have a shower. I haven't had anything except sponge baths and dry shampoo for a month, and they always do it while I'm drugged and asleep! I want to take a shower. Well, I really want a bath, but I'll settle for a shower."

"You tricked me," Krystal said in a mildly accusatory tone. "You just wanted to do all of this so you could see what you look like."

"The thought had occurred to me, but that's not why I went through all this," I told her, which was a half-truth. "I really am tired of just lying around and really do want a shower."

"I know you do, but you wouldn't have pushed yourself so hard if you didn't have something pushing you. Please, don't do that again. We're like sisters, remember? If you want something, ask me. Don't manipulate me. You're smarter than I am, and it makes me feel stupid if you do something like this."

Ashamed, I hung my head and mumbled, "I'm sorry. I didn't think you'd do it if I just asked. No one will let me look."

"Everyone's trying to protect you."

"The doctor said I can shower. No one can hide it from me much longer anyway."

"I think you should talk to Michael first."

"I'm an adult."

"An adult who's been through a traumatic incident that almost killed her. You're the social worker, Seneca. You know better than most people about stuff like this. Why won't you listen?"

"Because I'm stubborn?"

Leaning back against the wall, she muttered, "Michael is going to blow a gasket." Sighing, she directed, "Promise to keep your eyes closed until I say you can open them."

I promised and didn't open my eyes while I was in the shower. It hurt when Krystal washed the front of my body, but I knew there was no way around it. I wanted to feel truly clean, so I held onto the rails on each side of the stool and bit my lip in order to avoid a repeat of the *ow* mantra. The feeling I got from having my long hair shampooed and conditioned made up for the previous pain. With my eyes still shut, I asked Krystal if we could stay there for the remainder of the afternoon. She laughed and said the hot water would run out long before her shift was over.

When I was relatively dry, Krystal aided me in standing and stepping out of the tub. Thoroughly exhausted, I was thrilled to have accomplished my basic goals. I thanked Krystal as I secretly fought light-headedness.

All of this will get easier every day, I told myself. *Work on getting stronger, and it will happen.*

Krystal helped me to take a few steps then told me to stop where we stood and open my eyes. I stared at our reflection in the mirror. Krystal looked vibrant and healthy, and the mirror accurately showed that she'd lost more weight since my wedding. I, on the other hand, did not appear to be so vivacious or well.

Fading blue-black bruises speckled the front of me from my breastbone almost to my ankles, and dozens of healing cuts were visible. I saw the small scar on my neck where the surgeons had repaired my nicked vein and the larger scar near where the glass had almost punctured my lung. The scar on my leg where the artery had been lacerated was about eight inches long but seemed to be mending decently. I knew from my minimal medical training that I was actually healing at an extraordinary rate considering my injuries.

My main concern was how my appearance would affect Michael's physical desire for me. Would he ever want to have sex with me again after seeing me looking like that? Actually, I knew I'd looked much, much worse the previous month. Would he still want me when I was healed enough to make love to him or would he always think about me lying on the floor bleeding to death or picture me as the invalid I'd been for the last few weeks?

"Will you turn me a little so I can see my sides and back?"

"You know you can't turn your head enough to see the back, but I'll let you see the side where I'm not holding you."

What I could view of my side and back looked perfectly normal. It was almost surreal to see the disaster that was my front compared with the rest of my body. It did boost my spirits though and reminded me of what I would hopefully look like in the future.

As I stared at my bruised breasts, I said, "No wonder those hurt so much. They're extra-bruised."

"At least you have a good pair. They cushion the impact," Krystal half-joked. "Mine are so big that I probably wouldn't have been hurt at all anywhere else if the mirror had fallen on me."

I giggled and regretted it, as my ribs screamed for me to stop.

"Thank you so much for this," I told my friend. "I mean, thank you for taking such good care of me, period. But especially thank you for this. I needed to know."

We finished up in the bathroom then Krystal helped me return to bed. I ate a turkey sandwich, took a painkiller, and was eventually laid back and allowed to sleep.

I heard my Mommy and Poppy arguing violently about me. I couldn't understand why. As much as they fought, they didn't usually fight over me. Their confrontations typically involved money or jealousy. The trailer was so small, and I would lie awake at night listening to them fight then make up. Then there would be strange sounds of what I would later learn were those of passion. It was all extremely confusing to my young mind.

"Seneca?"

"Don't fight," I mumbled sleepily. "Poppy didn't mean it, Mommy."

There was a long pause. Fingertips moved my hair away from my face before lips lightly brushed the spot where my neck had been injured. I automatically reached my hand up and slid it into Michael's hair as I slowly came fully awake.

"Michael, where are we?"

"In our bedroom."

"I thought I heard my parents fighting. I must have been dreaming."

I felt Michael's hot breath on my throat as he sighed and admitted, "I was arguing with Krystal a while ago. She waited until

I came home even though the other nurse got here on time at 4:00. She told me what you did today, and I kind of lost it. I apologized to her before she left, and she said she'd expected me to be upset and took it all with a grain of salt. She held her own with me," he added, the respect evident in his voice. "I didn't expect her to argue with me. I know you haven't told her about what I used to be, but I get the impression she senses it. I didn't think she'd ever do anything that might make me angry. I mean I've...."

His voice trailed off, and I waited patiently for him to finish his sentence.

"I've killed people. I was very good at it," he said darkly. "It didn't matter that I didn't enjoy it and only killed out of necessity."

"Of course it mattered," I told him. "You sound like Tom."

"Thank you. That doesn't take away my culpability any more than it lessened his."

"I forgave you all your sins, remember? I'll always be here to forgive you and love you."

He moved his lips close to my ear and said hoarsely, "I killed a child once. Can you forgive me that?"

I felt one teardrop fall on my earlobe and another on my neck. Although it increased my pain, I brought my other hand up and placed it on the side of his head then urged him to tell me what had happened.

"I was in a dangerous place on a dangerous job. My target was an evil man who was working with his brother smuggling arms to people who were using them to kill our soldiers. He and I were in the middle of a transaction when someone ratted me out. Gunfire erupted, and I knew that this would be my only opportunity to stop him. Others had been trying for years without success, and I wasn't about to let him escape.

"I pulled, aimed, and fired my gun at the man, who was crouching and aiming at me. I'd just pulled the trigger when his little daughter ran out from somewhere nearby. She was four years old. The bullet hit her in the chest, and she...." He began to cry harder and said, "She looked right at me when the bullet hit her. She seemed so surprised. Then she fell to the ground. Her father didn't waste his chance, the bastard! He shot at me and almost got me in the belly. The next bullet I fired hit him between the eyes. He was dead in seconds."

"And the little girl?"

"I...I held her against me while she died. She didn't cry or ask me anything. She looked peaceful as she went, and all I could think of was that I'd ended the life of an innocent child. I killed her."

"You didn't mean to."

"I had killed a child. I was done."

"So, that's when you quit the military?"

"That's when I tried. They weren't very happy about it. They'd invested a lot of time and money in me, Rob, and John, and John had been killed the previous year. They tried to convince me to keep working, and I took one more assignment."

"And?"

"I got the job done, but I killed with anger. I wanted revenge for John, for that little girl, for all the people I'd seen die during my career. When it was all over, I was on the edge. My superiors realized if they didn't let me go and get me help that I could become a real liability. So, they did." He pulled away from me, reached for a tissue, wiped his eyes and blew his nose before saying, "I'm sure I'm listed in their files as Michael Benedetto, operative, businessman, and killer of little girls."

"Stop that! You didn't kill that child on purpose. It was an accident. You can't blame yourself!"

"Can't I? You told me, Nonno, and Diane the night the mirror fell on you that it was your fault your father died, which none of us believe. I can't feel guilt for taking the life of this child, but you can for whatever happened to your father?"

"It's different."

Michael looked like he was ready to explode although I wasn't certain if it was with anger, sadness, frustration, or a combination of the three. He slipped his hands behind my shoulders but was careful not to hold me too tightly. Then he kissed me hard. I could feel the tension and power coiled within him as it vibrated into me through his mouth, arms, and hands.

"Tell me what happened!" he demanded when he drew back from me.

"Michael, the nurse –"

"I told the evening nurse to take the night off, that I'd take care of you by myself."

"But –"

"What are you running from? Tell me! I'm your husband!"

"I can't! I'm terrified!"

"Of what?"

"Of remembering!"

"You blame yourself for something you can't even remember?"

"I don't *allow* myself to remember, at least not while I'm awake!"

"How do you do that?"

"I…I just do! I don't know how, but I do!"

He shook his head and said, "What the fuck?"

"Don't –" I began.

"Don't tell me I shouldn't swear!" he interrupted. "Stop avoiding the real issue!"

"I've lived like this for half my life."

"You almost ended your life last month because of it," he reminded me.

"Whatever you were running from in your sleep, you had to have been running pretty damn hard. The force required for you to hit that mirror and make it come away from the wall on top of you had to be –"

"I know! I know physics, remember?"

He grabbed my shoulders and asked fiercely, "What happened to your father, Seneca? How did he die?"

"It hurts too much right now!" I said desperately.

I realized he was not above using my weakened condition to wear me down. He'd determined I was going to tell him no matter what, and I had no choice. I couldn't even sit up by myself, much less walk away from him in order to escape his questions.

Even if I had been well, he wouldn't have let me go. He was way stronger than I would ever be, and he'd reached his limit when it came to being patient. He wanted to fix my problem and felt he couldn't because I wouldn't share it with him. I was boxed in and scared to death.

I knew Michael had years of training in how to respond to interrogation and how to interrogate others. I speculated as to how far he'd gone in order to get information out of adversaries. Had he used prolonged torture on captives? No, that wasn't Michael. However, I could imagine he was quite capable of roughing up an enemy to make him disclose vital information, not that I was afraid he'd ever strike me. I was well aware that he didn't have to. He'd been trained in how to get what he wanted, and I had no idea how to resist his tactics. It was a lose-lose scenario for me.

"Please," I begged one last time. "Don't do this to me. You don't know what you're asking."

He said nothing and simply waited. His hands were still on my shoulders, and his mouth was set with determination. The blue eyes did not reflect any of the usual sentiments they expressed for me like love, passion, excitement, frustration, kindness, happiness, or sadness. Instead, his eyes were cold, hard, and penetrating.

The field was calling to me, and I felt my heart pounding. I said Michael's name, but he said nothing in response. I began to shake and closed my eyes. He ordered me to open them. I refused.

"Look at me!" he growled. When I opened my eyes, he demanded, "What the fuck happened?"

"I want you to go," I pleaded. "Don't do this!"

Michael lifted me slightly, and I made a little mewling sound of distress. I thought it would stop him. It didn't.

"Did you watch someone stab him?" he asked. "Did he blow his brains out in front of you? Did you knock over a candle and set the trailer on fire? Was he —"

"He fell!" I screamed even though it caused me tremendous pain. "He fell from a work truck into the wood chipper when I tossed him his hat and the wind blew it and he reached for it and fell and fell in, and I watched it pull him in and heard him scream. There was blood everywhere, and he got ground up into little pieces before my eyes!" As I began to sob hysterically, I continued, "He'd motioned for me...for me to...to throw him the hat! I should...I should have climbed up on the truck instead! I shouldn't have tossed it to him when...when...when he asked me to! If I had gone up, then he wouldn't have fallen in and...and...and you can't imagine what it was like to see him die like that! People were...they were screaming, and I was screaming and then I ran! I ran as far and as fast as I could! I had to get away from seeing him and hearing him and...and...and then Mommy and some men found me and made me go home! I wanted to stay in the field! They wouldn't let me! And then no one would let me talk about it! I had to stay quiet!"

I clung to Michael as I cried. It was all I could do to hold onto him as I relived watching my father's horrific death over and over again. I buried my face against Michael's chest and beseeched him to somehow help me. Michael cradled me in his arms and said things to me that sounded comforting, but I couldn't make out his exact words over the sounds of my father's screams. When he tried to lay me back onto the pillow, I became frantic and held on tightly to the front of his shirt until he was dissuaded and simply held me. Eventually, I fell into an exhausted sleep.

I woke expecting to find myself alone in the bed. Instead, Michael lay beside me holding my hand and stroking my hair. I wanted to turn on my side to face him, but my ribs were already throbbing with pain and the rest of me was too stiff to move easily.

Turning my head slightly towards him, I asked, "What time is it?"

"4:00 a.m."

"Is the nurse here?"

"No. I canceled everyone for the weekend."

"But you said you need to work to catch up from all the time you took off when we were on our honeymoon and from when I was in the hospital."

"I'll work from home."

"But you haven't slept. You'll be tired."

"Yes, I will. It's not important."

"But –"

He told me to stop worrying about him, the business, and everything else. Then he kissed me and said that he was going to help me to the bathroom, get me food, and give me some pain medicine. That was precisely what he did, and I was completely worn out by the time I swallowed the pain pill.

"I don't think I can walk back to bed even with your help," I admitted.

"I'll carry you, but you have to wait for the pill to go down for thirty minutes, remember?" When I nodded, he dropped his head and said, "Seneca, I'm so, so sorry I pushed you tonight. I knew that whatever had happened to your dad had to be bad, but I had no idea it would be like that. I shouldn't have forced you to talk about it."

I didn't know what to say in response to this. A part of me hated Michael for what he'd done. Another part of me was grateful and relieved that I'd shared the memory with someone, anyone.

"I want to ask you something," Michael said. "If you don't want to answer me, then that's okay. I won't ever push you like I did earlier ever again. I swear it."

I stared at my lap and waited.

"I need to understand something you said. You told me after the accident that you couldn't talk about it, that you had to keep quiet. Why?"

My throat muscles constricted, and Michael had to remind me to breathe through my nose. I did and forced myself to take in air for a minute or two before looking at him and saying, "The grown-ups told me not to talk."

"What grown-ups?"

"All of them, except Mommy. Everyone was upset but they were also terrified about my telling anyone what had happened."

"Why?"

"The location was a big farm that made lots of money. They used mostly illegals to work on the farm, and if the authorities were called in, then the farm would probably be shut down since they were in violation of quite a few safety regulations, immigration laws, and child labor laws."

"So, the owners of the farm told you to keep your mouth shut after what you saw?"

"Not just the owners. The workers, too. Everyone was scared about losing what little income they had and of being found out. If I talked about Poppy's death, then they said they could all be deported or sent to jail. Mommy told them she didn't care, that someone had to tell somebody what had happened."

"But she didn't."

"There were threats made. She didn't have the money or wherewithal to get help. So, she finally told me that we couldn't talk about it to anyone except each other, and I couldn't talk about it to her. She still loved Poppy, even though she'd divorced him. I just didn't talk about it at all and made myself not think about it. Every couple of years, I'd dream about it. Then it would go away again."

"No one ever asked where your father went?"

"Everyone denied knowing what had happened to him."

"And you never got any counseling?"

I laughed bitterly and asked, "How do you get counseling for something that supposedly never happened, especially when you have no money to begin with?" I looked around the kitchen and said, "This house is the only good thing that came out of Poppy's death. After the owner of the farm died not too long ago, his wife's guilty conscience got the better of her. She found me and sent me a check as compensation for that thing that had never happened. I bought the house, built the garage, and invested the rest of the money to pay for insurance and taxes for the remainder of my life. I figured I deserved some security for once."

"You deserve more than that. I learned a lot about people and tragedy while I was in the military. One of the main things I learned is that every child who witnesses a parent's death suffers from PTSD. Those children need therapy and should be encouraged to talk about what they saw and the parent they lost. You were denied even those basic requirements for recovery. It's a miracle you didn't suffer from a complete mental breakdown."

"I couldn't do that to Mommy. I was all she had."

"Why didn't you get therapy as an adult?"

"After years of brainwashing myself to protect everyone else and my own sanity? I'm a social worker, Michael. I knew I needed counseling. I simply couldn't bring myself to go through with it. I was too scared."

"And now?"

"I'm still scared."

"Would you talk to my psychiatrist? You've done the virtual therapy with him about my problems. If he agrees to work with you, will you try to work through your own?"

The painkiller was making me sleepy. I nodded drowsily and agreed before asking Michael to bring me back to bed. As he did so, I requested that he tell Al, Diane, Krystal, Greg, Adiba, and Rakeem about the circumstances surrounding my father's death. I knew they would want to know what had caused Michael to dismiss all of the nurses for the weekend and couldn't bear the thought of having to revisit my childhood trauma with each one. I drifted off to sleep before I heard his answer.

When I woke again, it was late in the afternoon. Michael was sitting with his back against the headboard of our bed and was working on his laptop. As I stirred, he closed the laptop and put it on the nightstand then turned to me and asked how I was feeling.

"My body actually feels much better, and my mind feels sort of numb. Did you tell the others? Did you talk to Dr. Forrester about me?"

Michael explained that he had and that everyone was properly horrified by the revelation. The family and friends had all agreed not to talk to me about it unless I brought up the subject. The psychiatrist was more than willing to have sessions with me.

"Because my well-being impacts yours," I said sardonically. "I had a feeling he wouldn't refuse."

Michael bent down to kiss me and said, "I'm sure that's true to an extent, but he really does want to help you. He was very…concerned about you."

"When do I talk with him?"

"Every weekday at noon, unless you have a crisis and need to call him in-between."

"So, he's using his lunch hour to talk to me."

"Pretty much. He said if you wanted to call him this weekend then feel free. He'll start with you right away."

"He's that afraid for me?"

Michael nodded and said, "I don't think you realize how seriously damaging what happened is."

"I realize it," I said wearily. "Can we not talk about it anymore today? I want to do something…positive tonight."

"Like what?"

"I don't know. You need to work."

"Fuck work."

I'd rather you fuck me, I thought then blushed and turned my head so he couldn't see. *Is it my imagination or has Michael been swearing a lot more since we got married? I wonder why that is. Am I that much more frustrating as his wife or does he just feel more comfortable around me and can swear all he wants? Maybe I should ask him…*

"What do you want to do? Tell me."

I thought about his question for a long while then said, "I'd like for you to make us some dinner. It would be nice to eat on the lanai then go sit by the water or lie on a blanket and watch the sunset."

We'd just finished dinner on the lanai when the phone rang. It was Krystal.

"I have something exciting to tell you!" she announced. "Greg asked me to marry him! I think we're going to fly to Vegas in the spring and tie the knot! Will you and Michael come with us? I want you to be my Maid of Honor, and Greg's going to ask Michael to be his Best Man. We're going to ask Adiba and Rakeem to come to Nevada with us although we won't ask them to be in the wedding. I know they bowed out of yours, and we understand. We'd still like for them to attend."

"Michael and I would be thrilled," I told her. "Congratulations, Krystal. I'm so, so happy for you."

I told Michael the news as he cleared the table. He was happy for Greg and Krystal, and he said he'd be honored to be part of their wedding. While I sat in the rocker on the lanai, he went out to the beach and spread a blanket on the sand. Then, he carried me and lowered me onto the blanket.

I enjoyed the breeze and the sound of the waves. Kissing my temple, Michael asked, "What else can I do for you?"

"I want you to help take off my clothes so I can enjoy the beach as we did the night you proposed."

Michael aided me in undressing then stripped off his own clothing. He lay naked beside me and ran his fingers through my hair and kissed my shoulder. The fact that I could feel his erection pressing against my hip gave me hope that he might someday want to make love to me again. I decided to take the plunge and simply ask.

"Do you still want me?"

He stopped kissing my shoulder and propped himself up on one elbow then looked down at me in disbelief.

"How could you ever doubt that I'd want you no matter what?"

"Well, I have. I guess it's good we had sex more than once that last day before my accident, since it looks like it'll be a while before we can have regular sex again."

He smirked and said, "Regular sex?" As opposed to irregular sex?"

"You know what I mean."

"I want you every moment of every day. Nothing will change that."

Not feeling very confident at that moment, I turned my head towards the water. The sun was beginning to sink in the sky, and it looked as if it was going to be a magnificent sunset with pink and purple hues and fluffy clouds and the blue-green waves. I fell asleep lying next to Michael on the blanket and dreamed of my fifth birthday party and the Cookie Monster toy, of enjoying the cookie-shaped cake, of playing with the other children in the plastic pool, and of having a carefree day with both of my parents. It had been a fun birthday, the best I'd ever had. I stopped playing in my dream and stood in the pool looking around at everyone.

"Seneca! Seneca!"

I opened my eyes and mouth and immediately swallowed salty water. I choked and was disoriented and literally adrift. Waves lifted me up then pushed me down, and I couldn't get my bearings. I swallowed more water and felt my eyes burning with salt. I came up for air and coughed. A large swell pulled me under again, and I realized I was drowning. I had heard Michael's voice. Where was he? Had he seen me momentarily then lost me in the night waters?

A hand touch my arm before the waves carried me out further. I fought to rise to the water's surface, but there was only murkiness in the vast expanse of liquid surrounding me. I wasn't certain which way was up and had been weakened by my accident and the weeks of forced bed rest that had followed. In short, I didn't stand a chance.

I began to lose consciousness and ceased struggling. It felt good to float and let the water have its way with me. I was…I was….

Michael's mouth was on mine, and I suddenly felt the urge to…to breathe. I began to cough up water, and he quickly moved his mouth from mine and turned my head. My healing ribs protested as I threw up salt water onto the sand. I could feel waves rushing back and forth across one of my feet.

"What the fuck?!?" Michael yelled. "Seneca, answer me! What did you think you were doing? You're in no shape to be out in the Gulf right now, much less alone and at night."

"I didn't know," I insisted weakly. "I was dreaming I was in the kiddie pool on my fifth birthday."

"And that's what the Gulf of Mexico is?" he shot back. "A giant kiddie pool?"

"Where were you?" I demanded angrily, as I began to cry. "Where were you when I needed you?"

He began, "I went to the house to –" Then he stopped and gave me an odd look before asking, "When? When did you need me?"

I rolled onto my side, got to my hands and knees then stood even though it caused me pain. I barely noticed as I cried, "I needed you when I was hot or cold or scared or hungry or sad or despairing or when I watched Poppy die or when I held Mommy's hand as she died or when I went through my miscarriage or when I was so lonely! I needed you *always!*"

I was hollow and yet somehow filled with rage. I knew it was absurd to focus my fury on Michael. He'd known me for less than six months. There was no way he could have been there to help me through years of poverty, hopelessness, and pain. I didn't care. I'd needed him desperately.

Michael rose and walked towards me. The moon had come out from behind the clouds, and I could see the muscles rippling under his naked skin as he got closer. He came to stand in front of me and said, "I'm sorry, Seneca."

He was apologizing for something that hadn't been his fault, but somehow it made me feel better. He cupped my cheek in his hand, and I rested my palms on his chest. He lifted me up and carried me into the house. Bringing me into the bathroom, Michael stepped into the shower before putting me down. He washed both of us, being careful not to press too hard on my healing skin. Then I sat on the stool while he washed my hair. When we were dry, we got ready for bed but didn't put on any nightclothes. I was dangerously close to passing out from exhaustion and the aftereffects of my near-drowning, but I wasn't about to tell Michael that.

As it turned out, I didn't have to. Michael carried me to bed and placed me on top of the covers before gingerly bending my left leg and then moving my right. He carefully eased himself into me. He began to thrust in and out, but very gently. With each thrust, there was an apology.

"I'm sorry I wasn't there to cool you when you were miserably hot in the trailer. I'm sorry I wasn't there to make you warm when it was freezing. I'm sorry I wasn't there to comfort you when you were lying awake scared because your parents were arguing. I'm sorry I wasn't there to make sure you had enough to eat every day.

I'm sorry I wasn't there to cheer you up when you were frustrated by your lack of opportunity when it came to academics or your dancing. I'm sorry I wasn't there to get you help when your father died so horribly as you watched. I'm sorry I wasn't there to hug you when your mother died of cancer. I'm sorry I wasn't there to hold your hand when you miscarried your baby. I'm sorry I wasn't there during all those years when you felt so apart and alone. I'm sorry you were so hurt by life."

I began to cry and come at the same time. The climax was barely a tremor, but my tears were forceful. Michael pulled out of me without coming and took me in his strong arms. He held me against him and let me cry until I fell asleep feeling safe and secure. It was the most tranquil slumber I'd ever experienced.

Chapter Eighteen

I sat holding Tom's teddy bear in my arms and wondered if I should bring him to the memorial service we were about to attend. I had been pondering this question for the last half hour while Michael got ready in our room. I'd put on my warm, long-sleeved navy blue dress after I'd showered that morning.

I'd been planning the event for over a month. We had easily located Tom's grave at the end of September and decided to hold his memorial service on November 11th, Veterans' Day. I thought it would be the perfect way to honor Tom and other veterans whose service to their country had been forgotten or ignored. There had only been one flaw in my plan.

"I don't know what to do," I told Dr. Forrester during one of our early virtual sessions.

"I need clarification, please."

"I literally don't know what to do. I've never planned a memorial service or funeral before."

"What about when your mother died?" When I didn't answer, he prodded, "Seneca, we have to talk about these things, remember?"

"Michael won't let me forget," I said grudgingly.

"Because he wants you to get a handle on dealing with your PTSD as you should. Now, tell me about what the services for your mother were like."

"She was buried in a pauper's grave. The minister at her church coordinated a service, and everyone who knew her came. There were prayers and people telling me they were sorry. Then it was over."

"And what did you do for your father?"

I shook my head and couldn't find my voice. I was in the field and couldn't breathe. Michael was suddenly beside me reminding me to inhale through my nostrils and hold onto him for support. I buried my face against his chest although I didn't cry.

"Seneca, it's okay to talk about your father and his death," the therapist reminded me. "No one is going to hurt you or your mother. No one will be arrested or deported if you tell me about what happened. You don't have to be afraid anymore."

Without moving my head, I said, "We didn't do anything for my Poppy. How can you do something for someone when you can't even acknowledge his death?"

"Very true and very sad. We're going to fix that, but not today."

My curiosity was peaked. I looked at the computer screen but stayed tucked in Michael's arms. I considered how the psychiatrist would have me honor a man who'd been dead for fourteen years. The farm wasn't even operational anymore.

Forrester inquired, "What about your uncle and grandparents?"

"I was five the year my grandparents died, and I don't even remember going to their funerals. I was eleven when my uncle died, but my father and the minister took care of all the funeral arrangements."

"And your clients at Hearts at Home?"

"I attended plenty of funerals but never had to plan one myself. I want Tom's service to be special, but I don't know how to make it what he'd want."

"What do you envision?"

"Humility. Honor. Touching other people's lives."

The psychiatrist looked to Michael and said, "You and I are going to help Seneca with this, Michael. She needs to be in charge, but you're going to have to supply her with information and work on logistics."

And that was what Michael had done. He'd explained to me what military funerals and memorial services were like and different options that would be available to us. It hadn't taken us long to agree upon the details of the service, as he and I worked together with local organizations for veterans and with the Navy itself in order to arrange things. The veterans being served at John's Place had quickly assumed an active role in promoting the event and gave me helpful ideas or shared their thoughts on how this would help other veterans in the area.

"Seneca? Are you ready?"

I looked up at Michael, who was attired in his U.S. Naval dress uniform. With the exception of his medium-length black hair, he looked every bit the military officer he'd once been. I wondered if Tom's children had thought to bury him in his uniform.

"Are you going to be able to handle this?" Michael asked me as I stood and brought Teddy back to the bookcase.

"It's for Tom. I'll handle it. I've got lots of tissues in my purse."

He took me in his arms and kissed me before saying, "This is going to be hard, but it's going to be good for you and for everyone else, including me."

"I know. I just hope that more than a handful of people show up. I want to give Tom a proper goodbye with as many of his fellow servicemen there as possible."

"It'll be fitting even if it's only a few of us."

We rode in the SUV to the cemetery. The large parking lot was packed with cars, and we almost couldn't find a place to park. I figured lots of veterans' families must be making visits to their loved ones' graves in observance of the holiday. As we walked through the chilly November morning air towards Tom's gravesite, I could see that a crowd of at least fifty men and women were gathered there. The cemetery staff was busy setting up extra chairs as more people continued to arrive. Some veterans had parked their wheelchairs along the sides of the rows, and at least two-thirds of those present wore military uniforms. I saw people from every branch of the military in attendance, and the age group ranged from twenties to nineties from the looks of it. I recognized staff members and patrons from John's Place, but there were many strangers there as well.

Michael escorted me to the right front row of chairs, which had been reserved. Al, Diane, Adiba, Rakeem, and Krystal were waiting for us there. I took the empty seat beside Krystal that was close to the aisle. That left the chair next to me vacant for Michael, who had excused himself to talk with the military chaplain leading the event.

Over the remaining half hour before the start of the service, several dozen more attendees arrived. The cemetery crew ran out of chairs, so people stood off to the sides and behind the rows that were already filled. I was touched and had already used one tissue until it was limp and useless. I withdrew a fresh one as Michael came to sit beside me and took my hand.

When it was time for the service to begin, the Naval chaplain climbed up the few steps and walked across the platform that had been positioned under a large oak tree. A United States flag stood on one end, and flags representing each branch of the military ran the length of the raised area. All of our chairs faced this stage, and everyone who was physically able rose as the trim, middle-aged officer approached the microphone, introduced himself, welcomed us, and then opened with a prayer. Everyone who had a seat returned to it.

The chaplain spoke of Thomas Edison Langston, a decorated veteran with a strong sense of honor and a love for his country and its ideals. He talked of Tom's three decades of military service although he didn't reveal his role as an operative. Instead, he said that Tom was involved in "Communications." I gave Michael a sideways glance, but he didn't look at me. Was this some code word for operatives in the military or had Michael simply told this to the chaplain in order to conceal the true nature of Tom's duties?

The chaplain went on to talk of Tom's attainment of his Ph.D. and his dedication to his university students for the following twenty years. He mentioned many military and academic achievements and elaborated on Tom's passion for life, the arts, good food, and good friends. He didn't mention any of Tom's ex-wives or children.

The officer concluded by asking Michael to join him on the platform. I was confused. Whatever was happening, no one had told me about it. Why not?

I glanced at those sitting in our row. Krystal, Al, Diane, Adiba, and Rakeem also seemed perplexed but interested. There was an air of anticipation throughout the crowd.

Michael went to the microphone and withdrew something from one of his uniform pockets. He stood holding what appeared to be folded papers in his hands as he began by introducing himself and stating that he'd been fortunate enough to be Tom's friend for the last few months of his life. He credited me, whom he called Tom's "adopted daughter," with granting him the privilege of knowing such a brilliant, kind, and unflinchingly strong man. He then proceeded to say that he had something he wanted to read to all of those gathered, something Tom had given him on the eve of our marriage. Tom had asked him not to open the envelope until after his death, and Michael said he'd respected the older man's wishes. He now wanted to share Tom's missive with those present.

I reached for Krystal's hand and held it tightly as Michael unfolded the papers and started to read.

"Michael, if you're reading this, then it means I've kicked the bucket. It's about damn time. I've escaped from Death more instances than I can count, and I'm sure Death is ready for me to stop playing games with it. I'm ready, too.

"I don't know that I have much wisdom to share with you despite my long life. I've been a husband four times and a father four times. I seem to have failed each time. As you know, family life is often one of the greatest casualties of military service. It saddens me to know that I couldn't give my family what they needed from me, but I truly did my best.

"I was a good soldier and a good American. I did what I had to for the good of our country. I killed for Her and watched other soldiers and friends die for Her. Like most of us who truly know what it's like to fight for liberty, I developed scars inside and out. I suffered from PTSD and the knowledge that I'd had to take human lives in order to save human lives. I saw the world and lived in the world, and I hope I made a difference.

"I want you to know that you and every other soldier on this planet who fight for truth and justice have sacrificed a part of their souls but have gained an expansion of their hearts. No matter what cruelty exists, we soldiers will not rest until we've done some good. This might mean shooting down an enemy or playing baseball with children in war-torn areas who've forgotten what it's like to enjoy being carefree, even if it's only for a little while.

"What I'm trying to say is that you and all of the other true soldiers out there are true heroes, just as I am. I never thought of myself that way until I sat down to write you this letter. I always considered myself to be just a man whose job was to protect the lives and freedoms of all people, and I did it to the best of my abilities. I realized tonight that this is what defines a hero. I realized it's all right to be selfless and proud of ourselves simultaneously. We deserve to be honored and recognized for all that we've given for the good of the United States of America.

"Keep being a hero. Take care of your lovely wife and your family and friends. Keep helping other soldiers and their families. Never forget those who came before you and those who will come afterwards. We'll make the world a better place just by trying. Your dear friend, Tom."

I wiped at the tears on my cheeks and looked around. Almost everyone was crying, even the big, macho-looking men in their military garb. I was so proud – proud of Tom, proud of Michael, proud of every man and woman who had sworn to serve their country to the best of their abilities.

Michael stepped back from the microphone, and the chaplain came forward. He was wiping at his own eyes with a handkerchief and thanked Michael for sharing the letter before regaining his composure and offering a prayer for Tom and all veterans be they alive or dead. Then he asked those present to rise and honor Thomas Edison Langston and the other servicemen and servicewomen like him.

As if it had been choreographed, every soldier present brought his or her hand up in a salute. I was overwhelmed by the sight of this and wept as a seven-man honor guard stepped forward and fired a three-volley salute in unison with their rifles. Then a bugler played "Taps," while the crowd continued to stand at attention. It was hauntingly beautiful and sad, but it was also perfectly fitting for the occasion.

The majority of those attending lingered for almost two hours after the memorial was over. Stories were exchanged by the servicemen and servicewomen present, and those of us who had known Tom shared some of our own remembrances about him.

Michael and I drove to a nearby Italian restaurant where a table was waiting for us, Al, Diane, Rakeem, Adiba, and Krystal. Our collective mood was relaxed but somber. Krystal excused herself from the table to take a call from Greg, who had been unable to get the day off from his job as the manager of a large department store. When she returned, we all ordered pasta dishes in tribute to Tom.

"Adiba and I would like to say something," Rakeem announced once we'd placed our orders. "We have been waiting for the right time, and Adiba suggested that today was it."

"We're all ears," Michael offered.

"Tell us, please," Diane added.

"The first thing we would like to share is that we have decided to become U.S. citizens," Rakeem explained. "We have been thinking about this ever since we came to the United States, but we did not want to dishonor our heritage. We have come to realize that we can retain our pride in the country of our birth and have pride in our new country. Our daughter is both Iraqi and American, so we will be as well."

"I know myself what a difficult decision that is to make," Al confided. "I was an Italian who chose to become an American. I will tell you that I have never regretted it but also never abandoned my heritage. It is a part of me. That is the beauty of America. One can join the giant melting pot that is the United States and contribute from their place of origin to keep things fresh."

"That is our hope," Rakeem said.

"There is something else," Adiba told us. She seemed rather nervous, and I wondered what the problem was. She bit her lip then said, "I – we are going to have another baby at the end of April."

Surprised by how conflicted I felt upon hearing this news, I avoided looking towards Michael and hoped I concealed my jumbled emotions as I hugged Adiba. Everyone gathered wished the couple congratulations on both their decision to pursue citizenship and on the announcement of Adiba's pregnancy. As soon as I was able, I excused myself from the table and went to the bathroom where I locked myself in a stall and allowed myself to cry for a couple of minutes before wiping my face free of tears and returning to my family and friends.

After the meal, Adiba and Rakeem left to relieve the babysitter and spend the rest of the afternoon together. Al and Diane were headed to a friend's house for afternoon coffee, and Krystal was going first to the grocery store then to her home to cook a special low-fat dinner for herself and Greg. Michael and I returned to his SUV in the parking garage across from Whole Foods and sat in silence for a few minutes.

"Where do you want to go from here?" Michael asked before starting the SUV's engine.

"To the farm where my father died."

For a moment, Michael looked at me like I'd grown a second head. Then he said, "No way are we going there today."

"I'm going," I said resolutely. "You can come with me or stay at home, but I have to do this."

"Talk to Dr. Forrester first."

"He's off for the holiday, remember?"

"So, wait until tomorrow."

"No. I honored Tom today. I need to honor my father by at least acknowledging his death in some fashion."

"And what if you have the nightmare again?"

"I already know I'm going to have it tonight. There's no way around it."

"Therefore, you might as well just go to the scene of your father's accident and get it all over with at once?"

"Something like that."

Michael shook his head and clenched his jaw. I could feel the tension and frustration radiating from him, but I wasn't going to change my mind and he knew it. Finally, he grumbled, "How do I get to the farm?"

We were soon headed eastward. It would take us over two hours to reach our destination, and neither of us seemed inclined to talk. After an hour's drive, Michael asked, "What did you think of the service for Tom?"

"I thought it was exactly right. You?"

"Definitely."

After more minutes of silence, I volunteered, "That was very appropriate for Adiba and Rakeem to tell us about the citizenship thing today."

"Yes. Rakeem had told me a while back that they wanted to become citizens but didn't want to dishonor their ancestors by switching nationalities. We had a lengthy conversation about it, but then he never said anything on the subject again. I assumed they'd decided to wait."

"Speaking of waiting, I wonder why they waited so long to tell us about the new baby."

Michael stared at the road ahead and said, "Adiba probably got pregnant around the time you were in the hospital. Maybe she didn't want to say anything that might distract you from focusing on your recovery." Giving a half-shrug, he said, "Maybe they wanted to make sure that she was past the first trimester." Sighing, he said,

"Or maybe they just didn't want to upset us since they know we can't have babies of our own."

"I'm willing to bet everything on Door Number Three."

"Me, too. I saw your reaction when she made the announcement, and I could tell you'd been crying when you came back from the bathroom."

"I hope no one else could."

More silence followed. Suddenly, Michael asked, "What was it like to be pregnant?"

"Except for the sheer terror of knowing I'd made the biggest mistake of my life, it was great. I felt fabulous. No morning sickness or anything, just tons of energy."

"How far along were you when you lost the baby?"

"Sixteen weeks."

"How long did it last when you miscarried?"

"Most of a day."

"Did they give you anything for the pain?"

"Who?"

"The people at the hospital." When I didn't immediately answer, he prompted, "Tell me you went to a hospital."

"We were college students with no insurance."

"Was your husband there with you?"

"He'd already left for class and work. I skipped class and called in sick for my job. Then I paced around the apartment and kept moving from the couch to the bed to the bathroom. The pain and the guilt were terrible. I was glad and sad when it was over. I remember telling myself it would be different the next time I got pregnant. It never occurred to me there wouldn't be a next time."

"What did you name your baby?"

"Michael, it was tiny. I didn't have a clue if it was a boy or a girl."

"I *know* you, Seneca. Getting pregnant may have been a mistake, but I know you loved your baby and that you would have named it regardless."

I looked out of the passenger side window and said, "I named it John Henry."

"After John Henry "Doc" Holliday," Michael muttered. "Of course."

I pointed to a sign up ahead and said, "Turn left there."

"Seneca –"

"Please don't ask me anymore about John Henry today."

"I won't if you promise to talk about all this with Dr. Forrester during your next session."

"Okay. I promise. Now, take a right at the second road, then drive straight until you can't go any further."

Thirty minutes later, we were standing outside the locked gates of the deserted farm. It obviously hadn't been a working farm for at least a year. I slowly walked the perimeter of the fence with Michael close behind me. When I reached a certain spot about half a mile down, I pushed against a post in the fence. A small section swung back, and I walked through it.

"How did you know that was there?" Michael asked as he followed me onto the property.

"It was put there so illegals would have a way out in case the authorities came. As children, we used to play games with gates like that. We'd pretend they were the gates to secret gardens or the doorways to magical kingdoms."

Michael said nothing but put an arm around me as we walked towards the main farm buildings. When we got to the yard, I stopped and gently pushed his hand away then walked forward about twenty feet before pivoting and angling my head slightly upwards. I imagined my Poppy standing on the truck. He was grinning and motioning for me to throw him the baseball cap he'd worn that day. He looked happy, strong, and full of life.

I quickly turned and headed for the field where I'd run as a fourteen year-old girl. Michael stayed a respectful distance behind me, but I knew he was keeping a close eye on me and was thankful for it. So far, I was handling things fairly well. I knew that could change at any moment.

The chilly November afternoon was nothing like the hot summer day of my father's death. I didn't run and wasn't screaming or fighting to breathe. Instead, I was feeling rather detached.

I wasn't quite sure how long we stayed in the field. Michael leaned against a tree and gave me the space and time I needed to explore what had been my temporary refuge. An idea struck me, and I bent down and began to pick up pieces of palm fronds.

"Seneca?"

"I want to make a marker," I told Michael, as I examined a stick that I determined was too short for my purposes. "I'm going to make a cross out of sticks and lash it together with the pieces of palm leaves. We used to do it when I was a kid. I know it won't last, but it doesn't matter. Who knows what will happen to this place, period."

"We could get something more permanent in a cemetery," he suggested. "Perhaps something near your mother's grave."

"I haven't been to my mother's grave since the day she was buried. I don't think of her as being there." Looking up at him, I asked, "Do you go to your parents' graves?"

"No."

"What about your grandmother's grave?"

He shook his head and said, "I feel like you do. My Nonnie's not there. Why go talk to a piece of ground where her remains are? What purpose would that serve?"

I smiled tiredly and said, "I guess we're weird. Other people seem to take great comfort in doing things like that."

"Other people often do whatever their parents did just because they did it. I mean, I'm glad if it gives them comfort. It's just not my thing."

As I straightened, I asked, "So, we're agreeing that when we die, we don't want to take up extra space in some cemetery?"

"I'd like for my body to be donated to science."

Beginning to walk back towards the main buildings, I said, "That would be fine for me, too. I'll be dead, after all. Maybe someone can benefit from the study of what's left behind."

When we reached the yard, I sat on the ground in the same spot where I'd once stood and watched my father die. I held the sticks in position then lashed them together with the pieces of palm leaves. I'd been good at this as a child, and it appeared I hadn't lost my talent.

Michael found a flat piece of wood and used it as an impromptu hammer. My makeshift cross was soon embedded in the center of the yard. I took one last look around the area then reached for Michael's hand and told him we could go.

As we readied for bed that night, I asked, "Will you make sure I don't inadvertently hurt myself when I have the nightmare this time?"

"I will, because I'm not going to sleep. I'll work all night then catch a nap tomorrow."

"Michael —"

"Don't argue with me," he ordered. "Just sleep. I'll be here if you need me."

And he was. I came awake screaming and crying but also knowing that Michael's strong arms were around me. He was speaking soothingly to me and almost immediately handed me Cookie Monster. I quieted more quickly than I ever had before and was soon sleeping once more.

I woke to the sound of the clock alarm and found that I was anxious and sad, but I felt like I could function. I told Michael I wanted to go to work, and he didn't try to dissuade me although he did make me promise I wouldn't miss my session with Dr. Forrester and would talk with him about everything that had taken place the day before.

"I only have an hour with him," I reminded Michael. "I think this will take several sessions."

"I'm sure it will, but you have to hit the high points today."

"Such as?"

"Tom's memorial. Adiba's pregnancy. What happened when you lost John Henry. The visit to the farm. Your nightmare last night and your improved recovery time regarding it."

"I promise I'll mention all of that," I assured him. "Will you be in your office all day or do you have meetings elsewhere?"

"I'll be in all morning then out most of the afternoon. I'll be back around 6:00 if you want to wait for me. Then we could have dinner downtown."

I felt like I was on a roller coaster when it came to my emotions all morning, but I was able to handle things and do my job. I was inordinately pleased with this and hoped it was the start of a new trend. Maybe I was finally on my way towards moving on with my life after my Poppy's death.

I'd anticipated that I'd handle my session with Dr. Forrester as calmly as I'd handled the previous day's events. I decided afterwards that this had been a delusional assumption on my part. I sat in Michael's office and reviewed the details of the previous day while I sobbed and shook with the intensity of my emotions. I found it especially difficult to discuss my miscarriage, and I told the psychiatrist that I didn't understand this since I hadn't found it so challenging in the past.

"Had you ever told anyone your baby's name before yesterday?" he asked. "Did you ever share with anyone what it was really like when you experienced that loss?"

I shook my head. No one, not even my husband, knew I'd named the baby or what I'd endured during the hours of pain and grief.

"There are still things you haven't told anyone about that day," the therapist said frankly. "Tell them to me, Seneca."

I did. By the time our session was over, the box of tissues in Michael's office was empty, and I felt as though I'd cried out every drop of water I had in my body. The psychiatrist urged me to call him that evening if I needed to and told me we would talk the next day if he didn't hear from me before then. I thanked him and struggled to compose myself. It was time to return to work.

John's Place closed at 5:00, and the building was empty by 5:15. I continued to work in my office until 5:30 then shut off my computer and went to Michael's office to wait for him. I stood in front of the framed Frida Kahlo print and studied it for a while before going to the bookcase and selecting a book on the history of espionage. I was on page seventy-two when Michael entered the room and apologized for being late.

"I got absorbed in this book and don't even know what time it is."

He glanced at the cover and asked, "What page are you on?"

"Seventy-two."

"Ah, the section on ancient Rome."

"It's a really good book. I think I'll take it home and finish it this weekend. I could take a blanket out on the beach, wrap up, and read."

He smiled and bent to kiss me then put down the laptop in his hand and asked, "How was your day?"

"Terrible and wonderful. Yours?"

More routine than yours from the sound of it." Sitting on one corner of the desk, he asked, "Did you talk to Dr. Forrester?" When I nodded, he added, "And?"

"It was a lot harder than I thought it would be. He asked me to tell him things I'd never shared with anyone else and probably never will."

"Not even with me?"

"Not even with you."

"That's all right. I'm just glad you're talking to someone. I'm really proud of you."

"Thank you. I'm proud of me, too." Standing, I asked, "Do you mind if we just go home and have something light for dinner?"

"Fine by me. I never did get to take that nap I was planning on earlier today." Before I could tell him I was sorry, he stopped me and told me, "It's not a problem. I'll sleep late tomorrow."

"You mean until 5:00 instead of 4:30?"

"Maybe even 5:15."

"What about your run and time at the gym?"

"I'll work it in. It'll be fine."

We returned to the house, ate salads with cheese and some bread, and then Michael watched a program on the History Channel while I cleared the table and washed the dishes.

Once I was finished, I went to the living room. Michael was sound asleep on the couch. I left him where he was and didn't dare switch off the T.V. or do anything else that might wake him up. He needed uninterrupted sleep.

After changing into pajamas, I climbed into bed and resumed reading the book on espionage. When I turned the page from ninety-three to ninety-four, a piece of paper slipped out and fell onto my lap. I stared at it.

On the paper was a drawing of a heart with a knife plunged through it. The hilt of the knife protruded from the top, and the point of the blade extended out from underneath. Blood dripped from the heart. It was a gruesome image, and I wondered why Michael had stuck it in the book.

Maybe he inserted this as a bookmark. Then I thought, *Michael doesn't need bookmarks.*

I felt a sudden surge of fear. I sensed somehow that Michael hadn't put this paper in the book. It was a message, but from whom and for what purpose? I reflected on Esmeralda's predictions that Michael would go away from me for a time but not by his choice. She'd also said he would save my life, which he had when the mirror had fallen on me. She'd foretold that I would save his, but that hadn't happened, yet.

I thought of Michael's past life as a spy, of the enemies he might have, and of the box Tom had given me in case I was ever in danger. How many people might want to harm my husband even though he was no longer an operative? Would they want to extract secret knowledge he might have, kill him, or try to turn him against his country?

You're blowing this way out of proportion, I told myself. *It's a drawing on a piece of paper in a book. Show it to Michael, and he'll have an explanation.*

Chiding myself for overreacting, I replaced the paper where I'd found it and closed the book. I couldn't handle talking to Michael about anything else that night. I was struggling as it was. I'd ask him about it when I was in a better place to handle such discussion.

Michael came to bed soon afterwards, and we made love before our exhaustion got the better of us. When the alarm sounded the following morning, Michael remained sleeping with his body spooned against me. I was safe, secure, and loved. Everything was going to be fine, just like in my lovely dream.

In retrospect, I should have told Michael about the disturbing drawing right away. Instead, I kept putting it off. I finally put it off for so long that I forgot about it. If I'd immediately shared my find with him, then it might have spared many people, including me and Michael, from suffering, uncertainty, and tragedy.

I don't blame myself although I did for a long time. What happened in the years that followed was so shocking and unexpected that I had to fight to stay alive and protect those I loved, especially my husband. All I could do was have faith that John and Esmeralda's predictions were meant to come true and that everything *would* be all right in the end. That faith, along with support from family, friends, and an unlikely benefactor, kept me going when all seemed lost.

But that's another story….

The thrilling sequel to *A Lovely Dream* is *A Lovely Reality*. Filled with heart-pounding excitement, that book will be available in April of 2015. The gripping story will have readers pulse rates soaring as they follow Seneca and Michael's battle to survive an evil plot initiated by a murderous man from Michael's secret past. Innocent people will pay the price for what the psychopathic killer perceives as Michael's transgressions against him, and it will be up to Seneca to save the man she loves and to keep their children, family, and friends safe from harm.

ABOUT THE AUTHOR

Lauren Cutrera, who also writes under the name Barbara Cutrera, has published over 20 contemporary romance, romantic suspense, paranormal romance, mystery, and fiction novels. Diverse people and plots highlight her works, drawing readers into the characters' unique journeys as they navigate their way through their struggles and triumphs. Lauren and her husband, Budge, are the proud parents of a grown son. They live in southwest Florida and have a cute and naughty Yorkie, Hadrian, who sleeps next to Lauren as she writes each day.

Explore other published works by the author at amazon.com and goodreads.com

Check out all things Lauren (and Barbara) at www.laurencutrera.com

And connect with her there or on

Facebook: https://www.facebook.com/profile.php?id=100063631654302

Instagram: https://www.instagram.com/laurencutrera/

Pinterest: https://www.pinterest.com/laurencutrera/_saved/

OTHER BOOKS BY THE AUTHOR:

The Essential Elements Series

Kindred Spirits
Scorched Creek
Spirits Corner
Memory Lane
Homeward Bound

The Limitless Series

Sight Unseen
Better Left Unsaid
Unheard Of
Under Her Skin
Brain Storm
Out On A Limb

The Seneca & Michael Duet

A Lovely Dream
A Lovely Reality

The Gift Series

The Healer's Gift
Jordan's Way
Bound by Grace
The Nameless

The Real World Series

Over, Under, Across & Through
A Good Man's Life
Mercy
Unfinished Business (Final Chapter)

<u>Standalone Novels/Short Stories</u>

In A Manner of Speaking
Prim & Proper
Lucky
Compromising Positions
True: 3 Short Stories